SNOWFLAKES OVER STARR'S FALL

KATE HEWITT

B

Boldwood

First published in Great Britain in 2025 by Boldwood Books Ltd.

Copyright © Kate Hewitt, 2025

Cover Design by Head Design Ltd.

Cover Images: Alamy, iStock and Shutterstock

The moral right of Kate Hewitt to be identified as the author of this work has been asserted in accordance with the Copyright, Designs and Patents Act 1988.

All rights reserved. No part of this book may be reproduced in any form or by any electronic or mechanical means, including information storage and retrieval systems, without written permission from the author, except for the use of brief quotations in a book review. This book is a work of fiction and, except in the case of historical fact, any resemblance to actual persons, living or dead, is purely coincidental.

Every effort has been made to obtain the necessary permissions with reference to copyright material, both illustrative and quoted. We apologise for any omissions in this respect and will be pleased to make the appropriate acknowledgements in any future edition.

A CIP catalogue record for this book is available from the British Library.

Paperback ISBN 978-1-83603-261-8

Large Print ISBN 978-1-83603-262-5

Hardback ISBN 978-1-83603-260-1

Ebook ISBN 978-1-83603-263-2

Kindle ISBN 978-1-83603-264-9

Audio CD ISBN 978-1-83603-255-7

MP3 CD ISBN 978-1-83603-256-4

Digital audio download ISBN 978-1-83603-257-1

This book is printed on certified sustainable paper. Boldwood Books is dedicated to putting sustainability at the heart of our business. For more information please visit https://www.boldwoodbooks.com/about-us/sustainability/

Boldwood Books Ltd, 23 Bowerdean Street, London, SW6 3TN

www.boldwoodbooks.com

1

Jenna Miller didn't like the look of the guy as soon as he walked into her store. Popped collar on his polo shirt, cable-knit golfing sweater draped over his shoulders, the gold and silver links of a Rolex glinting on one tanned and muscular wrist. He slid expensive-looking aviator sunglasses onto his forehead, ruffling his nut-brown hair, as he glanced around at her store with narrowed eyes that flashed ice-blue, lips already pursed in obvious disdain.

Jerk.

Her shoulders had tensed, creeping toward her ears, as she stilled by the cash register where she'd been going through yesterday's receipts. It was a Saturday morning in June, the dust motes dancing through the drowsy air, caught by the warm sunlight, a perfect summer's day, although Jenna was already thinking about new stock, whether she should get in anything for fall, or even Christmas. She'd sold some fresh evergreen wreaths last year that had done pretty well, and she knew she always had to be thinking ahead.

But on this summer's morning she'd been enjoying the peaceful solitude of the store; it was only eight-thirty, and she hadn't had any customers yet, not that she'd had all that many lately, something that she was trying not to think about too much. Miller's Mercantile was a staple of Starr's Fall; it had been offering an array of basic groceries and hardware for over forty years.

That wasn't going to change, not on her watch, even if fewer and fewer people were coming through her doors. This man was, she told herself, a potential customer, and that was a good thing. She'd make sure it was.

He took a few steps into the store, glancing around, his lips now turning down in what was obviously dismay, or maybe even disgust. Clearly he was disappointed by what was on offer.

Jenna glanced around at the beloved and well-worn wooden shelves of admittedly slightly tired-looking grocery staples—bags of flour and sugar, cans of soup and beans, buckets of nails and screws. She'd added a few kitschy but appealing touches here and there—a barrel of pickles swimming in brine by the front door, an old popcorn machine. She offered every customer a free bag of popcorn; at least she did when she was able to get the machine working. It had been broken for a while, leaving a smell of stale popcorn and old oil in the air, but she wasn't sure people liked popcorn that much anyway. Maybe she'd get rid of it.

The man still hadn't spoken. Jenna wasn't even sure if he'd seen her. He stood in the middle of the store, about fifteen feet away, his hands on his hips as he continued to survey its offerings. Just yesterday Jenna had arranged a display of boxes of pasta on the end of an aisle; she thought it looked appealing, with a red and white checked tablecloth and the boxes stacked in a little pyramid.

She watched as the man surveyed the little display, his lip curling before he flicked his gaze away. He tucked one hand in the pocket of his Nantucket Red khakis as he strolled past the display in leather boat shoes without socks. Everything about him blared high-powered city type on a jaunt to the country, the exact kind of person Jenna tended to loathe—from far too much previous experience with one man in particular who was pretty much exactly like this one. Ryan had been younger, admittedly, and a bit flashier, but still. The two were cut from the same unfortunate cloth. Still, Jenna told herself, this guy was a potential customer, and she knew how to be polite.

"May I help you?" she asked in what she believed was a pleasant and friendly tone as the man continued to survey her store, his eyes narrowed.

Slowly he turned to face her. Jenna experienced a jolt then, unexpected and unwelcome, of awareness. *Physical* awareness, because, fine, the man was handsome. Hot, even, something she hadn't noticed when she'd been dissecting his clothing choices and deciding she didn't like him. Which, she could admit, was a tad judgmental of her, maybe even a *lot* judgmental, something she didn't like to think she was, but it was hard when this guy still hadn't spoken to her, as if she wasn't worthy of his notice when he was in *her* store.

Now his ice-blue eyes widened a fraction as he stared at her, seeming to take in her appearance and make his judgments just as she had with him. And she wasn't at all sure she liked that. She watched as his gaze raked slowly over her from head to toe, causing her cheeks to heat because, for heaven's sake, that look was thorough, and not in a good way.

And all right, fine, she knew she might not be at her best. She didn't get gussied up for a Saturday morning in the store. Her hair was in two long Pippi Longstocking-like braids, and she'd paired a flannel shirt, the sleeves hacked off, with a pair of old overalls with bright purple patches on the knees and butt. It was the kind of hippy lumberjack look she liked to embrace, but right now, underneath this man's scornful stare, she felt something close to embarrassment, and it made her furious.

How dare he make her feel that way? How dare she let him?

And he *still* hadn't spoken.

"Hello?" Jenna asked, her tone turning the teeniest bit pointed. "Do you need something?"

The man jangled some keys in his pocket as he arched one dark eyebrow. "I don't suppose you have smoked salmon in a place like this?"

Smoked salmon? *A place like this?* Indignation fizzed through Jenna, and she felt herself readying for a fight before she took a deep breath and managed to rein her temper back in. It was a fair question, she told herself, even if it didn't feel like one. She knew she was a little sensitive about any criticism of Miller's Mercantile, because her brother Zach had been criticizing it for months, if not years. He wanted to gentrify the store, offer expensive candles and artisan cheeses and cashmere blankets and who knew what else. So far, Jenna had held him off from turning the store into some kind of pretentious boutique, but the store's account books suggested something had to change.

Not like that, though.

"No," she answered in a clipped tone, "I'm afraid we don't. But we do have some canned tuna."

The man's nostrils flared and even though his expression was one of scorn, Jenna felt that jolt of awareness *again*. Why did he have to be so good-looking? Those bright blue eyes, the thick, wavy hair, its brown strands looking gold in some places where they caught the sunlight. He had the chiseled cheekbones of a male model and the muscled physique of a rugby player. Generic, she told herself dismissively. He could be any boring, blank-faced model on the cover of a Ralph Lauren catalog. Big deal.

"Tuna?" he repeated disbelievingly. "I'm not going to put canned tuna on my toasted sourdough."

Jenna let out a bark of scornful laughter before she could help herself. "Of course you're not," she agreed. "Well, if you'd like a breakfast alternative, may I suggest cornflakes? Very healthful. We do carry those. Or eggs." She tried to moderate her tone because she realized she was sounding a little snarky. "Scrambled eggs on sourdough are delicious... or so I've heard."

He raised both eyebrows then, his mouth quirking, looking amused in a disdainful way. This man had really cornered the market on smug superiority. "You've never eaten sourdough?" he surmised. "What a surprise."

Wow. He'd turned *toasted sourdough* into an insult. Jenna shook her head. He infuriated her, but weirdly, some small part of her was almost enjoying the exchange, the pointed intensity of it. "Welcome to Hicksville, Mr. Manhattan," she quipped. "Are you here on vacation?" She widened her eyes in mock dismay, resting one hand on her cheek. "Were the Hamptons overbooked?"

His mouth twitched in something *almost* like a smile although his icy eyes flashed with ire. "Let me guess, you've never been there?" he replied dryly. He jangled the keys in his pocket again. "Is there any other grocery store in this town?"

"Nope." She smiled sweetly. "If you want smoked salmon, I'd suggest the deli in Litchfield. It's only half an hour away. I bet your Porsche could make it there in twenty minutes."

He laughed, a bark of genuine amusement as his eyes glinted with something like appreciation. "How did you know I have a Porsche?"

Her smile widened, Grinch-like. "Just a guess."

They stared at each other for a long moment, a face-off. Jenna kept his gaze and did her best to ignore the alarming flutters in her middle. So he was good-looking. There were plenty of good-looking guys who were jerks. She'd had intimate experience with one in particular.

Then he dropped his gaze and shook his head as he looked around the store once more. "I don't feel like going all the way to Litchfield," he told her, an edge entering his voice. "So I guess I'll have to make do with whatever you've got in this place."

Somehow the way he said *this place* made her hackles rise again. He sounded so brutally dismissive. "Breakfast items are in the far aisle," she informed him stiffly. "Let me know if you need help finding anything else." She stocked orange juice in the admittedly small freezer section, but somehow she doubted this man wanted concentrate from a can, the kind you scooped out with a spoon and mixed with water. No doubt for him it was freshly squeezed from oranges flown in from Florida that very morning or nothing. Pressing her lips together, she turned back to the cash register and its receipts.

Jenna listened to his footsteps as he headed toward the far aisle, the weathered floorboards creaking under his boat shoes. He muttered something under his breath, and she thought she caught the word *unbelievable*. It was followed by a snort of something like disgust, which made her tense up, but she told herself she was not going to descend to his level. She'd be perfectly civil when he came back with his cornflakes, or whatever subpar item he'd chosen, because he couldn't have smoked salmon on his toasted sourdough. Good grief, the guy was practically a parody of the overprivileged city type, and of course he had no idea that he was. He'd be asking for avocadoes next, along with tomato juice and a celery stick for his Bloody Mary.

Jenna continued counting yesterday's receipts, only realizing she had not kept any of the amounts in her head when the man returned and thumped a box of generic-brand cornflakes onto the counter with more effort than was needed.

"These expired two months ago," he informed her flatly.

A flush rose to Jenna's face—she tried hard to check everything she stocked was within date—and she glanced at the top of the box, April of that year clearly stamped on top. Oh, dear.

"I'm sorry about that," she told him as politely as she could. "Did you see any other boxes that were in date?"

In reply, the man simply shrugged, and Jenna bit the inside of her cheek before continuing in the same solicitous tone, "Why don't I go check that for you?"

She slipped out from behind the counter, conscious of the man's silent stare on her retreating back—the purple patches on her butt feeling very noticeable all of a sudden—as she headed back to the breakfast section of the store. It only took one glance at the cereal boxes stacked on the shelves to realize he must have taken one from the very back of the shelf. Every other box she saw was in date.

What a jackass.

She took one of the in-date boxes and returned to the cash register, placing it on the counter with a little more force than necessary.

"There we are," she announced. She discovered she could still sound sweet while gritting her teeth. "This one doesn't expire until next year... just like all the other boxes on the shelf. You must have found the only one that was expired." She flicked her gaze to his to find him eyeing her with something like a smirk. "How unlucky of you."

"It wouldn't have happened if you kept track of your stock," he answered shortly. "Considering the size of this place, it shouldn't be too hard." Before Jenna could reply to that zinger, he nodded toward the receipts. "You don't have a computer, I'm guessing? Or even a calculator in this place?"

There were those three words again—*in this place*. Like she was living in a hovel. "Actually, I do my adding up on an abacus," Jenna returned dryly as she rang up his box of cereal. "And I scratch the numbers into a stone tablet. That will be two sixty-five."

"I wouldn't be surprised," the man returned as he handed over a platinum American Express card that had some heft to it; in fact, it wasn't even *made* of plastic, like any normal credit card. She took a not-so-secret pleasure in handing it straight back to him.

"I'm afraid I don't take American Express."

He let out a huff of disbelieving laughter, scowling at the same time. "Why am I not surprised?"

"I don't know," Jenna replied sweetly. "Why aren't you?"

He shook his head slowly in seeming disbelief. "Do you treat all your customers this way?"

"Only the rude ones." The words slipped out before Jenna could stop them. Okay, she needed to remember he *was* a customer, no matter how obnoxious he seemed. She took a deep breath and let it out. "Sorry," she managed grudgingly. "But you got my back right up with your—your snotty attitude about my store." As far as apologies went, she realized, hers had pretty much sucked. "Do you have another credit card?"

Wordlessly, his mouth compressed, which somehow emphasized his lean cheekbones, he handed over another credit card.

"Are you here on vacation?" Jenna asked as she put the credit card through the machine, which was ancient and usually took several minutes, but most people in Starr's Fall used cash. At least at her store, and the ones who used a card didn't mind having a few minutes' chitchat while their card was approved. It was practically a ritual.

Not this guy, apparently. He was still scowling as he replied in a clipped voice, "No. Not on vacation."

"Visiting someone?" she asked, a little too hopefully. *Please don't let him be...*

"Actually," he informed her coolly, "I moved here a couple of days ago."

For a second, Jenna couldn't keep the horror from her face, and the man noticed. "That's quite the welcome," he remarked with a rasping, humorless chuckle. "And I thought countryfolk were meant to be friendly, helping each other out and all."

"Maybe don't buy into corny stereotypes," she shot back, and he shook his head.

"There's no pleasing you, is there? Well, don't worry, it's not like I'm going to try. You won't catch me in this dump a second time. Litchfield it is." He drew himself up as he finished, "Frankly, I'd travel all the way back to New York to avoid encountering such a... such a..." He paused, clearly at a loss, while Jenna stared at him, wondering what on earth he was going to say. "Such a *shrew* like you again," he finished, a little uncertainly, like he wasn't sure he'd landed on the right word.

"A *shrew*?" Jenna didn't know whether to be outrageously offended or scornfully amused. "What are you, Shakespeare?" she asked, and he just blinked at her for a second before he remembered to glare.

Amusement gave way to anger as she glared back. If he never darkened her door again, it would be too soon. All right, she could have been a *little* friendlier, but he'd been sneering at her store from the moment he'd crossed the threshold. Stupid city idiot. They were all alike.

At least you treat them all the same.

She pushed that little voice away as the man suddenly burst out in exasperation, "How long does that damned machine take?"

"It's just about finished," Jenna informed him icily. She took the card out of the machine, glancing at the name on its front. Jack A. Wexler. She thrust the card at him as the receipt began to print out, another laborious process.

"Would you like the receipt?"

"No," he stated flatly, and without another word, he grabbed his box of cornflakes and marched out of the mercantile, making sure the screen door banged hard behind him.

"Jerk," Jenna muttered to no one. Saying it out loud didn't make her feel much better. She glanced back at the pile of receipts and then pushed them away, annoyed as much at herself as at Jack Wexler. Well, almost. She knew she shouldn't have been so snippy, rising to his stupid bait time and time again, but men like him *really* got her back up—privileged, arrogant, so sure of their own effortless charms. And she *wasn't* stereotyping, she told herself, even though she knew she pretty much was.

But Jack Wexler had shown his colors several times over in the space of ten minutes. At least if he made good on his promise she'd never see him again, although she had to wonder why an obvious city type like him had moved to Starr's Fall. It was far off the beaten track when it came to ex-Manhattanites. They usually didn't venture past Litchfield, and they thought *that* was the boonies.

Never mind. She was putting it—*him*—out of her mind right now.

There was enough to be occupying her time, anyway, dealing with the store. Now that her brother Zach had started his own furniture restoration business out of the back barn, Jenna managed the mercantile pretty much on her own... which was how she liked it.

Zach had struck out on his own because he hadn't felt the store was big enough for both of them, and in truth it hadn't been. Jenna knew she might have been the *teensiest* bit controlling when it came to managing this place, but it was because it mattered so much to her... and it was all she had.

Which was a somewhat depressing thought, and not one she wanted to dwell on overmuch. She was nearly thirty-nine years old and Miller's Mercantile was pretty much her life. Not her *whole* life, of course. She had a great group of friends; in fact she was meeting Annie Lyman for dinner tonight at Starr's Fall's only diner, The Starr Light. And then there was Laurie and Liz and Maggie and Zoe... but why was she thinking this way, as if she had to add up all the good things in her life like a column of numbers, making sure the profits were more than the costs?

It was stupid Jack Wexler, Jenna knew. Being so scornful about her store and sneering at her, calling her a *shrew*, of all things, like something out of Shakespeare. That had been some serious misogyny there, and none of it was any reason to feel like her life was lacking, because it wasn't. So, Jenna told herself, she simply wasn't going to think about him anymore.

A couple of hours later, her equanimity was mostly restored. Stacking shelves, ordering inventory, chatting with a few friendly customers, familiar faces she knew and liked... it all grounded her in the reality of her life, which she enjoyed. She *liked* being part of this community; she enjoyed being known. She'd chosen to come back to Starr's Fall after a whirlwind year in San Francisco and two more miserable years in New York, attempting to make a dead-on-arrival relationship work, and this town had helped to heal her. Jack Wexler might think he was above her country ways, but she'd had her time in the city, too, and she'd turned her back on it for good.

But why was she thinking about Jack Wexler again?

By late afternoon, the store was empty, the summer air still and drowsy, and Jenna pulled out her laptop—she had all her accounts on a spreadsheet like any normal business-minded person of this century; she just liked counting the receipts, seeing the tangible evidence of her profits, something she wished she'd mentioned to Jack Wexler—to work on the store's website. Her friend Laurie, who ran Max's Place, Starr's Fall's new pet store and bakery, had convinced her that she needed one.

"Everybody looks online first, Jenna," she'd told her. "You have to have a *presence*."

And so Jenna was, slowly and painfully, navigating her way through one of those websites-from-a-box jobs, pointing and clicking and trying to make it look personalized. It was, she'd discovered, a lot harder than Laurie had made it sound, but she knew she needed to make some changes to how she ran things, and a website was one she could handle.

After an hour of tinkering, she went on Google to see if the website came up in the search for Miller's Mercantile; Laurie had said that "search engine optimization" was important, and Jenna could see why. She wasn't a *complete* technophobe, after all. She scrolled as much as the next person, but making websites felt like a whole other level.

As she scrolled down through the hits—an article in *The Litchfield County Times* when they'd had their twenty-fifth anniversary, years ago—she suddenly stilled as six words jumped out at her. *Worst Store in the Whole Area.* It was a review on TripAdvisor, and it had been made that morning. Sucking in a hard breath, she clicked on it and read the single scathing paragraph.

> Went here for some basic groceries but never again. Store is badly stocked with subpar items that are past their expiration date, and the woman at the counter was one of the rudest and most unpleasant people I have ever encountered, insulting me personally multiple times, and for no reason. I moved to Starr's Fall for the community and was sorely disappointed by one of my first experiences of it. Hopefully someone in the town will start another grocery store and put Miller's Mercantile out of business, as it surely deserves. If I could give it less than one star, I would have. Do NOT recommend!!

Jenna blinked, reeling from what felt like an intensely personal attack. She felt both hurt and painfully exposed, like Jack Wexler—because he had obviously written the review even if the username was simply *A Concerned Resident*—had peeled back a layer of her skin. All right, she'd been snippy, but then, so had he. Could he not see that?

Of course he couldn't.

The hurt—she had tears stinging in her eyes, and she *never* cried—was fast morphing into a far more comforting fury. Anger she could do, especially when she was not in the wrong. At least not as much as Jack A. Wexler made her out to be.

Pursing her lips, Jenna typed out a response to the review.

> I'm so sorry you had such a negative experience, Mr. Wexler, but perhaps next time you could make fewer offensive comments about my person, my business, and my inventory before you've barely crossed the threshold. Amazingly, you managed to find the one box of expired cereal in the entire store. I hope you found your smoked salmon, zooming over to Litchfield in your Porsche, while this "shrew," as you called

me, continues to serve the good people of this wonderful community.

She pressed publish before she could overthink it, smiling grimly as it appeared on the screen.

This, Jenna thought, was war.

2

By the time Jenna was walking into The Starr Light that evening, she found she was still fuming, although she was trying to hide it. She'd stopped by Your Turn Next, the town's new boardgame café, to rant about Jack Wexler to her brother Zach and his new girlfriend, Maggie, who ran the place. Unfortunately, she'd had an uncomfortable feeling they'd been more amused than outraged on her behalf, which was incredibly aggravating.

All right, Zach, of all people, knew she had something of a temper; he'd been living with her for pretty much his whole life. But they hadn't seen and heard just how obnoxious Jack Wexler had been. She also hadn't told them about the one-star review online, because she'd been too annoyed—as well as embarrassed. Miller's Mercantile had few enough online reviews as it was, so Jack Wexler's one-star had seriously lowered her overall rating. Considering she was trying—albeit not as hard as she could or even should be—to attract new business, this development was fairly worrying, and yet she knew there was nothing she could do about it.

Let it go, Jenna told herself for the umpteenth time, but the problem was, that review was still up there, and as long as it was, she knew she would feel furious—along with stupidly hurt, which made her feel even more furious. Why should a man she barely knew have that kind of power over her? She'd worked long and hard to make sure *no* man had that over her ever again, and it was incredibly aggravating that a stupid stranger did.

There was no winning, she reflected gloomily. She just hoped Jack Wexler steered clear of her, because she was certainly going to steer clear of him.

Her friend Annie Lyman was already seated in a deep vinyl booth in Starr's Fall's only diner when Jenna arrived. Rhonda, the owner, pouring coffee from behind the counter, gave Jenna a wink and a wave as she came in.

"The usual for you girls?" she called, and Jenna smiled a little tiredly.

Her usual was a gin and tonic and she felt she was going to need it. "Thanks, Rhonda," she called back, and slid in the booth opposite Annie, who was perusing the menu avidly, even though Jenna was pretty sure she also ordered the same thing every time —a double bacon cheeseburger with extra fries.

"Hey," she said gently. "How are you?" Annie's mom Barb had been diagnosed with Parkinson's just over a year ago, and she'd been steadily declining ever since. It was heartbreaking to watch her friend's mother slowly but surely lose her abilities—fine motor skills had gone first, then speech, and then walking. She'd moved into hospice care just a few weeks back, a pale shadow of herself, although amazingly still in good spirits. The last time Jenna had visited her, Barb hadn't been able to speak or even lift her head from the pillow, but she'd smiled, and that beatific curving of her lips had just about broken Jenna's heart. The palliative nurses thought it was likely to be no more than a matter of months.

Jenna knew Annie was finding it incredibly tough. She and Barb had run Lyman Orchards together for the last ten years, ever since her dad had died. They were best friends as much as they were mother and daughter; Annie had always been fiercely protective of Barb, and watching her suffer without being able to do anything about it had to be tearing her apart.

"Well, you know." Annie answered Jenna's gentle question as she pursed her lips, her gaze fixed on the menu. "Could be better, could be worse, I guess." Her lips trembled for a second until she pressed them together. "It is what it is."

Grief, Jenna thought, had to be hard no matter what form it came in, or how much time you had to prepare yourself for it. Not that she'd experienced this particular kind of grief; her own parents were fit and well, living in Florida, having retired from running Miller's Mercantile four years ago. And not that she'd grieve them all that terribly if they were gone, which was a horrible way to think, but there it was.

They'd been emotionally absent from her life for a long time now. There had been no big drama or hostility, just what had felt like a lukewarm love on their part, that had drifted into a vague indifference on both sides as she'd grown older. Her parents had had far more interest in each other and their business than the two children they'd raised; at least it had always felt that way to Jenna, and never more so than when she'd limped back from New York, a shadow of herself, and her parents hadn't even noticed how much she'd been hurting.

She grieved the relationship she'd never had with them, she supposed, but that was a different kind of pain, more like a scar than a wound, and one she was well used to.

"Tell me something funny that happened to you today," Annie commanded abruptly. When she looked up from the menu, her eyes gleamed with unshed tears and Jenna's heart ached for her. She'd been friends with Annie since she'd been tiny; although Annie was a few years older than her, they'd always got along, and when they'd both settled in Starr's Fall, two decidedly single women in their thirties, they'd developed an even stronger bond. Although Annie wasn't single anymore, Jenna reminded herself a little morosely. She'd starting dating Mike the Mechanic back in April; you could spot them a mile away, as Mike was six four and Annie nearing six feet, both with full heads of wild gray hair. They were simultaneously the most improbable and perfect couple ever.

"Something funny...?" she repeated musingly. The only thing Jenna could think about that happened today was her unfortunate encounter with Jack Wexler, and that definitely *hadn't* been funny. But maybe she could make it funny, for her friend's sake. "Well," she began, propping her elbows on the scarred table, "I met the biggest jackass in all of northwestern Connecticut today. Does that count as funny?"

"Only if he did something stupid rather than annoying," Annie quipped with a wobbly smile. "Did he?"

"If you count asking for smoked salmon in Miller's Mercantile as stupid, then yes. He wanted it for his toasted sourdough, would you believe?"

Annie let out a gurgle of laughter. "Toasted sourdough! Did he seriously say that?"

Jenna nodded, heartened by Annie's incredulity. "Yup."

"That's both stupid *and* annoying," Annie decided. "Was he rude about it?"

"*So* rude," Jenna replied decisively. She found she was enjoying this retelling of the whole Jack Wexler episode—instead of coming across furious and, well, *shrewish*, she re-imagined herself having risen above it... for Annie's sake. "This guy practically has privilege tattooed on his forehead," she continued, settling into her story. "You should have seen the clothes he was wearing—boat shoes, the popped collar, the Rolex, the sweater thrown over his shoulders. *And* he drives a Porsche. Like, try not to be so basic, dude. We *get* you're rich. You don't need to scream it."

"Good grief." Annie shook her head, her eyes glinting with amusement, which made Jenna feel a whole lot better. She would gladly throw Jack Wexler to the wolves for her friend's sake, and after all, hadn't he done the same thing to her, by writing that horrible review? The memory of it still made her burn, even as she was trying to make light of the whole thing for Annie.

"So did he just storm out of the store or what?" Annie asked.

"He bought some cornflakes because he said he couldn't be bothered to go all the way to Litchfield. But he kept calling the store 'this place' like it was some dirt-floored hovel, and he told me he'd never come back. He also called me a *shrew*, before he slammed the door on the way out and roared off in his Porsche."

She didn't actually know if he'd roared off or not, but it sounded about right.

Annie shook her head, marveling at Jack Wexler's sheer nerve. "A shrew? Seriously? What a jerk."

"That's not even the worst of it," Jenna continued, leaning forward. The wound was still raw, but she needed to tell someone, and Annie was her best friend. "He wrote a one-star review on Google, absolutely trashing the place. And *he* had been the rude one."

Annie's eyes widened. "Okay, now he sounds like a total ass," she stated definitively. "Nothing funny about that. Is he here on vacation?"

For a second Jenna hesitated, as she recalled, slightly uncomfortably, that Jack Wexler *lived* in Starr's Fall now. He was, more or less, her neighbor, and she wasn't one to create bad blood.

But he'd started it, and he'd written that review... even if she'd been a little rude in return.

"He just moved here," she admitted. "Unfortunately."

"Who just moved here?" Rhonda asked as she plopped down two generous gin and tonics onto their table. "And why is it unfortunate, may I ask?"

"Do you eavesdrop on everyone's conversations," Jenna teased, smiling, "or just ours?"

"Oh, everyone's," Rhonda informed her airily. "But only if they're interesting. So who are you trash-talking, girls? Should I be concerned?"

"Just this big jerk who's moved to Starr's Fall," Annie told her with relish. Clearly she was enjoying having something to focus on other than her dying mom, but Jenna experienced a *slight* twinge of unease at the thought of spreading such notions when Jack Wexler *had* only just moved here. But then she remembered that wretched review, and she hardened her heart. He deserved every bit of it and more.

"Oh?" Rhonda's penciled-in eyebrows improbably rose. "And what big jerk is this?"

"This guy who came into Miller's Mercantile," Annie said, and Jenna tried not to wince at the sound of her friend's voice ringing out through the whole restaurant. "What was his name, Jenna?"

"Umm..." Fine, the die was cast, and he really did deserve it. "Jack Wexler."

Annie nodded solemnly. "He's some blowhard from the city who complained about Miller's Mercantile because it didn't have *smoked salmon*." She rolled her eyes, her salt and pepper curls bouncing around her flushed face. Two sips of gin and tonic and her friend was already well on her way to a serious buzz, Jenna noted with affection. Annie had never been able to hold her liquor, and Jenna suspected she needed a bit of liquid relief at the moment.

"Jack Wexler..." Rhonda mused. "I'll make a note of it if he comes in here. If my eggs Benedict isn't good enough for him, then I don't know what is."

"He gave Jenna's store a one-star review online because of it," Annie continued boisterously, and this time Jenna did wince. She didn't really want that information spread around, for the sake of her store, rather than Jack Wexler.

"Now that does sound like a jerk," Rhonda agreed, her eyes narrowing. "Of the first order. I know how much a one-star review can hurt, trust me. I had some jackass in here once who one-starred me because I didn't give free refills on *wine*." She planted a hand on one bony hip, her peroxide-blonde ponytail flipped over her shoulder. "Maybe I should ban this Jack Wexler from the premises. If he's going to be the type to look down his nose at every joint in this town—"

"He is," Annie insisted, taking another sip of her drink. "He certainly sounds like it."

Jenna was starting to feel slightly alarmed. As much as she'd disliked Jack Wexler, she didn't want to be accused of black-balling him in all of Starr's Fall before he'd barely set foot in the place. Plus, she had a feeling that would just make him double down on trash-talking her store. "I'm not sure—" she began.

"No Jack Wexlers allowed!" Rhonda crowed with a cackle that ended in a smoker's cough, and Annie actually applauded. She had good friends, Jenna thought, dear, *loyal* friends, but maybe they'd taken this a touch too far, both for her sake and because Annie was clearly in desperate need of a distraction, and Jack Wexler was it.

"Well, he *has* moved here, so maybe we should be a little..." she began feebly, only for the words to die on her lips as she caught who was coming through The Starr Light's swinging doors, his ice-blue eyes narrowed in now-familiar derision, sunglasses slipped up onto his forehead just as before even though it was nearing dusk.

Oh, no.

"What?" Annie asked, taking in the undoubtedly horrified expression on Jenna's face. Then she followed her frozen gaze to the man still standing in the doorway, surveying the diner like a king might survey his domain.

"Oh," Annie breathed. "That's *him*! It must be. He *looks* like a jerk."

"Is it?" Rhonda craned her neck to clock Jack in the doorway, her eyes narrowed in preemptive scorn. "Well, I'll tell him right now what I think of him." She started to sashay over to him, and swiftly Jenna grabbed her arm. She could not be responsible for running a new resident out of town, even one as odious as Jack Wexler.

"Rhonda, he's a *customer*," she hissed. "And if you antagonize him, he's just likely to give you a bad review, too—"

"I'd like to see him try—"

"Plus," Jenna whispered as a flush crawled up her throat, "I might have been a little rude to him. Just a little."

"You?" Annie scoffed disbelievingly. "Rude?"

Rhonda, however, hesitated, which was a little humbling. "Well, I'll see what he's like," she groused. "But he's out on his ear if there are any complaints, let me tell you."

Jenna watched, feeling a jumbled mixture of anticipation and trepidation, as Rhonda strode toward her newest customer. He'd changed from his ensemble earlier and was now wearing a gray quarter-zip fleece that looked expensive and very new, paired with similarly crisp-looking jeans. He'd also exchanged his boat shoes for a pair of hiking boots, also clearly new. He'd probably taken the price tags off that morning, Jenna thought cynically. He was so much of a city boy, it was kind of ridiculous.

He was, she noticed, still gazing around the diner with the same narrow-eyed assessment to which he'd subjected Miller's Mercantile.

"May I help you?" Rhonda's voice rang out, sounding more than a little aggressive, and Jack jerked back a little, clearly startled by her tone. Oh, dear. Jenna knew Rhonda was a little defensive of her. Years ago, when she'd first limped back to Starr's Fall with a broken heart, wounded pride and a soul-deep cynicism that all men had to be lying cheats, Rhonda had commiserated with her over a bottle of wine late at night in this diner, the sign flipped to closed.

Jenna couldn't remember half of what she'd blubbed to Rhonda two or three glasses in, and she cringed a little now to think of it, because she tended to keep her emotional cards close to her chest. Rhonda, however much a gossip she liked to be, hadn't let Jenna's secrets slip. At least, Jenna hoped she hadn't.

Just like she hoped Rhonda didn't make Jack Wexler Starr's Fall's public enemy number one, even if he deserved to be. She'd told herself she was going to rise above his slurs and sneers, but right now it was feeling like she hadn't at all. She might have even brought the whole episode a little lower.

"I was hoping for a table," Jack told Rhonda in a voice that bordered on arctic. "If that's not too much to ask?"

"And will you give me a one-star rating if it is?" Rhonda returned in the same aggressive tone, and Jenna closed her eyes. Rhonda was known for refusing customers service, it was true, but she usually waited until they'd first done something objectionable.

Sensing someone's gaze on her, Jenna opened her eyes to find Jack Wexler staring right at her, his narrowed gaze like a laser, freezing her in place. Jenna felt as if her heart had stopped beating, the whole world had stopped moving, as they stared straight at each other for several long beats.

Then Jack snapped his gaze back to Rhonda, and Jenna tried to remember how to breathe.

"I don't think I'll bother," Jack replied, his cut-glass tone carrying through the whole diner, and then he turned on his heel and walked out, the door banging behind him.

"*Well*," Rhonda announced, like his behavior proved everything she'd thought about him and more.

There were only a handful of customers in The Starr Light, but they were all buzzing with speculation about the scene. Jack Wexler had clearly made his name in the town, and not in a good way. The question was, Jenna wondered morosely, how much of it was her fault?

She didn't want to be the kind of person who created drama. She'd had enough in her life, heaven knew, and she was trying to keep things on a more even keel, especially since she and Zach had had a falling out. They'd managed to recover their relationship, and Jenna hoped it was on its way to being stronger than ever, but this...? She really didn't need a Jack Wexler in her life.

Jenna glanced once more at the diner's door, firmly closed, dusk settling over Main Street. It seemed, she reflected, she didn't have one. Jack Wexler was nowhere to be seen.

3

Jack strode down Starr's Fall's Main Street, his heart pounding with fury as he reflexively clenched and unclenched his fists. It was so obvious what that woman had done back there. She'd gone and badmouthed him to everyone in this town, and all because *she'd* been rude to *him*.

All right, he might have been a *little* rude to her, but she'd been downright annoying, and she'd deserved that review. Mostly. *Maybe.*

Jack let out a long breath, doing his best to get his heart rate to slow. God help him, he didn't need *another* heart attack three months after the first one. And he certainly didn't need people like Jenna Miller—he'd learned her name when he'd searched the store up online—making his life even more miserable than it already was.

Why had he moved here again? For the rest and relaxation, a chance to recover after losing not just his health, but his business, his life, his whole purpose?

And the trouble was, that *wasn't* an exaggeration, which had been a major part of the problem.

Jack let out another long, low breath as he came to a stop in front of his car. Jenna Miller had nailed that—it was this year's Porsche Spyder, definitely a boy-toy kind of car, but he'd needed the pick-me-up after his endless hospital stay, and hell, he could afford it. Why not? Although, it had to be said, when parked between a battered sedan and a rusty pickup truck, his flashy convertible was looking a little showy and ridiculous... but so what? He wouldn't apologize for having made money. A *lot* of money.

Even if it had nearly killed him.

With a groan, he pressed the key fob, causing the beep of the Porsche unlocking to echo up and down the empty street, its headlights flashing. He slid inside, resting his hands on the leather steering wheel as he took a few more deep breaths. His heart rate was beginning to slow, but now his stomach hurt, both because he was hungry—the food options in Starr's Fall were *severely* limited—and because he suspected his damned ulcer was flaring up. Again.

Just another symptom of the high-stress life he'd reveled in for nearly twenty years. All gone, in one literally heart-stopping second, when he'd collapsed in the middle of the most important business meeting of his life, with the biggest and riskiest company he'd ever invested in about to go public. He'd reaped a multimillion-dollar profit, not that he'd been able to enjoy that moment of triumph. He'd been in Beth Israel Hospital, getting a stent put in and fighting for his life.

Sighing, Jack pressed the ignition, and the Porsche roared to life. He wasn't going to waste another second of his time fuming over Jenna Miller. She'd looked like some kind of crazy cat lady, with her patched overalls and sleeveless plaid shirt, her hair in two long auburn braids like she was sixteen instead of probably pushing forty. Not that she'd looked middle-aged; there had been something youthful about her golden-green eyes, the spattering of freckles across her cheek and nose. And even the overalls hadn't been able to hide her curvy but athletic figure.

Jeez, why was he thinking like this? About *that* woman? Clearly it had been a while since romance or anything like it had been a possibility in his life, if he was checking out women like Jenna Miller.

Jack pulled away in the car with a pleasingly loud roar, an effective *screw you* to the good people of Starr's Fall who had already decided to kick him to the curb, although unfortunately he didn't really have anywhere to go besides home. He'd just bought a three-million-dollar property on Bantam Lake, a few miles outside of town. But from now on he wouldn't be going into Starr's Fall; judging from what Jenna Miller had said, Litchfield was more his vibe. Even if it was half an hour away.

But that didn't solve his problem *now*, which was that he was hungry. He wasn't about to drive all the way to Litchfield, but he did remember passing a pizza place on the edge of town. Pizza was definitely something he wasn't supposed to eat; his doctor had given him a strict diet to deal with the effects of the ulcer and the heart attack, and Jack had not liked the look of it. It involved a lot of leafy greens and not nearly enough to disguise them with.

Besides, he'd been so good for the last three months, sticking to the boring diet, filtering out every temptation and enjoyment in life. One slice of pizza wasn't going to kill him. Hopefully.

He pulled into the strip mall outside of Starr's Fall, noting the two empty storefronts as well as the pizza place, which was a hole-in-the-wall joint with bright halogen lighting and a depressing lack of atmosphere. Hopefully he wouldn't get food poisoning.

"Wow," the guy behind the counter greeted him as Jack strode into the place. "Nice ride."

"Thanks," Jack said shortly. "I'll take..." He scanned the offerings and then, feeling reckless, said, "One large pepperoni pizza."

"Spicy or extra spicy?"

"Spicy, please." He didn't have a death wish, despite how much this day had sucked. After his unpleasant encounter at Miller's Mercantile, he'd visited his mother—always a painful occasion—and then gone for a gentle hike—as per the doctor's orders—and ended up getting blisters from his new hiking boots. He'd had to hobble his way to The Starr Light, where he'd been *hoping* for a decent meal. Instead his day had gone from bad to worse. Well, maybe the pizza would make it better.

"You on vacation?" the pizza guy asked.

It was a valid assumption, Jack knew, but it still irritated him. "No," he replied, trying for a reasonable tone. "I live here."

The guy's eyes widened. He wore a greasy baseball cap backward and sported a very patchy beard that mostly hid his pimples. He scratched his cheek thoughtfully as he gazed at Jack, who stared levelly back. "New here?" he finally asked, and Jack just nodded. He really wasn't in the mood for some kind of heart-to-heart.

Fortunately, the guy decided to finally make his pizza—this was clearly a one-man operation—and Jack retreated to the window, sliding out his phone to check for messages.

Nothing. He'd been in Starr's Fall for three days and no one had checked in once. No one had checked in after his first week in the hospital, either. He'd run a company with over a hundred employees and not one of them had bothered to ask how he was, whether he was settling in, or if his health was okay.

Not that Jack had actually expected them to; he knew what Wall Street was like. A couple of years ago, Michael Banner—someone he'd worked very closely with and would have, at least in a matter of speaking, called a friend—had discovered

Buddhism and retired early, cashing in his stocks and moving to Bermuda. Jack hadn't sent him a single text to ask how he was. Such a notion hadn't even crossed his mind.

Banner had been out of the game; he'd become instantly irrelevant. You didn't stay on top in the finance world by chasing after has-beens, not even if they'd been your friends. *Especially* not if they'd been your friends. Better to create a little distance, show people you absolutely were not about to try to find yourself or join an ashram.

Jack started to swipe to check his NYSE app, but then he stopped himself. No point going down that route. His heart couldn't take it, in more ways than one.

"Hey, mister? Your pizza's ready."

"Thanks." Jack swiped his credit card—he didn't even bother whipping out his platinum this time—before taking the box and heading outside. It was a beautiful summer's evening, the air soft and dusky, the sky a twilit violet with the first stars starting to glimmer on a horizon fringed darkly with evergreens. For a second, he imagined himself in the Hamptons—like Jenna Miller had so nastily joked—at the beachfront mansion he'd once rented with a bunch of friends. He couldn't remember much about that trip, to be honest. It had been whiskey-soaked and drug-fueled, although he'd kept himself from the latter. Unlike a lot of the guys on Wall Street, he'd never dabbled in the hard stuff. It hadn't mattered in the end, though. He'd still had to call time at just forty-two years of age, in the prime of his career.

Three months on, it remained a bitter pill he continued to choke on.

The drive back to his sprawling house on the lake took ten minutes, and Jack felt his mood plummet with each one. What did he have to look forward to? Eating a pizza alone that would probably cause him heartburn, if not something worse, and then a couple hours of mindless TV when he'd never been one for television, anyway. There had never been enough *time*.

But that frantic, busy-busy buzz of life that had kept him constantly on his toes, blood pressure soaring, excitement always fizzing as he looked to close the next deal... it was all gone. Some guys, like his former friend Michael, had been glad to re-evaluate their priorities. Slow down and savor whatever it was they wanted to savor. Jack, however, did not appreciate the opportunity. He just wanted his old life back, in every aspect, even the stress and accompanying ulcer. He'd thrived on it, all of it.

Out here in the boonies, there was nothing to thrive on. There was nothing, period.

He unlocked the back door of the lake house he'd bought after one look online and strode through the yawning mudroom to the even bigger kitchen. It was far too big a house for one person, although he'd always liked airy spaces, and the floor-to-ceiling picture window overlooking the lake, so close you almost felt as if you were walking on water, had been a definite selling point.

Still, it wasn't like he was going to host parties or even have anyone over. There was no one *to* have over; the friends and colleagues of his old life had already forgotten him. As for his new life? Well, his welcome to Starr's Fall had not exactly been heartening, to say the least.

Jack tossed the pizza on the kitchen table that seated twelve and had been carved out of a single piece of oak—he'd hired an interior decorator to furnish the entire place, giving her carte blanche because he hadn't cared—and glanced longingly at the empty drinks cabinet. Strictly no alcohol for the foreseeable, his doctor had said, unless he wanted to wind up on the operating table again. Jack had obeyed him so far, but what he wouldn't do for a single malt whiskey right about now...

With a sigh he turned to the picture window, taking some small solace from the view of the lake, an evening mist settling onto its placid surface in ghostly shreds, the shoreline across the stretch of water dense with dark evergreens. Loneliness swept through him like an empty wind, rustling and rattling and leaving nothing behind but a deep, painful longing for what was... and what would never be again.

Improbably as well as irritatingly, his mind drifted once more to Jenna Miller. Back at the diner she'd been seated in a booth with another woman—Jack hadn't taken in the details, but he'd seen that much. Clearly enjoying roasting him to all and sundry, too. She was probably the toast of the town, he reflected sourly. Born and bred here, loved by everyone, defended to the death, yada, yada, yada.

Flipping the lid of the box and reaching for a slice of pizza, he wondered what she was doing now.

* * *

By six-thirty, Annie needed to get back to her mom and Jenna was heading back to Miller's Mercantile, feeling disconsolate and a little restless. No matter how much she kept telling herself that Jack Wexler had made his own bed, and he could now darned well lie in it, she still felt... not *guilty*, no, but uncomfortable. A little, at least, although she wasn't even sure why, because he really had been rude.

And good-looking. For some reason, she kept remembering just how much.

But it wasn't even Jack Wexler who was making her feel this way, Jenna knew as she let herself into the empty house behind the store where she'd lived for most of her life. It was the loneliness that she'd kept at bay for the last few years but was always crouching at the door, waiting to rush in and take up all the space if she gave it a second's chance.

Whenever she felt this way, she trotted out the laundry list of reasons why it was unreasonable to do so. She had good friends, a great brother—even if they'd been at odds occasionally—and, well, not a *thriving* business, but at least one that was limping along, and that she enjoyed. Many people had less, a lot less, and she had never been one for self-pity. At least not overt self-pity; like the loneliness, it could creep in by the back door and take up irritating residence.

But she didn't want to do that now, even if Jack Wexler—and yes, this was about him, sort of—had as good as held a mirror up to her own life and forced her to stare at her reflection. *Look at you, you rude, washed-up shrew of a woman. Who would ever love you, never mind like you? You're pathetic.*

All right, he hadn't said all that, but he might as well have. He'd certainly been thinking it, and now Jenna was too, which felt pretty miserable. She'd spent a lot of time doing her best to stop thinking these kinds of thoughts, back when she'd come back to Starr's Fall, emotionally bloodied and bruised and trying her hardest not to show just how much. Ryan Taylor hadn't just broken her heart, he'd crushed her confidence, her sense of self. She'd done the one thing she'd sworn she wouldn't and tried to make a man her everything, searching for that stupid fairy-tale romance that growing up she'd watched from afar. Her parents might have had it, but she didn't want it, and she wasn't going to go looking for it ever again.

Neither was she going to talk about it or confess her feelings of loneliness to any of her good friends, because that would be pathetic *and* make her feel worse.

So here she was, in a dark kitchen, pulling her laptop toward her and stupidly clicking on TripAdvisor to look at that review again. Why was she torturing herself this way? Not that there was much else to do...

With a sigh, Jenna read through it again—she had it practically memorized by now—and noticed, glumly, that there were two new likes. Who had liked such a piece of vindictive garbage? Was it someone who had been to her store? Someone she *knew*?

The prospect was even more dispiriting. She'd made Miller's Mercantile her whole life for the last few years, since her parents had retired. She and Zach had been running it together, but she'd put her soul into this store in a way he never had. Maybe because she hadn't let him, but still. Reading those words of Jack Wexler's, even knowing they must have been fired off in a temper, *hurt*.

And they also made her wonder if maybe she was doing something wrong. The store's profits had been slipping for well over a year. They didn't get the tourists in Starr's Fall to justify turning it into some high-end gift shop like they had in Litchfield, and now that Instacart delivered to the town, it was only the old-timers and loyalist townspeople who bought their groceries here. What could she do? What did she *want* to do?

Sometimes, in her bleaker moments, Jenna considered jacking it all in. Selling her share in the store and hightailing it to Bermuda or the Bahamas or one of those places. The money would last at least a year or two, and after that, well, maybe she'd have an epiphany. Or she'd open a surf shop or something, not that she'd ever surfed, or had even wanted to.

Jenna let out a gusty sigh as she closed her laptop. How could she be thirty-eight years old and still not know what she wanted to do with her life, or even who she *was*?

Bizarrely, and uncomfortably, her thoughts drifted back to Jack Wexler. Again. Why on earth had a guy like him moved to Starr's Fall? And those new hiking boots and fleece... They kind of screamed midlife crisis. Had something happened to him? Maybe that was why he'd been in such a mood, because now that she thought about it, he'd seemed irritable coming into the store, even before he'd asked about the smoked salmon, and she wasn't sure it had been just run-of-the-mill snobbishness. Or was she giving the guy too much credit?

Remember what guys like that are like, Jenna, she told herself. *They're ruthless. Heartless. Liars...*

She didn't usually need the reminder. In fact, Annie would say that she thought about Ryan way too much, considering it was ten years since they'd broken up. Or, to put a finer point on it, since he'd ruthlessly dumped her when she'd been forming the word *yes*, thinking he might propose after waiting with bated breath for two years, tying herself into knots to be the woman he wanted, to absolutely no avail.

Yes, it *still* hurt, even if it shouldn't. Maybe it always would.

As for Jack Wexler? Jenna was determined not to give him another thought.

She pushed her laptop away and headed into the store that adjoined the house, treading the old wooden floorboards in the dark, breathing in its familiar smell of dust and wood polish, pickles and popcorn. Not the most tantalizing aroma, but Jenna loved it. Maybe she would get the popcorn machine working again, she thought. The machine smelled enough as it was, and it was a cute and unique thing to offer. Maybe she'd even stock smoked salmon, like a joke, and advertise it in the window. *Goes great with toasted sourdough!*

The thought made her snicker, and she decided she felt better.

The Jack Wexlers of the world were *not* going to bring her down, she told herself. Not back then, not now, and not ever.

4

THREE MONTHS LATER

Something had to change. It was a fact that had been dogging Jenna for months, maybe even years, but she knew she finally had to face it now as she stared at the spreadsheet of sales for August and the numbers didn't remotely add up. There weren't that many numbers to begin with; sales had been dipping steadily month on month for longer than she was comfortable acknowledging, even if she had to now, because the money, what there was of it, was running out.

If she kept on the way she was going, Jenna reflected glumly, Miller's Mercantile might be forced to close its doors by Christmas, if not sooner. She'd known this, at least on some level, for a while, but now it was smacking her in the face, and it *hurt*. Her stomach felt as if it were lined with lead, and she had to swallow hard as she closed her laptop and stared into space, her mind too blank to think of options.

It had been a good summer in many respects. She'd had fun with friends, spending long, lazy evenings at Laurie's or Annie's, or hanging out with Zach and Maggie and her son Ben at Your Turn Next, the boardgame café Maggie had opened on Main

Street. There had been hiking up to Starr's Fall's eponymous waterfall, and a day out at the beach on Bantam Lake, admiring the gorgeous lake houses with their own shore frontage.

Annie's mother Barb was, amazingly, still hanging on, which had given Annie a new sort of energy, even though everybody knew the end was inevitable, as it was, Jenna supposed, for every person on this earth. Still, she'd enjoyed it all, and she'd been both glad and grateful for the needed affirmation that she really did *like* her life in Starr's Fall. Plus, she hadn't seen Jack Wexler once, which made her wonder if he'd limped back to New York in his shiny new hiking boots. *Good riddance*, she'd thought, with only a small pang of uneasy guilt. Back in July she'd noticed that his awful review had been taken down… Had someone complained or had he suffered a crisis of conscience? She didn't know, but she was glad it was gone.

And now it was fall, one of her favorite times of year, the sky a deep blue and the air crisp, the leaves turning orange and red and crunching underfoot. Really, life, overall, was pretty good… if only her business wasn't failing. If only she knew what to do about it.

As if on cue, her annoying little brother, who had known Miller's Mercantile was struggling for longer than Jenna had, sauntered through the front door of the store.

"Hey, sis." Zach gave her a lazy smile as he fished a pickle out of the barrel by the front door and bit into it with an audible and juicy crunch. "How's life? Haven't seen you in a few days," he remarked around a mouthful of pickle.

"Life is fine," Jenna replied, unable to keep a certain glumness from her tone.

Zach cocked his head. He was, Jenna knew, ridiculously good-looking, which had once made her—freckled, red-headed and slightly overweight—resent him, but she'd learned to if not love her body, then at least like it, and she no longer begrudged Zach his effortless boyband looks. "Life is fine, but...?" he prompted as he swallowed his bite of pickle, clearly clocking her sour emphasis.

"I'm going to have to close Miller's Mercantile by January if something doesn't change," she admitted reluctantly, bracing herself for his inevitable told-you-so, even if it was just in the form of a cocked eyebrow. "And no matter what you think, Zach," she couldn't help but add, "selling a few ridiculously priced candles is *not* going to fix things."

He took another bite of pickle, looking bemused. "That was never my suggestion, you know."

"I know," Jenna grumbled. "It was all artisan-this and fancy-that. Right?"

Zach shook his head slowly. "I still don't get your beef with quality." Jenna pressed her lips together rather than reply and he continued, his eyebrow now raised just as she knew it would be. "Is it really just because some rich jerk messed with your heart ten years ago?"

"And now I feel pathetic, so thank you for that," Jenna replied tartly. Her heartbreak summed up in one pithy sentence, so she felt like a teenaged girl who still couldn't get over her crush. "There might be a personal element," she conceded, "but it's also common sense. We don't get the tourists Litchfield does, we never have, so what's the point catering to them?" She'd had precious few gracing the store over what were meant to be the most touristy months of summer.

"*You* don't get the tourists," Zach corrected her, "because Miller's Mercantile looks like a cross between a goodwill donation center and a defunct Texaco."

Jenna flushed. There *was* an old gas pump in the parking lot that her parents had bought in the hopes it might be put to good use—it never was—and Jenna hadn't managed to get rid of it. It was kind of cool in a retro way, but it was also an eyesore and took up way too much space. As did the sagging sofa on the front porch that looked like a breeding ground for fleas. Zach had said he'd shift it for months, but Jenna had put him off, because she liked the idea of a sofa on the porch. Just not that one.

"Seriously, Jenna," Zach said, gentling his tone. "I really don't get it. Why are you so resistant to change? Any change?"

Jenna shook her head. "It's not worth going into now," she stated, "because I know I *have* to change if I want to keep this place open. Whether I'm resistant or not"—and she had been, she knew that full well—"something's got to give. I just need to figure out what—and how."

"And you don't want to go with my artisanal take?" Zach pressed, wiping his pickle-juiced hands on his well-worn jeans. "Inviting local artists and craftsmen? Having demonstrations, workshops..."

Jenna heard the enthusiasm in his voice, but she knew she didn't share it. "Zach, that sounds like something you could do with your furniture restoration business," she told him with a weary smile. "It would probably be amazing, but it's your thing, not mine. I don't need to piggyback on your dream." And the truth was, Zach's business was doing way better than hers, not that she was comparing them. Much, anyway. But far too often when cars pulled up to Miller's Mercantile, it was to go to Miller's Furniture Restoration, only six months old, in the barn behind. Jenna had lost count of the confused frowns and wrinkled brows of would-be customers stepping into the store and saying, "Sorry... I'm looking for the furniture place...?"

She'd learned to smile as she pointed them in the right direction.

"All right." Zach was, as ever, equable. "So what's *your* dream?"

It was a fair question, and one she didn't have an answer to. Once, she'd had dreams. Big, rosy, romantic dreams of finding that fairy-tale love and living in New York, having the career and the marriage and everything that came with it. All that had come crashing down around her. And yes, maybe it was pathetic to still feel bruised after *some guy messed with her heart* ten years ago. But it had *hurt*. And it had made her very reluctant to trust just about anyone—or anything—again. Too good to be true almost always *was*. Including artisanal workshops and expensive candles.

"My dream," Jenna told him in a tone that was meant to close down the conversation, "is to keep this place going, whatever it takes."

"Seriously, Jenna." Zach's expression had gone all soft and, Jenna feared, somewhat pitying, which she really could not stand. She was the older sister, the responsible one who had it all together. She definitely did not need her little brother feeling sorry for her. Ever.

"I am serious." She rose from behind the counter, grabbing a crate of bottles of laundry detergent she'd meant to stack earlier. "Just because you chased your dream of furniture restoration doesn't mean I have to follow suit. Leave it, Zach." Her voice held a note of warning, and thankfully Zach heeded it.

"Have you got plans tonight?" he asked instead. "There's a Scrabble tournament at Your Turn Next. It's also Nacho Night. Five-dollar cover and all the nachos you can eat. Maggie makes a mean salsa. Why don't you come along?"

Nachos and Scrabble. There could be worse things, Jenna reflected. A lot worse things. And, more because she didn't want Zach feeling sorry or, heaven help her, *worrying* about her rather than actually wanting her to go, she shrugged her assent. "Sure, I'll go. Why not?"

* * *

That evening, Jenna was strolling down Main Street, enjoying the September sunshine that set the lampposts afire as twilight began to darken the edges of the sky to violet. The leaves of the maples lining the street were tipped scarlet, and yet the air still held the drowsy warmth of summer. Jenna loved this time of year, when everything felt as if it were on the cusp; it reminded her of her school days, of sharpened pencils and fresh paper and a sense of optimistic possibility that in truth she couldn't remember feeling in a very long while.

She'd figure it out, she told herself, trying her best to hold on to that fragile, fleeting sense of optimism that the weather had given her. She'd find a way forward for Miller's Mercantile. Maybe more staples for the average townsperson, some extra decorations at Christmas, a section of prepared meals for the hurried homemaker, or...

Her mind sputtered out like a pickup truck on empty. She just couldn't think what else to do. She had tried various ideas over the years, admittedly in a cautious and hesitant way that hardly counted, but *still*.

Once she'd done a partnership with a deli in Torrington to provide readymade sandwiches, but they'd been so expensive and if no one bought them on the day, she'd had to throw them out or eat them herself—and the loss. She'd eaten way too many Italian subs and had gained ten pounds as an added kicker.

Experimenting could be expensive. And she'd long ago learned not to try to be something you're not, which was why she was so resistant to gussying up the mercantile like it was a Litchfield deli.

No, she'd have to think of something else... she just didn't know what yet.

Suppressing the sigh that came too readily to her lips, Jenna opened the door to Your Turn Next, surprised by just how many people were up for Scrabble and Nacho Night. Her friend Liz, who ran Midnight Fashion, Starr's Fall's premier—and only—fashion boutique, was there, already swilling what looked like a margarita. The boardgame café didn't have a liquor license but customers were allowed to bring their own, and Maggie generously didn't even charge a corkage fee. Liz looked like she'd made about four liters of margaritas, judging by the filled soda bottles on the floor next to her.

Annie was there too, with her boyfriend Mike, both of them taking up the whole of a three-seater sofa. Jenna also spied Joshua and Laurie, a couple so cute they surpassed nauseating and went straight to sublime. Jenna would have been envious except she was too happy for them—Laurie and Joshua had both suffered some seriously hard knocks in their lives, with Joshua's mother dying when he was a teen and Laurie growing up in foster care. How could anyone begrudge them their happiness?

Maggie's fifteen-year-old son Ben was hanging out with some of his friends from high school, including Bella Harper, whose parents Lizzy and Michael, new to the town a few years ago, ran the bakery The Rolling Pin. Jenna half-wondered if a romance might one day bloom there; love was in the air for lots of people, it seemed, just not for her.

"Hey, Jenna," Maggie greeted her warmly from behind the counter. "What can I get you? Latte, cappuccino, mocha...?"

"Margarita," Jenna decided. "If Liz is sharing."

"She certainly brought enough," Maggie replied with a

twinkle in her eye. Maggie was another person Jenna was glad to see so happy. She'd moved to Starr's Fall back in January, a year after she'd been widowed. She and her son Ben had so clearly been bruised by life, and it had been Jenna's own brother Zach, ten years younger than Maggie and a gamer like Ben, who had helped them to heal. Zach and Maggie had been a couple now for coming on three months, and they tended always to look very loved up.

But Jenna wasn't envious. Oh, no. She gave Maggie a quick smile before plopping down on the sofa next to Liz. Liz was divorced, happily bitter about it since her husband had run off with another woman and she'd lost their marital home to boot. She was also a wonderful gossip.

"Hey, Liz," Jenna greeted her. "Mind if I have some of that margarita?"

"Of course!" As ever, Liz sounded ebullient. "Small, medium, or large?"

"What do you think?"

Liz hooted as she reached for a big red plastic cup. "That kind of day?"

"That kind of life," Jenna replied before she could think better of it as Liz started to pour.

"Oh now, now, none of that," Liz admonished sternly as she handed Jenna a very full cup. "If women like us start in on the self-pity, there's no pulling us back from the brink."

Jenna paused mid-sip as she stared at Liz. *Women like us?* Liz was fifty-three. Jenna was thirty-nine, just last month. She'd had a birthday dinner at The Starr Light with Annie, Zach, Maggie, Laurie, and Joshua, and it had been very nice indeed. She might be getting older, but Jenna didn't like how Liz had just lumped them together like they were in a postmenopausal divorcee club together.

Was that how everyone in Starr's Fall saw her? Not that she minded being lumped with Liz, not exactly anyway. Liz was svelte, elegant, with diamonds or pearls always winking in her ears, her hair in a glossy silver bob. But still... Jenna wasn't quite there yet, was she?

"I didn't know you liked to play Scrabble," she remarked to Liz, in an effort to change the subject, as well as the nature of her thoughts.

"I don't," Liz replied blithely. "But there's a very eligible bachelor who likes to play, so I thought, why not?" She waggled her eyebrows as she gave a playful shrug.

A very eligible bachelor? Jenna felt that space between her shoulder blades prickle with suspicion. "And who might that be?" she asked in as neutral a tone as she could manage.

"His name is Jack Wexler and apparently he's good-looking *and* loaded," Liz replied with enthusiastic alacrity. She was always eager to dish the gossip, and this was clearly a motherload. "Made a fortune on Wall Street as a venture capitalist and then moved here."

Jenna made some sort of scoffing sound. "So what's he doing in Starr's Fall?" And why, she wondered, was she so surprised that Jack Wexler was still here? He'd said he'd *moved* here, after all. Just because she hadn't seen him didn't mean he'd disappeared. She'd just stupidly hoped he had.

Sort of, anyway, because the truth was, over the course of the summer Jenna had done a number of covert looks around whenever she'd been out and about in town, wondering if she'd glimpse those distinctive Nantucket Red khakis, that head of nut-brown hair. Not sure what she'd do or even how she'd feel if she did see him, but in any case, she never had.

"It's a nice place to retire to, I guess?" Liz replied with a shrug. "I haven't met him yet, but I'm hoping tonight's the night." She let out a hoot of laughter as she took another sip of her margarita.

"I've met Jack Wexler," Jenna told Liz, simply because she knew it was bound to come out at some point and she'd rather that she was the one to control the information.

"You have?" Liz's eyes rounded. "I have to say, he seems to be a very private man. I heard that he moved here in June, but no one seemed to see hide nor hair of him until last week, when he started coming in here to play Scrabble."

"Really?" He hadn't struck her as the Scrabble type, and she wondered if he'd gone away for the summer, after all.

"How did you meet him?" Liz asked.

"He came into Miller's Mercantile back in June." Jenna congratulated herself for not adding that he'd acted like a complete jerk.

"Oh, of *course*..." Understanding lit Liz's eyes. "*That* was Jack Wexler. Makes sense." Clearly she'd heard the gossip, which came as no surprise. "Not quite the place for smoked salmon, is it?" she remarked teasingly, which stupidly stung, just a little. Liz was only pointing out the obvious, but Jenna would have rather she phrased it differently, more along the lines of how Annie had reacted, thinking Jack Wexler was an idiot for wanting salmon in the first place. Not, of course, that there was anything wrong with wanting salmon... which maybe she should have considered when Jack Wexler had walked into her store asking for it.

Goodness, but she was feeling muddled about everything, and she'd only had one sip of margarita.

"So you think Jack Wexler is going to come tonight?" she asked Liz.

"Zach said he was. They've become buddies, apparently. Jack plays Scrabble with him."

Her brother played *Scrabble* with Jack Wexler? And hadn't

thought to mention it? Especially when she'd complained about Jack Wexler after their first interaction back in June? Although, come to think about it, that was probably why he hadn't mentioned it. In any case, after that showdown in The Starr Light, Jenna was pretty sure tongues had wagged for some time about the mysterious Jack Wexler and why he wasn't welcome. Zach probably hadn't mentioned it because he hadn't wanted to incur her ire. She could, Jenna knew, be a little grumpy sometimes, especially with her brother.

"Hmm," was all she said to Liz, and she took a large sip of margarita. She couldn't quite figure out how she felt about seeing Jack Wexler again. He probably wouldn't remember her, she told herself, even as she suspected he would. And would he be as rude as he had been before? Would *she*?

Whatever happened, it would be in front of half of Starr's Fall, which was a less than appealing prospect. She'd prefer her dramas play out privately, if they had to happen at all.

Maybe she'd ignore Jack Wexler, Jenna thought, only to realize that could come across as passive-aggressive. No, she'd take the high road, she decided, as she'd meant to when she'd first met him, and be perfectly polite, maybe even friendly, if she could manage it. She'd be friendly *first*, so he couldn't claim he'd been the one to extend an olive branch. Which was kind of a competitive way to think about it, but so what? She'd still be friendly.

Satisfied with this, Jenna sat back and took another sip of her margarita, only to nearly choke on it when she saw who was already walking through the door of the café. Wearing khakis, a pressed button-down shirt in Oxford blue under a gray fleece vest, it was Jack Wexler himself, in the flesh... looking as rich and privileged and *hot* as ever.

5

Jack eyed the crowd in the café warily; the last time he'd come in here it had just been Zach, and they'd played a very pleasant game of Scrabble. He wasn't sure how he felt about meeting what looked like half the population of Starr's Fall, but he'd promised Zach he would come, and the truth was, he was finally trying to make an effort to get to know people. Not that it was easy, or even that desired, at least not *all* the time, but three months on from his move, he was starting to feel a little... dare he admit it, he didn't want to, but *lonely*. He was actually lonely.

It had been a long, hard summer, starting with that stupid pepperoni pizza he never should have eaten, that had had him driving himself to the emergency room in Torrington at midnight, and then staying in the hospital for nearly a week with a bleeding ulcer. He'd spent the rest of the summer recuperating, barely venturing out besides visiting his mother, and meeting no one. So much for the brand-new life he'd hoped to make for himself here. Those three long summer months had given him plenty of opportunity to realize he needed to stop resisting these unwelcome changes to his life. To resolve to be different. This was his life now, whether he wanted it or not, and he needed to make the most of it.

"Jack!" Zach bounded up to him, reminding him of a golden retriever in human form, all shaggy hair and wide smile. Jack was grateful for the younger man's friendliness; he knew he hadn't been all that reciprocal, no matter that he *was* trying. Sort of.

"Hey, Zach," he greeted him.

Zach clapped him on the shoulder. "Glad you made it, dude."

"Yeah." Jack managed a smile as he felt all the curious gazes in the room fixedly trained on him. The good people of Starr's Fall were not subtle when it came to strangers, and even though he'd technically been living here for three months, he was still very much one. Maybe he always would be.

Zach rocked back on his heels as he gave him a considering look. "How are you feeling?"

In a weak moment last week, Jack had confessed some of his health troubles. "Yeah, I'm okay." There was, Jack feared, nothing more boring or pathetic than a middle-aged man detailing the woes of his digestive system. He had no intention of doing so ever again.

"Great." Zach seemed as willing to skip over the medical check as he was, and Jack could hardly blame him. "Who can I introduce you to?"

Reluctantly, Jack's gaze skimmed over the crowd as he did his best not to meet anyone's eye, before it came to a sudden screeching halt on an all-too-familiar face. Jenna Miller.

She'd been sipping her drink, but she stilled as he stared at her, unable to look away even though he wanted to. That woman had practically had him blackballed from town, all over that stupid review, which he'd taken down months ago, in a fit of admittedly uncharacteristic remorse. He didn't think he was a vindictive person, but she'd made him feel as if he was with the reply she'd written to his own review; every word seemed to vibrate with both fury and hurt.

Now he stared at her, taking in her hair, wild waves of auburn that tumbled halfway down her back. She had the same freckles he remembered—*why* he'd remembered, he had no idea—spattered across her nose and cheeks, and her hazel eyes were wide and clear, her gaze fixed on his. Her lips parted as she slowly lowered her cup.

Zach followed Jack's gaze and remarked, "I think you know my sister already, right?" There was a thread of laughter in his voice that suggested he knew about the whole Smoked Salmon Incident. Good grief, Jack regretted that whole episode, mainly because it had followed him like a bad smell.

Not that he'd been out all that much, but when he had, it had seemed as if everyone in this town had heard of it, and thought *he* was the ridiculous one for assuming Miller's Mercantile might stock smoked salmon, of all things. Jack didn't know if that reflected badly on him or on the store, but either way he wanted to move on. He had absolutely no desire to be the smoked salmon guy of Starr's Fall.

It was bad enough, he'd discovered, owning a Porsche in this place. That had been commented on just as much, so much so that he'd taken to parking it on the outskirts of town and walking in. Easier all around, even if it left him feeling disgusted—with himself. Why did he care what these backwoods hicks thought of him?

Except somehow he did. Sort of, anyway. And, to be fair, no one here was really a *hick*, despite his initial unfriendly assumptions.

"I didn't know she was your sister, but we have met briefly," Jack replied, tearing his gaze away from Jenna, and Zach chuckled all too knowingly.

Snowflakes Over Starr's Fall 49

"Maybe you need a proper introduction."

Somehow Jack found himself steered in Jenna's direction, and he was not a man who let himself be steered. He did the steering generally, quite forcefully too, but life had thrown him a serious curveball in the last six months, and now he found himself docilely following behind a guy, he had to be honest, he probably wouldn't have hired to work in his company's mailroom.

Jack stopped so he was standing right in front of Jenna, the whole café having fallen silent to witness this exchange. He might actually hate small-town life, Jack reflected as he gave Jenna a tense smile. She looked up at him, a small, answering smile playing about her mouth, her eyes glinting with humor as if she knew how uncomfortable this made him and was enjoying that fact. Of course she was. She was the one who was at home in this crowd, who knew everyone and called them friends, not him. Not remotely. Not yet, anyway.

"Nice to see you again," he forced out, sounding completely unenthused by the prospect, and Jenna let out a gurgle of skeptical laughter, her head cocked to one side so her hair flowed past her shoulder in a tumbled river of red-gold.

"Is it really?" she teased. At least she sounded friendly, but Jack still winced. Could they not put that one blasted conversation behind them? "I know we haven't met properly," she continued, "but I have a feeling you probably know my name."

"Jenna Miller," he duly acknowledged.

"And you're Jack Wexler." She cocked her head to the other side, pulling her hair around one shoulder as she smiled at him, her eyes glinting gold. She seemed far less shrew-like than he remembered, which was an uncomfortable realization. "Nice to see you again," she parroted, a laugh in her voice, with a look that felt like it was just for him, almost, but not quite, as if she were flirting. Still, despite that unsettling thought, Jack felt a pulse of relief go through him. *No drama here*, he wanted to tell all the folks with their necks craned and their eyes out on stalks. *Move along.*

"Nice to see you again," he said, stupidly for a second time, like he was a robot who had one dialogue setting, and then he gave a nod and started to turn away. Job done.

"*I* haven't met you," the woman sitting next to Jenna remarked in a strident tone as Jack reluctantly turned back around. "Liz Cranbury. I run Midnight Fashion, the ladies' boutique in town." She held out a slender, well-manicured hand as she fixed him with a disconcertingly beady eye beneath a sleek silver bob.

"Jack Wexler," he said, dutifully taking her hand. "Nice to meet you."

"Would you like a margarita?" she asked, nodding to a soda bottle filled with a lurid red liquid on the floor next to her. It looked like something you'd see at a frat party and choose *not* to drink.

"I'm very tempted"—he was not—"but unfortunately I'm on a strict no-alcohol diet," he told her, wishing he didn't sound so tediously boring. "Sorry."

Jenna, he felt, was still watching him, although he wasn't willing to risk looking at her again. He moved along, murmuring a few random hellos aimed at no one in particular before he headed back to the coffee bar, where Maggie, whom he'd met a few times now and found reassuringly friendly and normal, gave him a sympathetic smile.

"Starr's Fall can sometimes feel a little like a lion's den," she murmured. "But you just ran the gauntlet, so good job. Peppermint tea?"

He nodded in relief. "Thanks, Maggie." He rested one elbow on the counter as he surveyed the scene from a comforting distance. Thankfully, the excitement of his entrance had abated, and everyone was back to chatting, with only the occasional, half-interested look thrown his way, almost in dismissal.

Jack exhaled slowly. It had been a long time since he'd been in any kind of social situation, and he felt both uneasy and awkward, sensations that he was not accustomed to. Back in his old job, his old *life*, whenever he'd come into a room, he'd commanded it. He hadn't bothered with small talk because time was money, and he was making a lot of it... and everyone who mattered had known that.

But all that was gone, and he had to figure out who he was without it... if anything. Sometimes he felt like a cipher, an emptiness inside him like a whistling wind and nothing more. It was not a good feeling.

"Hey."

Jack turned, blinking in surprise to see Jenna standing next to him, brushing a strand of wavy auburn hair out of her eyes as she gave him what looked like a sheepish smile.

"I just wanted to apologize properly," she told him frankly, her tone friendly but also resolute, like this was something on her to-do list she needed to get out of the way so she could move on with the better things in life. "For our... interaction... back in June. I was a little snippy then and I'm sorry for it."

"Apology accepted," Jack replied stiffly. He could feel all the eyes in the room on them, avidly. "I, ah, wasn't the friendliest person myself, in that situation."

"Well, I guess you really wanted smoked salmon," she replied with a wry smile, and he forced a smile in return, although in truth everything about that interaction—and the frustration he'd felt since for this new, unwelcome life of his—still chafed. He'd felt it particularly that morning back in June, when he'd read the news right before heading into her store and seen just how much

Wall Street had moved on without him. Adam Lassiter, the new CEO of Wexler Capital, had been hailed as a hero, and the name of the firm changed to Legend Investments, which was so stupid and basic and completely erased him from the firm he'd founded. It had smarted, a lot, and he'd let that anger and hurt carry him into the store and his stupid spat about smoked salmon.

He wasn't about to explain any of that to this woman, though. Let her think he was just a jerk who'd wanted a particular product. Who cared?

"Something like that," he agreed neutrally.

"Did you ever find any in Litchfield?" she asked, and Jack wondered why on earth they were *still* talking about smoked salmon.

"No." He paused and then admitted with deep reluctance, "The truth is, I've been out of action for most of the summer." He gave her a tight smile and in answer to her obvious confusion, explained, "I ended up needing surgery for a bleeding ulcer. Trying to avoid going down that route again, so I'm being very careful." He looked away, embarrassed that he'd mentioned it, *again*. Good grief, he was sounding so very tedious. He needed to get some hobbies. Some *more* hobbies, since playing Scrabble had become one, mainly by default, because it felt like there was so little he could do these days. That needed to change.

"I'm sorry to hear that," Jenna replied, sounding genuinely contrite. "That sounds painful."

It had been excruciating, but as he really didn't want to talk about it, he just shrugged. "Water under the bridge, anyway, in regard to that episode?" he asked. "I'd love it if the residents of Starr's Fall could conveniently forget all about it, but I have the sense that isn't going to happen, at least not anytime soon. They all seem to possess the memory of an elephant."

Jenna chuckled, and Jack found he liked the sound of her laughter, rich and throaty. "You're right there," she agreed. "This town doesn't forget *anything*." A small sigh escaped her as she looked around. "I love everyone here to pieces and they all have hearts of gold, but sometimes it can feel a little... suffocating."

Curious, Jack shifted his stance to move a little closer to her. "You lived here your whole life?"

Jenna nodded. "Bar three years in the city—first San Francisco, then New York. I worked in marketing." She made a face. "Not that you'd know it."

He cocked his head. "Why wouldn't I?"

She shrugged, the collar of her sweater sliding over one freckled shoulder. She was wearing as colorful an ensemble as she had the first time he'd met her—a rainbow patchwork skirt that swept the floor paired with chunky hiking boots with bright red laces and an oversized cable-knit sweater that looked as if it had belonged to a fisherman about fifty years ago. A very large fisherman.

"Just that if I had a better head for it, Miller's Mercantile might be doing better than it is."

Jack wasn't surprised the store was struggling, considering what a dump it had looked like when he'd walked in there, but he was surprised that Jenna had admitted it. She seemed like the prickly, proud, and yes, a little shrewish type... At least she *had*. He didn't know what to think of her anymore.

"Anyway," she said quickly, and he could tell she wanted to move past that admission, which he suspected she hadn't meant to make. "What brought you to Starr's Fall?"

"Retirement," he replied succinctly, and her eyes widened in surprise, because hopefully he didn't look *that* old. "Health reasons forced my hand, unfortunately." Here he was, talking about his health problems again. Someone shut him up, *please*.

She nodded her semi-sympathetic understanding, her eyes still bright with curiosity and something that almost looked like confusion. "And you picked Starr's Fall because...?" she prompted, with a lilt of incredulity in her voice that annoyed him. Was it so strange that he'd come to this place? Was he *that* much of a city slicker?

He thought of his mother, whom he'd seen that morning. She'd been sitting by the window, a blanket over her bony knees, her hair, once so perfectly styled, in flyaway wisps about her wrinkled face. She'd called him Frank. He wasn't about to go into any of that with this woman. "It was convenient."

Jenna let out a laugh, the sound even more disbelieving. "I don't know anyone who thinks Starr's Fall is convenient. Not anyone who's lived here, anyway." She eyed him consideringly, as if she suspected he was lying, and Jack felt his body tense, his hands begin to curl into fists. With effort, he kept them flat and loose.

"Well, it's convenient to me," he replied shortly, and then cursed himself for yet again sounding like a jerk. Jenna was just being friendly, and maybe a little bit nosy, but he knew he was overreacting. Even so, he was not about to explain why he'd moved here to Jenna Miller, with all the emotion that entailed. They might have made up, but they weren't *friends*. Not even close, especially the way she was acting now, all snottily superior, because she was a Starr's Fall old-timer and he wasn't. At least, that was what it felt like.

"Surprisingly so, I think," she replied with a new coolness to her voice. "For such a city slicker like yourself." There was the faintest hint of a sneer to her voice, and mentally Jack shook his head. Had he actually been starting to think this woman was nice? For a little while there, it had almost seemed as if they could get along, which meant it was time for a reality check.

"So what are you going to do about your store?" he asked, sounding, he knew, a little aggressive, and Jenna jerked back.

"Excuse me?"

Jack shrugged. She'd touched too many raw nerves in the last few minutes, and when that happened he went on the attack. It felt good, in a way, almost the way he used to feel when he was closing a deal—that surge of adrenaline, the thrill of satisfaction. He was in control again. "You said it yourself," he reminded her. "That it wasn't doing great."

"I said it could be doing better than it is," Jenna corrected quickly, an edge entering her voice. "As just about any business could, I might point out."

Jack let out a scoffing laugh that put her back right up, he could tell, and perversely he was glad. "Come on. That place? Smoked salmon aside, it looked like it was on its last gasp. When's the last time you turned a profit—2005?"

All right, that might have been a *little* harsh, even if it seemed like it was pretty much true.

Jenna's eyes narrowed to golden-green slits. "And here I was, thinking you might be an okay kind of guy, since you took down that review—"

"I took down that review because you were trash-talking me all around town," he cut her off, and then added, an edge entering *his* voice, "And for no other reason."

She let out a huff of hard laughter, her eyes sparking with what Jack suspected was genuine hurt. "Noted," she bit out. "Thanks for the clarification."

"You're welcome." He sounded as sarcastic as he felt. They glared at each other for a full five seconds, while the whole room seemed to melt away, and there was nothing but Jenna Miller and her fury-filled eyes, that stupid sweater *still* sliding off one shoulder.

Then, with a choking sound as she suppressed whatever she'd been tempted to throw at him, she stormed off, back to the sofa, where Liz What's-Her-Name had been, Jack feared, watching their whole exchange with an unbecoming avidity.

Okay, he really did hate small-town life, if this is what it was. He turned back to the counter to find Maggie giving him a commiserating smile.

"Jenna's... passionate," she remarked diplomatically, and Jack's mind immediately filled with the kind of images Maggie was definitely *not* talking about. What was *wrong* with him? "Here's your tea," she added, proffering a mug.

"Thanks," Jack bit out, and then, realizing how ungracious he sounded, he gave her a shamefaced smile. "Sorry."

Maggie gave a small, wry laugh. "Don't apologize to me, Jack," she told him. "I'm on your side. Everyone here is lovely, whether you believe it or not, but small-town life definitely takes some getting used to."

It certainly did, Jack thought grimly. The question was, did he even want to get used to it?

6

Jenna flung herself on the sofa next to Liz, her heart thundering, her hands clenched into fists. Okay, Jack Wexler was just as much of a jerk as she'd first thought he was. No, *more*. How dare he tell her that her store was on its last gasp, even if it was? And that stupid barb about 2005?

"Well, well, well," Liz remarked. "What was all that about?"

Jenna had to take several deep breaths before she could make herself reply. "I was trying to offer an olive branch to that man but next time I won't even bother," she said tersely. Not that there would even be a next time. She'd make sure there wasn't.

"Oh, really?" Liz took a sip of her second margarita, looking amused. "From over here it looked like you two were flirting."

"*What?*" Jenna felt a full-body flush sweep over her in a tide of heat as she shook her head so violently her ears almost rang. "Absolutely not."

Liz's smile was teasing as she lowered her glass. "Are you sure about that?"

"Of course I'm sure!" Jenna replied indignantly. "He insulted me and Miller's Mercantile again. The guy is a complete *ass*." Her voice rang out a little too loudly and with a pang of unease, Jenna wondered if Jack could overhear her. Well, who cared? He deserved to be called every insult she could think of.

"So the lady doth not protest too much?" Liz quipped. "Good, because then I might have a chance."

"You want to date Jack Wexler after what you've seen of him?" Jenna demanded. Not to mention that Liz had to be ten years older than Jack, although Jenna supposed that didn't matter too much. Maggie was ten years older than Zach, and they were certainly making it work. But the thought of Liz and Jack dating... well, she didn't like it, for some reason.

"I certainly want to get to know him better," Liz replied equably. "He's uber rich, good-looking, dresses well, and doesn't seem to me to be as rude as you think he is. He came over here to introduce himself, after all, and I thought he seemed pretty friendly, in a reserved kind of way."

"Hmph." Jenna reached for her empty margarita glass and thrust it at Liz for a refill. She was not going to say anything more about Jack Wexler. She wasn't even going to think about him.

Liz laughed as she poured Jenna some more margarita. "The look on your face!" she exclaimed. "What can I tell you, the sparks were definitely flying over there when you two were chatting. But as long as you're sure you're not interested..."

"Trust me," Jenna interjected darkly, "I am *not* interested." She glanced back at Jack, intending to give him a full-on glare, but he was talking to Maggie and not looking at her, which was, perversely, aggravating. Never mind. She really wasn't going to think about him.

"Aren't we meant to be playing Scrabble?" she asked Liz, a little peevishly. "And having nachos?"

"Suit yourself," Liz replied. "I'm just enjoying watching the world go around."

Jenna suppressed a groan as Liz trained her gaze on Jack, who was leaning against the counter, smiling at something Maggie had just said. When he smiled, Jenna couldn't help but notice, he looked different. Lighter, the lines of care drawn from nose to mouth and fanning out from his eyes had softened. How old was he, she wondered. Forty? Forty-five? Not any older than that, surely. He certainly looked fit enough, even if he'd been ill. She could see the bulge of the bicep of the arm he had braced against the counter, the sleeves of his button-down shirt rolled up over strong forearms. Not that she was looking, of course. He'd just caught her eye.

"Well, I'm going to play Scrabble," she declared, and got up to find a board.

Most of the people there, she realized as she took a Scrabble box from the shelves lining one wall, did *not* seem to be there to play Scrabble, or any other game. They were happily chatting and laughing as the first platter of cheesy, jalapeno-scattered nachos came out, ignoring the boxes of Scrabble lying about.

Resolutely, Jenna took herself off to a table for two in the far corner and started setting up the board. She'd play by herself if she had to, but she had no intention of fanning the flames of speculation when it came to Jack Wexler, by chatting about him or to him. Definitely not to him.

"Ah, are you playing?"

Jenna looked up, having just put seven tiles on her rack, to see Starr's Fall's unofficial matriarch Henrietta Starr standing imperiously in front of her, her gnarled hands clasped on the head of an ivory-topped cane of burnished mahogany. "It appears that you might be the only one," the elderly woman quipped with a small, shrewd smile. "Do you have a partner?"

Jenna gestured to the seat across from her. "You're welcome to join me."

"Thank you," Henrietta replied with gracious hauteur, and she perched on the chair, her back ramrod straight, her ankles neatly crossed, her eyes seeming icy-blue—the same shade as Jack's, almost, Jenna couldn't help but notice—in her wrinkled face.

Jenna knew Henrietta Starr more by sight than any interaction she'd had with her over the years. The old lady had been more or less housebound for decades, although Jenna could still remember when she'd been a little kid, and Henrietta had appeared, dressed magnificently in belted suits with narrow skirts and padded shoulders, a fox-fur stole draped over the ensemble, to cut a ribbon or judge a contest on the town green. There had always been something commanding and frankly a little intimidating about the woman, and there still was, even though she had to be over ninety, and now looked tiny and wrinkled and alarmingly fragile. The fire in her eyes, that sense of remote confidence, remained the same.

"Do you play Scrabble very much?" she asked as Henrietta laid her cane to one side before taking her own tiles.

"I have in the past," she replied with dignity. "And Maggie, the proprietress of this establishment, plays with me on occasion. We're both equally terrible." A smile split her face like a crack in a plate and Jenna found herself smiling back. "Poor Maggie thought I believed myself to be a champion, but trust me, my dear, I am well aware that my better days are far, far behind me."

"Well, it's a relief to hear about your Scrabble-playing abilities," Jenna told her, "because I'm probably equally terrible."

"You run Miller's Mercantile, don't you?" Henrietta remarked as she carefully arranged her tiles. "I remember when your parents bought that old place. It must have been forty years ago now."

"Forty-two," Jenna confirmed with a small smile. She realized she was a little curious as to what Henrietta Starr had made of her parents—Dave and Polly Miller had been only twenty-seven when they'd bought the falling-down farmhouse that had become the general store. They'd been hippies twenty years too late, with chickens wandering through the kitchen and cannabis smoke wafting through the air, or something like that judging from the stories they'd told.

By the time Jenna had come along they'd cleaned up their act a little, but the store had remained the lovably ramshackle place it had always been and that Jenna was reluctant to change... even though her parents had been happy enough to leave it—and her and Zach—behind and embrace their new retired life in Florida, something Jenna found unsurprising considering their history but still managed to hurt. *Children* were supposed to be the ones who blithely flew the nest, who forgot to call home, who guiltily sent a card several weeks past a birthday, *not* the parents, and they hadn't even sent a card, anyway. Her mother had left a voicemail.

"How time flies," Henrietta replied dryly, "except when it drags."

Jenna smiled in rueful acknowledgment at that. She imagined time might drag a little for a woman who was mostly housebound, waiting out her years alone. She knew Laurie visited her, which was very good of her friend. Maybe she should, too.

"All right," she said cheerfully as she glanced down at her tiles. "Let's see how good you are."

"I told you I was dreadful," Henrietta replied imperturbably. "Are you still running that store?"

Jenna glanced up. "Yes," she replied frankly, "or trying to." Somehow it was easier to talk honestly to the no-nonsense Henrietta Starr than it was to the obnoxious Jack Wexler. She could admit her struggles to Henrietta more than that smirking man.

"I'm afraid I don't shop there anymore," Henrietta told her matter-of-factly, without so much as a hint of apology. "It's too far out of town for me to walk."

"I think you do shop there, actually," Jenna replied with a small smile. "Doesn't Laurie Ellis do some shopping for you?" She knew Laurie dropped by the mercantile once a week at least, to pick up a few cans of soup and other staples for Henrietta.

Henrietta drew back, looking startled. "Is that where she gets my shopping?" she exclaimed. "Well, then, let me tell you, dear, you could do with a little more variety in your merchandise, and in particular, your soup."

"Oh?" Zach had complained about such things before, and it had rankled Jenna considerably, but somehow she couldn't be offended when Henrietta said it, maybe because she recognized something of herself in Henrietta—or more aptly, Henrietta in herself. They were both plain-talking, independent people—and she'd probably end up an old spinster too, Jenna thought on something of a sigh. For some reason, her glance moved back to Jack; he was chatting to Zach now, looking serious as he swept his hair back from his eyes with one long-fingered hand. Resolutely she turned back to her companion. "I'll keep that in mind," she promised. "What kinds of soup would you suggest?"

"Something with a little *heft* to it," Henrietta replied with feeling. "If all you're eating is soup, you want it to feel like a meal."

"That's certainly understandable," Jenna replied with a smile. "I'll see what I can do."

"Good," Henrietta replied tartly, and then turned to her tiles.

More varieties of soup, Jenna reflected wryly as her partner began to lay her tiles on the board. Somehow she didn't think that was going to be nearly enough to save her store.

* * *

A week passed with Jenna coming up with no new ideas, at least none that she felt had any traction. She considered turning part of the store into a café, but she feared she was too far out of town to get the necessary foot traffic, and there were several coffee places already—besides the boardgame café, Laurie's pet shop and bakery, and also Joshua's bookshop all offered coffee. The Rolling Pin, too, had an espresso machine up and running. For a town the size of Starr's Fall, there were certainly quite a few coffee options.

Then she'd considered turning over a section of the store to home goods—blankets and pillows and the odd chair, maybe, but didn't people just get that kind of stuff online? She already had a hardware section that got a little business, although not really enough to justify it.

The trouble was, Jenna didn't actually *know* what the good people of Starr's Fall wanted in a general store, besides Henrietta Starr wanting some hefty soup, anyway, and in her heart of hearts she was afraid that Miller's Mercantile might have already had its heyday. People liked the convenience of the big Stop & Shop in Torrington, where you could get everything you wanted and more under one roof. Miller's Mercantile was never going to be that, but what *could* it be?

She still had no idea.

Jenna was trying not to feel too glum as she walked into town one cool evening in late September, the sky violet and starry, the crispness in the air reminding her that it was almost October. It was the night of the Starr's Fall Business Association's monthly meeting, an occasion Jenna usually enjoyed but which she was now semi-dreading, because someone was certain to ask how the mercantile was going, and admitting failure was not a pleasant thing to do.

The church basement where they had the meeting was already bustling when Jenna walked in five minutes early. Laurie was there, chatting with Michael Harper, Lizzy's husband, who was co-chair this year, and Zoe, the twenty-something who ran the town's only ice cream parlor, The Latest Scoop, was laughing with Liz Cranbury, while Maggie and Zach slid into chairs at one end.

The Business Association had been a ladies-only event for years before Joshua Reed had finally joined last year, giving up his ensconced curmudgeonly status as the town's bachelor bookstore owner—Laurie had helped with that—and then just a few months later, her brother Zach had rocked up, the proud new proprietor of Miller's Furniture Restoration. Michael Harper had joined his wife in chairing, and while Jenna was glad the men had joined, both for their sakes as well as that of the association, she missed the girls-only vibe; plus, as everyone knew, she didn't like change.

When was she going to start embracing it? Maybe not until she was forced to turn the "closed" sign on the mercantile—forever.

"Hey, Jenna," Zoe called over to her, flicking her bright pink hair out of her eyes. Zoe was twenty-eight and, at least to Jenna, impossibly cool. She wished she could be the kind of person to rock pink hair and a nose ring, but she just wasn't, and she'd come to accept that. Still, every time she caught sight of Zoe with her laid-back, uber-confident attitude, Jenna felt a little pang... of something. Not strong enough to be actual envy, but definitely something. Maybe it was just getting older. She would be forty in less than a year, and there was no escaping that, or how she'd wished her life had turned out a little differently by this point. It was what it was, Jenna told herself as she steeled her spine. No use being sorry about it. As Liz said, self-pity wasn't a good look on a woman her age... or to be fair, on anyone.

"Hey, Zoe," she called back with a smile, and then greeted the others around the table. Annie was usually in attendance but had been missing the last few to spend time with her mom. Still, it was a good showing. Just as Lizzy Harper, the new chair, came to the head of the table to start them off, Rhonda breezed in with a cocky grin for everyone as she plopped herself down at the end, fanning her face.

"I power walked here and I'm a little hot," she explained cheerfully. "Also I was checking out the nice set of wheels parked in front of the church." She let out a wheezing cough. "*Someone* won the lottery."

Nice set of wheels? Alarm pinged through Jenna as Lizzy banged the gavel to call them to order. There was only one person in Starr's Fall who had a car that answered to that description, and he had no business being here...

"Meeting come to order!" Michael called cheerfully. Jenna had been the Business Association's chair last year, but over the summer it had moved to Lizzy and Michael, and Jenna had told herself she was glad. She didn't need the extra hassle of running Starr's Fall's sometimes-struggling association, but as Michael banged the gavel again, clearly enjoying the mini power trip, something in her chafed, just a little bit. She was used to being in charge, but it was just as well she wasn't, she told herself, as she needed to focus on her own business.

"All right, ladies and gentlemen, let's get started," Michael began. "Tonight we need to discuss the Fall Festival next week, then we've got Winter Wonderland to organize in December, plus the continuing issue with the streetlights, and any ideas we might have to beautify our lovely Main Street, including the empty storefronts."

He paused, looking around the table with eyes that were bright with enthusiasm. "Now, before we begin with all that... I'm thrilled to say we have someone new joining us today, to act as a consultant to the association. He comes with plenty of experience and wisdom from working on Wall Street for twenty years, starting his own venture capital firm, investing in new and innovative technologies and businesses, *and* he lives right here in Starr's Fall! I'm sure everyone will be thrilled to welcome..." He paused to take a breath, and Jenna tensed instinctively, because she just *knew* what was coming next... "*Jack Wexler* to our group!"

Then, like he was a celebrity arriving on a talk show, Jack strolled in from the hallway, giving everyone a lazy wave before he joined Michael at the head of the table, looking relaxed and assured in a crisp white button-down shirt, open at the throat, and well-ironed khakis. The Rolex Jenna had seen before glinted on one wrist, and as he leaned back in his folding chair and crossed his legs, Jenna saw he was wearing designer loafers of what looked like Italian leather with no socks.

Such a rich guy cliché, she thought, her lip curling before she made herself iron out her expression to something approaching neutrality. So Jack Wexler was going to advise all the residents of Starr's Fall how to operate their businesses. Great. Just what she needed right now.

Her lip curling again, Jenna folded her arms, sat back in her seat, and waited for what *wisdom* Jack Wexler would no doubt smirkingly impart.

7

Jenna Miller had an expression on her face that would curdle milk—lip curled, eyes narrowed, arms folded, head cocked to one side like she was seriously skeptical about anything he might say before he'd even spoken. Jack kept his expression friendly and relaxed as he flicked his gaze away from her. Lizzy Harper had invited him to this meeting, and he was going to do his utmost to be helpful to those attending, no matter what Jenna Miller thought about it.

Admittedly, he'd been reluctant when Michael had first floated the idea to him, at the boardgame evening last week. "We could really use an injection of energy into our little group," he'd told him with enthusiasm. "And as someone with so much experience..."

Not that he'd even talked up his experience. He'd asked him what he'd done before moving to Starr's Fall, and he'd told him, end of. When Michael had, with obvious interest, pressed for more information, Jack had given it to him—just the facts, no humble (or otherwise) bragging. And when he'd practically begged him to come to their little Business Association meeting, he'd agreed, because it seemed rude not to and, the truth was, he was going a little crazy with the boredom and isolation.

He should have realized Jenna Miller would be here... and looking like she was spitting nails.

"Jack...?" Michael prompted, and belatedly he realized he was supposed to speak. Michael seemed to be waiting for him to impart some serious pearls of wisdom, like he had the magic formula for financial success in his back pocket. And once he might have, but now, stupidly, considering the way Michael had just bigged him up—and he hadn't even mentioned all his accomplishments—he felt nervous. That, he suspected, was down to Jenna and the look on her face.

Jack gave the room a friendly smile, making sure his gaze skimmed right over the woman glaring at him from the back right of the table.

"Before I say anything myself," he told them all, "I'd love to hear from you, and what your experiences have been, operating a small business in Starr's Fall. What are the advantages, the challenges?" He raised his eyebrows, smile still in place, although he could *feel* Jenna fuming. "What excites you about having a business here, and what worries or even frightens you? What's happened in the past, and what is your vision for the future?" He could feel himself getting into the rhythm of what he was saying, his voice falling into that upbeat and confidently coaxing tone that had won over so many would-be investors. It felt good, getting back into it, even if he was just advising a bunch of small fish in a very small pond.

How the mighty have fallen.

He could imagine Alex, his old nemesis from Axios Investments, snickering at the sight of him sitting here, like he was at the head of an important board meeting in some gleaming tower on Wall Street, instead of in a church basement that smelled like gym socks and stale coffee.

Never mind. These were, he'd discovered over the last few weeks, kindhearted and decent people—at least bar one, who was now openly scowling at him. He almost felt like telling her to be careful, because her face might freeze that way. He could imagine his mom saying that to him once upon a time, a thought that made him ache with sorrow and so he pushed it away.

"Anyone?"

"An advantage is definitely the community here," Laurie volunteered with a warm smile for the whole group. "I moved here a year ago, totally on my own, and everyone was incredibly welcoming and supportive. The number of people who turned up for my grand opening..." Her eyes brightened with emotion as she looked around at everyone assembled. "It still makes me choke up. People *want* businesses here to succeed—"

"Well, save that adults-only store that guy from Torrington tried to open, next to where that new pizza place is," Rhonda chimed in darkly. "We didn't want that kind of thing going on here, let me tell you. He was selling VHS tapes out of his trunk in the parking lot before we had him move on." She dropped her voice to a conspiratorial whisper as she explained to Jack, "We had Mike, the town mechanic, give him a friendly nudge. If you've ever seen Mike, you'd know how that went."

"All right," Jack replied, both startled and amused and trying to hide both emotions. "Thank you."

"Rhonda, that was twenty-five years ago," Liz interjected good-naturedly. She turned to Jack with a smile. "I didn't even live here then, but I know that nothing like that has happened since." She tucked her silver hair behind her ears. "But I agree with Laurie. The community here is great in terms of support. But..." She hesitated, glancing around at everyone almost in apology. "Sometimes people can be a little stuck in their ways. I get it, because no one wants Starr's Fall to change—"

"Except we want the empty storefronts to be filled," a young woman with a shock of bright pink hair chipped in. "Not all of us are against change, Liz."

Jack saw the pink-haired woman give Jenna a friendly but rather pointed smile, and he realized that there was history here. History he must have accidentally stumbled into when he'd walked into Miller's Mercantile.

"I know that," Liz replied, also with a glance at Jenna, "but pretty much everyone in Starr's Fall likes tradition. There's the way things have always been done, and that's just accepted and not to be discussed." She gave a little shrug. "I've been here for over twenty years, and I still feel like a newbie sometimes. What about you, Michael? You and Lizzy have only been here a couple of years. Do you feel like that?"

"In some ways, yes," Michael replied. Jack knew he and his wife ran The Rolling Pin, which was a much more upmarket establishment than Miller's Mercantile and seemed to do a fairly brisk trade in baked goods and coffees. Jack thought there were some ways in which they could expand, but he hadn't shared them with the Harpers yet. "Certainly there's a protocol in place for a lot of things," Michael continued. "The first time Lizzy and I judged the cake walk we didn't rig the music right, and we got an earful."

Laurie laughed. "I remember Jenna telling me about that." She glanced at Jenna, eyebrows raised, smile still in place. "Jenna, what do you think? You've been in Starr's Fall longer than any of us here, except for Rhonda and Annie." She turned to Jack. "Annie Lyman's a lifer, too, but she's not here tonight."

Jack nodded, waiting for his nemesis to speak. Jenna looked like she was chewing her tongue, no doubt in an effort to keep from spitting out something snarky about him. Jack found he enjoyed her fluster.

"Yes, Jenna," he chimed in, all solicitude. "I'd love to know what you think." He smiled as he met her narrowed gaze with a deliberately pleasant one of his own, suspecting it would annoy her more.

"What I think?" Jenna finally said, unfolding her arms and sitting up straighter. "I think we don't need some New York hotshot telling us how to turn Starr's Fall into something it's not and never will—or should—be."

Her words landed with a figurative splat, making everyone blink and recoil, just a little. She'd spoken flatly, without any overt hostility, but she'd definitely soured the mood, and, Jack saw, she realized it, shifting in her seat as color came into her face and she glanced away. Jack almost felt sorry for her. Almost, but not quite.

"Oh, come on, Jenna," Michael finally said in a jovial, cajoling kind of voice. "I think we could certainly take some advice, at least."

"And what kind of advice does Jack Wexler want to give?" Jenna asked with acid sweetness. She turned back to face him. "I'd love to hear it."

"Before I give any advice," Jack replied, instinctively mimicking her pseudo-sweet tone, "I'd love to hear from *you*. What challenges do you face with Miller's Mercantile?" He kept her gaze as her face flared redder and her beady gaze turned into a full-on glare. Jack waited. Maybe he shouldn't be, but he found he was enjoying putting her on the spot.

* * *

Jenna shifted in her chair, willing the flush she could feel scorching her face to die down. Of course Jack was enjoying tormenting her like this. She could see it from the way his mouth kicked up at one corner, in a telling smirk. He was going to make her squirm... but she wouldn't let him.

"Well, like everyone else, I face all the challenges of a twenty-first-century world with everything available online," she stated evenly as she kept his ice-blue gaze. "These days it seems like people want things to be cheap, convenient, and quick, and I'm not sure Miller's Mercantile can be all three, although I have always tried to keep the prices low. You might not know it, Jack," she continued conversationally, "but over 10 percent of the residents in this part of Connecticut are living below the poverty line, and another 10 percent are hovering around it. Admittedly, we have our fair share of ex-urbanites and celebrities who come here for a taste of rural life, rocketing around the countryside in their Porsches and Beamers, but the average resident is struggling to make ends meet, and so my store, shabby though it might seem, reflects that."

She stared at him, and he stared back, a glint of something that almost seemed like admiration but was probably just amusement in his eyes. For a long moment no one spoke, and Jenna could feel the curious gazes of every single person in that basement boring into her as they watched her and Jack's exchange like it was a tense tennis match.

"Fair enough," he finally replied equably, "but then you're only catering to 20 percent of the population, and as you are running a business, not a food bank, you might want to think about the other 80 percent, if you'd like to stay afloat. What do *they* want? How can you make Miller's Mercantile appealing to all, or at least most, of the residents of Starr's Fall and the surrounding area?"

"If I knew the answer to that question," Jenna returned tartly, goaded into it and wishing she wasn't, "I would be doing it. Obviously." And if that was all the advice he had, it wasn't very helpful.

"I think we're all wanting the answer to that question," Michael interjected with a rueful laugh. "We're all struggling, one way or another. Times are hard, and like Jenna said, people don't have a lot of extra money to spend. We need to give them a reason to come to Starr's Fall in the first place and spend money here, not just in one place, but all over."

"Which requires working together, to make sure Starr's Fall as a place is an appealing shopping proposition," Jack agreed. "From what I've seen on the Main Street, there are some great novelty stores—the boardgame café and the pet store and bakery in particular are out of the realm of the ordinary, certainly." He smiled at both Laurie and Maggie in what Jenna expected was an attempt to show he didn't mean it as a criticism. "Most people will travel some distance for a novelty store," he continued. "But it helps to have some anchors in place, as well." He glanced around the room. "Have you ever been to a quaint little town that's *all* antique stores and kitschy boutiques, but no pharmacies or hardwares? If you don't like the kitschy stuff, there's nothing for you there, and that's the kind of situation you want to avoid in Starr's Fall. You want to make sure there's something for everyone on the Main Street, including covering the essentials, like with Miller's Mercantile, for all demographics."

"But that's what I've been *doing*," Jenna burst out, frustrated now. He was reading from her hymn sheet like it was rocket science and he was the only one who understood it. "I've kept a firm commitment to the basics, and that hasn't been working all that well." She glared at him like it was his fault, but he just smiled.

"So maybe you need to re-evaluate what that firm commitment looks like," he suggested.

"You think?" Jenna shook her head, annoyed as well as exasperated. "Well, if you have any bright ideas, do let me know."

She'd meant it as a put down, but Jack surprised—and aggravated—her by saying in that same pleasant voice, "Actually, I do have some ideas. But we don't need to take up the Business Association's time by going through them. Why don't we talk after the meeting?"

Jenna stared at him for a full five seconds before she finally managed a jerky nod. "Fine," she said, and then grudgingly added a very belated, "Thank you," simply because it seemed expected.

Michael took back control of the meeting and as they started talking about next week's Fall Festival as well as making plans for the Winter Wonderland Weekend in December, Jenna wondered what kind of advice Jack Wexler was going to give her. Would he be all condescending, telling her how to run the store his way, which might work in Manhattan but not in small-town Connecticut? The prospect was already making her grit her teeth, but, Jenna acknowledged, he *had* had a lot of success in business, and she was getting desperate, so… maybe she should keep a semi-open mind. She'd listen to him, anyway, even if she suspected she wouldn't want to hear his advice.

Sure enough, as the meeting broke up an hour later after tabling further discussion about the Winter Wonderland Weekend to next month, Jack ambled up to her, all relaxed ease and careless confidence, which set Jenna's teeth on edge before he'd even spoken.

If he really had run his own venture capital firm, she reminded herself, he might have some ideas about how to run a business. He just didn't have a clue about Starr's Fall… or her.

"I feel like it's time to bury the hatchet," he told her without preamble. They were standing off to one side of the basement, but Jenna knew everyone had to be holding their breath, trying to listen in. "I think it's three times now we haven't got off to a very good start, and I have to take at least partial responsibility. I certainly could have been a lot more tactful in how I spoke of your store, and for that I'm sorry."

"Well," Jenna managed after a second's startled pause, because she hadn't expected such an upfront apology, "I appreciate people who call it as they see it."

"Even if you see it differently?"

His eyebrows rose in query and something compelled Jenna to admit, "I don't see it that differently, to be honest. I know Miller's Mercantile is struggling. I know it looks like it might be on its last gasp, and you were right, it pretty much is. I just don't like some snooty out-of-towner saying so." She smiled to show she was joking—sort of—and Jack gave a theatrical wince.

"Snooty out-of-towner? Guilty as charged, I guess. Was it the Porsche that gave it away?"

"And the Rolex, and those loafers." She pointed at his feet. "Although they're better than the brand-new hiking boots you wore when I saw you in The Starr Light. Did they give you blisters?"

"Yes, bad ones. I had to limp all the way back to my Porsche."

Jenna pursed her lips. "Oh, dear."

"Your sympathy is overwhelming." His mouth twitched in a smile as he cocked his head, looking amused rather than offended. "Why do I feel like I'm a terrible cliché?"

Jenna gave him an innocent look, eyebrows raised. "Because you are one?"

"And you're not?" he countered, and she let out a huff of laughter.

"Let me guess. Crazy cat-owning spinster who is as quirky as the shop she runs?"

His mouth curved and his eyes glinted, and Jenna was... affected. She tried to ignore the flutters that had started up in her middle. "Do you own a cat?" he asked.

"No."

He laughed softly, the sound seeming to wind its way around her senses. "Well, not that cliché, I guess."

"But another one?"

"You tell me." It was, Jenna reflected, starting to feel like they were flirting... and she didn't mind.

Whoa, Jenna. Remember that it's a guy exactly like this one who broke your heart and worse, destroyed your confidence? You want to go there again?

Not that she had any intention of anything happening between her and Jack. A little innocent flirting was one thing...

"Tell you what," Jack said, one hand tucked in the pocket of his pressed khakis, the epitome of relaxed confidence. "Why don't you come to dinner one night this week and we can discuss how I think you could improve the mercantile? I'll do my best not to sound like a know-it-all, and I won't even charge you my usual management fee."

Jenna was reeling from realizing she'd just been asked on the approximation of a date, so it took her a moment to ask, "And what is your usual management fee, out of curiosity?"

"Two percent of the invested funds I'm managing."

"Considering what's in my bank account, you wouldn't be getting much," Jenna replied. Had he really just asked her to *dinner*? Jack just smiled, waiting for her response, and a sudden, heady feeling of recklessness gripped her as she lifted her chin. "But in any case, dinner sounds like a better offer for both of us, so if you really did mean it, then I accept."

8

Accepting what amounted more or less to a date in front of a good portion of the town's population was not, Jenna realized, very wise. Especially when the date was with Starr's Fall's most eligible bachelor, and it wasn't really a date in the first place. At least, Jenna was not letting herself think it was a date, because, she told herself, she and Jack didn't even like each other. He was just going to be offering some business advice that she probably wouldn't even appreciate, and then they'd go back to ignoring each other. The thought brought equal amounts relief and disappointment, which was aggravating in the extreme.

It was also exasperating how interested just about everyone in Starr's Fall was about the prospect of said date. She and Jack had agreed to meet at six-thirty on Wednesday, a mere two days hence, but in those two days Jenna had more business come through the store than she'd had all month. Everyone wanted to know what was going on with her and Jack, and Jenna decided they might as well pay for the privilege.

"I only answer questions from paying customers," she told

Zoe Wilkinson, who had come in to hear some dirt and good-naturedly bought a loaf of bread and a gallon of milk.

"So did Jack Wexler really ask you out? He was talking so quietly we couldn't actually overhear," she complained as she handed Jenna a twenty. "Doesn't he have an amazing voice? So low and rumbling. Very sexy."

"He's old enough to be your father," Jenna admonished, and Zoe rolled her eyes.

"Only if he had me when he was fourteen. He's forty-two."

"How do you know that?"

"It's called Google? His profile's online. Do you know he made his first million when he was twenty-three? There's an article about him in *Forbes*."

"Wow, stalker much?" Jenna teased. "And no, it's not a date. We're having dinner to discuss how I can keep this store going. If he made his first million when he was that young, he'd better have some good ideas." Something Jenna had realized in between deciding she disliked Jack Wexler and feeling like she could flirt with him was that he actually might have some good advice. No, he didn't know Starr's Fall, but he clearly knew business. And yes, she did have a serious chip on her shoulder when it came to rich know-it-all guys, but Jack wasn't Ryan, and she had no intention of dating him, anyway. More to the point, he most likely had no intention of dating her.

Even if they were having dinner together.

"Well, keep me posted," Zoe said as she gathered up her milk and bread. She gave an apologetic grimace as she glanced around the store. "This place is really kind of cute. I should come in here more, but I tend to rely on Instacart."

"As does everyone else," Jenna agreed with a sigh. "Don't worry, I won't hold it against you. Much."

She'd had more or less the same conversation with what felt

like half the residents of Starr's Fall, some of them asking more obliquely, others demanding to know outright.

"Can you take photos of his house?" Liz Cranbury asked as she bought some lettuce and a bell pepper. "Discreetly, I mean, on your phone. It's that huge place out on Bantam Lake that that famous architect built for himself but then got divorced and moved to LA, do you remember? I've heard it's fantastic inside."

"I am *not* taking photos of his house," Jenna told her.

"I'm so jealous," Liz replied. "As much of you seeing the house as dating Jack Wexler."

"I am *not* dating Jack Wexler—"

"You guys flirt by fighting," Liz cut her off. "It would be annoying if it wasn't so cute." She held up one manicured hand. "And don't worry, I won't step in. Girls' code and all that. But try to get a photo of at least one of the bathrooms, okay? He'll never know."

Somehow, knowing Liz's penchant for gossip, Jenna suspected he would. And she was not taking creepy photos of Jack Wexler's bathroom, although she was almost as curious as Liz to see the interior of the big house on Bantam Lake. No one had seen the inside of it.

By Wednesday evening, when Jenna was closing up the store to get ready for her non-date, she'd had enough of the speculation and suggestions. At least she'd profited from it, she told herself as she headed to the house to change. If gossip about her social life kept people coming to the store, then maybe she should think about having more of one.

Her stomach fluttered with nerves and more than a little anticipation as she headed upstairs. Since this wasn't a date, it begged the question what she should wear. She was most definitely *not* getting gussied up; the very last thing she wanted was for Jack to think she'd made some kind of effort for him. But she wasn't sure she wanted to rock up to his door in her usual eclectic outfit, either. What to do?

A hammering on the kitchen door had Jenna stilling, one hand on the knob of her bedroom door. More hammering. And then a voice.

"Jenna Miller, open up. I walked all the way out here to keep you from embarrassing yourself, and I'm not going away without fulfilling my duty."

It sounded like Zoe Wilkinson, who was not someone Jenna would expect to come knocking on her door. She liked Zoe, and they were friendly, but Zoe was ten years younger than her, and they didn't really hang out all that much, per se. Slowly Jenna walked back downstairs and opened the door.

"Zoe..." She shook her head slowly at the sight of the young woman standing on her doorstep, looking resolute. "What are you doing here?"

"Helping you get ready for your hot date," Zoe replied. "I realized you were probably going to wear your patchwork skirt and call it fancy, and I figured you needed an intervention. Not to say," she added quickly, "that I don't like your style, because I do. You totally rock the I-just-got-out-of-bed boho look. But... I feel like you need a little extra zing, when it comes to dinner with Jack Wexler. Liz agreed, and so did Annie. Laurie and Maggie, too. And Rhonda was the one who mentioned it first, so... I was nominated to come help you out."

"Does every single person in town know I am having dinner with Jack Wexler?" Jenna demanded. "*And* are they all really talking about my wardrobe?"

"Yes," Zoe replied instantly. "Everyone knows about the date, anyway. Only the women are talking about your wardrobe. Are you surprised?"

No, she wasn't, but she was flustered. She didn't like the

thought of everyone up in her business, especially her *romantic* business, and especially when she hadn't had any romantic business in ten years, save for a few very dispiriting blind dates she'd prefer to forget.

"Thanks for the mercy mission," she told Zoe dryly, "but I have no intention of making an effort for Jack Wexler."

"Correction," Zoe replied, "you don't want to *look* like you made an effort. Totally get that. But actually make an effort? Yes, you do."

"Well, all right," Jenna admitted somewhat grudgingly, because she had a point. "I guess."

"Let's go upstairs and have a look at our options." Zoe was already heading toward the stairs. "I've never been in your place. It's so quaint, isn't it?"

Jenna glanced around at the forty-year-old furniture her parents had bought in yard sales. "Yes," she agreed. "Quaint."

With great foreboding, she followed Zoe up the stairs. By the time she had, Zoe had already found her bedroom and was surveying the state of her closet, hands planted on her slim hips.

Jenna had very uncertain feelings about having anyone in her bedroom, never mind Zoe Wilkinson, who yes, was someone she liked, but not someone she knew all that well. And who, it had to be said, had a certain style all her own. Right now she was wearing a fitted bright purple t-shirt with an artful rip along the hem and a pair of black jeans with shredded knees. Both garments clung to her slender figure, and Jenna wouldn't be seen dead in either. It was a great look for Zoe, but she really wasn't sure this was the person to give her fashion advice. But then who was?

"So we've got some options," Zoe called over her shoulder as she freely rifled through the scant items in Jenna's closet. "Fortunately, Liz Cranbury came through with this." She reached down to the leather backpack she'd dropped at her feet and pulled out a Midnight Fashion bag which she thrust at Jenna. "It's gorgeous."

Jenna took the bag and peered inside with some trepidation. There, folded up with tissue paper, was a deep red sweater in softest cashmere. She pulled it out and examined it; it was gorgeous, but it was also very sexy. The deep v-neck, on her generous figure, would be... indecent.

"All you need is a pair of bottoms—jeans without patches, preferably, or maybe some black pants?" She peered in the back of her closet and pulled out a pair of wide-legged black pants Jenna hadn't worn since she'd lived in New York. "These are perfect!" Zoe ran a hand along the fabric admiringly. "And they look expensive."

"They were." Stupidly, Jenna found her throat had gone a little tight. They were just a pair of pants, for heaven's sake, but they reminded her of everything she'd once tried so hard to be... for a man. She didn't want to do that again, and certainly not with Jack Wexler.

"I think they're a little too fancy," she told Zoe. "And I'm afraid this sweater, beautiful as it is, is going to make me look like Jessica Rabbit."

Zoe raised her eyebrows. "And that's a bad thing?"

"Considering this isn't a date—"

"I know you keep saying that," Zoe cut across her, "but I just don't believe you."

"Well, you should," Jenna replied slightly tetchily. She'd always admired Zoe's feistiness, but less so right now. "I'm not sure I even like Jack Wexler as a person, so why would I go on a date with him?"

"Lots of people go on dates with people they're not sure they like," Zoe replied, the voice of reason. "That's why they go on the dates."

Jenna just shook her head. She wasn't about to argue the point yet again. She'd done that enough over the last two days. "Not the pants."

"Okay." Zoe put them back. "Fair enough. What about a pair of jeans?"

Jenna sighed. The sweater was soft, and beautiful, and she realized she didn't want to rock up to Jack's big house on Bantam Lake looking the way he'd expect her to—like a colorful mess. But did she want to look sexy?

"Just own it," Zoe advised, as if she could read Jenna's whole thought process. "Stop worrying about what Jack Wexler thinks."

"I'm not worried about what Jack Wexler thinks," Jenna retorted automatically. Zoe arched a skeptical eyebrow, and Jenna sighed. "Fine. I'll try on the sweater."

Since Zoe didn't seem interested in giving her privacy, and Jenna told herself she wasn't a prude, she pulled off her t-shirt right there and grabbed the sweater. As she pulled it over her head, she savored the softness of the cashmere, even as she acknowledged it was pretty snug.

"*Va-va-voom*," Zoe remarked in appreciation as Jenna pulled it down over her hips. "You look amazing. And yes, a bit like Jessica Rabbit, although that reference is a *little* dated, but it's a good look, trust me."

Jenna eyed her reflection doubtfully. If even her references were dated, was she too old for this? The sweater was tight, although not as tight as she'd feared. She wasn't showing yards of cleavage, just a generous hint of it. With a pair of normal-looking jeans, she supposed it wasn't an outrageous outfit, but would it look like she was trying to impress Jack?

"Don't overthink it," Zoe advised. "And remember, Jack is not that dude back in New York or San Francisco—or wherever—who was obviously a douchebag."

Jenna jerked her gaze from her reflection to stare at Zoe in shock. "You know about him?" She had never told Zoe about Ryan. She hadn't told *anyone* about Ryan, except for Rhonda, and Annie, and a little bit to Zach. Okay, three people was clearly three too many.

Zoe shrugged her assent. "I know the basics. I think everyone does, Jenna, to be honest. You remember this is Starr's Fall, right?"

"I know, but..." She shook her head slowly. She'd thought she'd kept her private life private, but clearly she'd been fooling herself. Why wouldn't people know about that old heartbreak, when they seemed to know everything else? "What do you know?" she asked Zoe, steeling herself for her reply.

"Only that you dated some rich guy who led you on and then broke your heart. Typical city slicker." She shrugged, her eyes alight with interest. "You can tell me the details, if you like. I won't pass them on."

"No, thanks." Jenna had no intention of imparting those painful details to anyone. Zoe, and apparently the rest of Starr's Fall, knew enough, and while she knew everyone would be sympathetic, she still didn't like them knowing. "It was a long time ago."

"Exactly, and your date is in less than an hour. You're going to wear the red sweater?"

Jenna glanced at her reflection again, torn between wanting to be exactly who she was and no one else and needing to show Jack Wexler—and everybody else—that she could in fact be different. She was overthinking this, she decided with exasperation. It was just a sweater, after all, and a very nice one at that.

"Okay," she relented. "I'll wear the sweater." It had been very generous of Liz to gift it to her, after all.

"Great. Now we can move on to hair and makeup." Zoe reached for her backpack. "I'm thinking understated and sophisticated, barely there but beautiful. We'll style your hair in glossy waves and do a *tiny* bit of contouring and lip. What do you think?"

Considering Jenna never wore makeup or did anything with her hair, that sounded like a lot.

"I don't know…"

"Come on." Zoe withdrew a set of straighteners from her bag. "You have the most gorgeous hair, Jenna. With a little styling, you'll look like Julia Roberts. One look at you and you'll be able to knock Jack Wexler over with a feather."

Now *that* was a prospect that had some appeal. She'd like to surprise Jack, Jenna realized. She'd like to show him how he'd underestimated her. Suddenly, this whole evening took on a different complexion—not one of her being prickly and defensive, doubling down on what she'd already said and done, but bowling Jack over with how different she could be.

"All right," she told Zoe recklessly. "Bring it on."

9

Jack eyed the bottle of red he'd bought in Litchfield—Starr's Fall did not have a liquor store, which was something that clearly needed to be addressed—wondering if he should open it. He was still marveling at the fact that he had, in a moment of utter recklessness, invited Jenna Miller to dinner. And she, in what he suspected was a similar moment of recklessness, had accepted. Not only that, but they'd done so with an *audience*, which meant all of Starr's Fall was talking about tonight before it had even happened.

Not that Jack had been privy to those conversations. He'd kept his head down, visiting his mother and doing what now amounted to work—reading and checking the stock market, somewhat compulsively even though he was trying to monitor himself—in the house rather than venture into Starr's Fall and face the speculation. Still, he was pretty sure it was happening, and he didn't know how he felt about it—or the woman in question.

He was attracted to Jenna, he could acknowledge that much. Whether he *liked* her or not remained to be seen, but he was starting to suspect that when she let down her defenses she might be funny and smart and interesting. He'd enjoyed their little bit of banter at the end of the Business Association meeting, if that was indeed what it had been. He still wasn't sure.

But was it going anywhere, even somewhere casual? Did he want it to? And never mind him, did Jenna? He wasn't even sure he wanted to be thinking this way. He'd always been a planner, an overthinker, at least in business. But in relationships? He hadn't had enough of them to know.

Jack glanced at the bottle again and then, in another moment of recklessness, reached for the corkscrew. Life was short and his lately had been incredibly boring, so... why not? He was just giving the corkscrew a final twist when the doorbell rang.

He finished opening the bottle, putting it to one side before he quickly checked his reflection in the hall mirror. His wardrobe was full of the same kind of clothes—hand-tailored suits for work and expensive khakis and button-down or polo shirts for leisure. He'd chosen a pale green button-down shirt and navy-blue khakis for tonight, but now he wondered if he looked like a boring businessman. Maybe he *was* a boring businessman. Plus, he'd nicked himself shaving, like he was some teenager, and the cut was obviously apparent and embarrassing. She'd think he was nervous, and he *was*, which was just stupid.

He'd made million-dollar deals, Jack reminded himself. He'd met celebrities and socialites, he'd dined in their penthouses and partied on their yachts, he'd traveled the world three times over, staying at five-star hotels in every city that mattered. He did *not* need to be nervous about having dinner with some crazy cat-loving spinster from Starr's Fall, although they'd already both agreed that was not who Jenna was. Whatever. She wasn't someone he needed to be *nervous* for.

The doorbell rang again, a slightly more insistent press,

which made Jack smile. That was so Jenna. With a spring in his step, he went to open it.

"Hey," he greeted her, managing to sound relaxed, before he caught sight of her and his jaw nearly dropped. He'd become used to seeing Jenna Miller in her usual get-ups—hippy skirts, plaid shirts, oversized sweaters, overalls, hiking boots. She was not wearing any of those tonight.

Tonight she was wearing a soft red sweater that hugged her curves and gave him a tantalizing glimpse of her generous cleavage. She'd paired it with slim-fitting dark blue jeans and black leather ankle boots, and her hair fell about her shoulders in soft, shimmering waves of red-gold. She looked... stunning.

"I can see you're as surprised by my appearance as I am," Jenna told him with a wry laugh. "Zoe Wilkinson sabotaged me. She came over an hour ago and insisted on giving me some kind of makeover." She handed him a bottle of wine which, at first glance, was of surprisingly good quality. "From my parents' cellar," Jenna explained, correctly clocking his look. "They were collectors, once upon a time."

"Thank you," Jack replied when he'd finally found his voice. That sweater was... amazing. "Come in."

Jenna gave him a fleeting, teasing smile as she stepped across the threshold into the foyer, tilting her head back so her hair flowed down her back as she took in the soaring space. "I hope you realize that the entire population of Starr's Fall thinks we're on a date?" she remarked, seeming unfazed by the prospect. "If you glimpse a pair of binoculars in the bushes outside, you'll know why."

"I suspected there might be a fair amount of spurious interest," Jack replied, closing the door behind her. He decided not to address the date comment directly, not yet anyway. "Would you like a drink?"

Jenna turned to face him, her hair bouncing around her shoulders like a shampoo ad, her eyes glinting green and gold, her mouth curved in a small, expectant smile. All right, he'd been attracted to her, but it had been somewhat grudgingly, almost against his will, and only because, Jack had told himself, he'd spent the last six months in virtual isolation.

Now he felt the full throttle of that attraction overwhelm him. Jenna Miller was gorgeous.

"What's on offer?" she asked, and for a second he thought she meant something else entirely.

"I just opened a bottle of red wine," Jack replied after a second's pause, his voice only a little strangled, "and there's white in the fridge."

She cocked her head to one side, so her hair flowed down nearly to her waist. "I thought you couldn't drink?"

"I've been given the all-clear, for rare occasions only. I decided this is one of them."

She laughed, the sound soft and musical. "Wow, I'm honored. Then yes, I'll have a glass of red, if it's open. Thank you." He led the way into the kitchen, and she followed, looking around in obvious interest. "Everyone is as curious about this house as they are about our dinner," she remarked. "I hope you're willing to give me the full tour?"

Jack reached for two crystal wineglasses from a set of twelve the interior designer had chosen, along with everything else. "If you'd like."

He poured the wine and then handed her a glass, clinking it with his own before he took a sip. Jenna did likewise, her eyes dancing over the crystal rim.

"This is all feeling very civilized," she remarked as she lowered her glass. The wine had made her lips look even redder.

"It's indeed reassuring to know we can be civil to each other,"

Jack replied in agreement. "I'll have you know, I'm not actually a big jerk. At least I don't like to think of myself as one."

"And I'm not actually a shrew," Jenna replied lightly before teasingly parroting, "At least, I don't like to think of myself as one."

Jack gave a little rueful wince of acknowledgment as he remembered how he'd actually called her a shrew. That had been a hard day, getting used to a life he'd never asked for and still wasn't sure he wanted. "That was very rude of me to say," he told Jenna. "As was writing the review. I don't think of myself as vindictive, either, but my adjustment to rural life was... bumpy."

He'd basically been dragged into it kicking and screaming. "If you don't make some changes, Jack," his doctor had said, "you'll be dead in five years, if not sooner." Jack had been lying in a hospital bed, having just recovered from surgery and practically seen the Grim Reaper standing in the window. He'd taken the doctor seriously... eventually.

"Well, we've covered that ground before," Jenna told him lightly, "so no need to go over it again. Let's view this as a clean slate, for both of us." She mock-narrowed her eyes at him. "But if you trash my business tonight when you give your well-meaning advice, we might need to start over yet again." Before he could reply to that, she held up one hand, slender and long-fingered, as she gave a laughing grimace. "I'm just kidding. Sort of."

"It feels personal to you," Jack told her. "I get it."

Jenna frowned as she dropped her hand, her gaze moving over him curiously. "Do you?"

"More than you might realize." He paused before admitting a little uncomfortably, "Before I moved here, my venture capital firm was my life. It *was* my personal. I didn't have anything else. So if someone criticized it, it felt like a personal attack. I didn't always take it well. I, ah, have been known to have something of a temper."

Jenna gave a small smile at that, before eyeing him thoughtfully. "That must have been hard, when you had to retire."

"It wasn't ideal." He felt an alarming thickening in his throat, and he gave her a quick, brisk smile as he nodded toward the rest of the house. "How about that tour?"

* * *

Jenna followed Jack out of the huge kitchen—Liz would have definitely enjoyed a photo of the soaring space, with its marble island as big as a putting green, not that Jenna even knew how big those were—and wondered about what Jack *hadn't* said. He'd moved the subject on pretty quickly, and it was obvious he didn't want to talk about having to retire.

Jenna had to respect that. She didn't particularly want to talk about the painful episodes in *her* life, and it must have been a massively wrenching change for Jack, to exchange the high-powered world of business for small-town life in Starr's Fall. She still didn't completely understand why he'd made such a move—surely he could have stayed in the city if he'd really wanted to—but maybe he would tell her in time.

She was starting to appreciate that Jack Wexler might not be the stereotypical, overprivileged rich guy she'd first made him out to be. At least, he was more than that.

And, it had to be said, she'd enjoyed the way his eyes had widened at the sight of her when she'd arrived. Zoe had been totally right about the sweater. It was a particularly empowering feeling, to know she could make a man like Jack Wexler look at her in such obvious and undisguised admiration. It didn't mean anything, of course, and she was pretty sure this still wasn't a date.

But... her feminine confidence had taken a bruising over the last few decades, and it was nice to get a little of it back, however briefly. She'd also appreciated just how nicely Jack Wexler cleaned up, but then he pretty much always looked good. When she'd caught sight of him looking so freshly ironed and fantastic, and yet with that little nick on his jaw that made her think he must have cut himself shaving, which made her like him all the more—well, she'd reacted with a fizzy sense of expectation. This might not be a date, but it was starting to feel like one.

"This place is pretty huge," she remarked as Jack led her through the enormous foyer, complete with a massive chandelier, marble floor, and a double staircase curving up to a landing. "Do you get lost in it?"

"I only go in a few rooms, to be fair," Jack replied. He opened a pair of bi-fold doors that led to an equally huge living room, with white leather sofas scattered artfully in front of a massive stone fireplace laid with a few tastefully varnished logs. Everything about the house was built on a grand scale—it was a cross between a castle and a ski lodge, and it could probably sleep twenty, if not more. Jenna thought she would feel lonely, rattling around in all those rooms, beautiful as they were. Did Jack?

"Why did you buy such a big place?" she asked curiously. "Do you have six kids tucked away upstairs, or are you just planning on hosting huge house parties?" She smiled playfully. "Invite your jet-setting friends over every other weekend?"

He laughed wryly, although his eyes suddenly looked sad, the corners drooping, and she half-wished she hadn't made the joke. "Nope," he said as he ushered her out of the room. "No kids and no house parties. And"—he paused as he closed the doors with a click—"no jet-setting friends, as it happens."

"What about all your city friends, though?" Jenna pressed, wanting to know more about him. "They must like to travel, even if it's just to northwestern Connecticut."

"The funny thing about those," he told her as he walked across the foyer to the dining room, which was equally impressive with a table that looked like it seated sixteen, "is that they tend to be *city* friends. Once you lose your status there, they're not so interested."

Ouch. "Is that what happened?" Jenna asked quietly. She was surprised to feel a stirring of pity as well as sympathy for him. She certainly knew what it felt like when someone dropped you. Hard. She just had assumed Jack, with all his success and self-assuredness, didn't.

He stared at the empty table, a stretch of ebony that was made for dinner parties it didn't seem like he would ever have. "Pretty much," he replied with a shrug, his gaze sliding away from hers. "I've become irrelevant in that world, now that I'm retired. I get it, because when people left Wall Street, I treated them the same way. When your work is so intense, and it's basically your whole life, well, it's hard to remember the people who got out of the rat race." He sighed and then smiled, although it didn't quite reach his eyes. "I'm trying not to take it personally."

"Still..." She thought of his remark when they first met about how small towns were supposed to be so welcoming, and a sharp pang of guilt assailed her at how nasty she'd been. Had he still been reeling then, from such an abrupt change in his life? "You know, now I really feel like a big meanie," she confessed suddenly, the lightness dropping from her voice. "Being so rude to you before. It sounds like you could have used a kinder welcome. I should have been more understanding.".

Jack shrugged. "I think I deserved it. Well, some of it, anyway. Besides, clean slate, remember?" He smiled down at her, his eyes crinkling, and when Jenna breathed in, she inhaled the scent of his cologne, which smelled citrusy and expensive and made her head spin. Jack moved past her to step out of the dining room. "Next up is my study, which is a room I actually use, so it might be a little more interesting than these set pieces." He gestured similarly to the room they'd just left.

"Well, now I'm really curious," Jenna teased. She was flirting, she realized, and she didn't mind.

Jack led her down a narrow hallway to the study, a classically male room, all leather and mahogany, with nautical maps gracing the walls. Jenna stepped closer to study one. She'd assumed the whole place had been decorated by some anonymous interior designer, as Jack had intimated; it had that feel, elegant but somewhat soulless. But these maps, she saw, were well-used and wrinkled, with routes outlined in red marker.

"What are these?" she asked as she turned around to glance at him. "They don't look like they were chosen by some woman in a white silk pantsuit named Helena, or whoever did your interior decorating."

He laughed softly as he stepped closer to her. "Actually, her name was Pippa, and I don't remember what she wore." His shoulder was almost brushing hers, and Jenna felt a tingle up her arm as if it was. "These are maps of the sailing trips I've taken over the years, with my dad."

"You sail?" she asked, before wincing at how dumb a question that obviously was.

"Yep, although not too much recently." He grimaced. "Too busy."

"But with your dad…?"

A shadow came over his face as he glanced back at the maps. "Yeah, my dad and I used to go on a sailing trip every summer. We started with day sails and then moved up to some bigger trips. When I was little, I loved it. Highlight of the whole year, hands down. But then I became a teenager..."

"And you didn't love anything," Jenna filled in gently. She remembered those angst-filled days.

"Yeah, especially not something as boring as messing around on a battered old boat with my old man." He sighed, his eyes still shadowed with regret. "He died when I was in my twenties, and I always regretted not having gone on one more sail with him. I'd always said I would, but then I'd put it off. I started sailing solo, kind of in his memory." He nodded toward some of the other maps. "Not too often, but I liked taking the time out."

Jenna stepped closer to one of the maps to trace the line in red with one finger, impressed. These were not short journeys. "You sailed all the way from New York to Florida?"

Jack laughed softly, sounding both bemused and proud. "Yeah."

Jenna turned to face him, even more impressed. "And you sail alone?" she clarified. That sounded brave... and lonely. Kind of like living in this house... but maybe Jack preferred it that way.

He nodded. "All my trips were solo."

That took some skill, as well as courage. "Wow, I'm impressed," she told him sincerely.

"Well, it was kind of my downtime. So I could get away from it all, you know, for just a few days."

"Seriously. I guess when you decide to do something, you don't do it by half." He gave a slightly abashed, smiling sort of shrug that was kind of adorable. "So, what's your next big trip?" she asked.

"Well, I don't think there will be one," he replied after a moment. "Not for a while, anyway. Can't exactly sail solo for four or five days when you might keel over with a heart attack." Jenna thought he'd tried to sound flippant, but he hadn't quite managed it.

She frowned. A heart attack sounded way more serious than anything she'd been envisioning, although considering he'd been forced to retire, maybe she should have expected something like that. "I thought you'd had an ulcer?" she asked uncertainly.

"Well, that too, but trust me, there is nothing more boring than some worn-out middle-aged man droning on about his health problems, so..." Gently he touched her shoulder to steer her out of the room, and Jenna resisted the impulse to shiver under that light touch.

"I wouldn't call you worn out," she teased as they walked back to the foyer, sensing that Jack wanted the conversation back on lighter footing. "Especially since you've sailed around the world. Also Zoe informed me tonight that you made your first million when you were, like, eleven or something."

He chuckled at that, which she was glad of. She realized she didn't like seeing that look of sadness in his eyes, like some essential spark had gone out. "A little older than that, but all that's in the past, so..." He shrugged his powerful shoulders. "Worn-out middle-aged man it is."

"You still can't convince me." She realized she sounded flirtatious again, and she took a sip of wine to cover her own confusion. All right, she was attracted to this man, mainly because he was gorgeous and way more interesting than she'd first given him credit for. But beyond that? Did she even need to think beyond that, at least for now? Maybe she should just enjoy this evening for whatever it was... even if that felt kind of terrifying, all of a sudden.

"Do you want to see the upstairs?" Jack asked, with absolutely no innuendo in his voice, but Jenna blushed anyway. Considering the recent nature of her own thoughts, she didn't think she could handle seeing Jack Wexler's bedroom, even if she was intensely curious about it.

"Maybe later," she said, and then realized how *that* sounded. She could feel her face turning as red as her sweater.

Jack laughed softly, his blue, blue gaze moving slowly over her. "I'm guessing that didn't come out the way you meant it to."

"No," she agreed with a shaky laugh as every part of her tingled, "and the unfortunate thing about being a redhead is your blush gives you away every time."

"I like it," Jack told her. His gaze was still resting on her, thoughtful but also... admiring? At least it felt like it, and it was making her blush all the more. "It's like an emotional monitor."

"Yeah, one I can't control."

"All the better," he assured her. "A little honesty is refreshing. When I was working on Wall Street, everyone was so devious and manipulative, always out for the main chance. It was a seriously cutthroat world. I loved it, but now that I've been out of it for a little while... well, I still miss it, a lot even, but I wonder if I should." He shrugged, seeming almost embarrassed by the admission, like he'd said more than he'd meant to. "Anyway, enough philosophizing," he continued with a quick smile. "You came here to talk about business, right?"

Jenna made a face. "I think I'd prefer talking about philosophy." And she wanted to learn more about him, because he really was far more interesting than she'd realized. "I have a suspicion you're going to tell me my store sucks, and you'll probably be right." She sighed, feeling dispirited for the first time that night. As exciting as it was to have Jack look at her in admiration, and to feel like they were flirting, the truth remained... Miller's Mercantile was going down the drain.

"I certainly wouldn't say it like that," Jack told her as they walked into the kitchen. He'd laid one end of the huge oak table for two, complete with plates, silverware, glasses, and linen napkins. It looked both intimate and elegant.

"Full disclosure," he called back as he headed to the oven. "I didn't feel, considering our history, that I could buy anything readymade at the deli in Litchfield, so I actually made dinner, which you might regret. I'm not a great cook. In fact, I'm not a cook at all. I strictly ate take-outs for most of my adult life."

"You cooked?" Jenna was both touched and impressed. "I'm honored."

"As long as I don't give you food poisoning..." He took a covered cast-iron dish out of the oven and lifted the lid to eye its contents dubiously.

Jenna put her wineglass on one end of the enormous marble island. She was enjoying the sight of Jack Wexler with a pot in his hands, looking adorably uncertain. "What did you cook?"

"Mushroom barley risotto. I had a sudden crisis about whether you were vegetarian. And full disclosure, as I've droned on about before, I have to be careful about what I eat." He grimaced, and she laughed softly.

"I eat everything, but risotto sounds delicious." She really was touched that he'd cooked for her. It was just about the last thing she would have expected from what she'd thought Jack Wexler was.

He was surprising her in all sorts of ways tonight, and she'd only been here for half an hour. What, Jenna wondered with a thrill of anticipation, would the rest of the evening hold?

10

Jenna watched, her elbows propped on the counter, as Jack moved around the kitchen, first stirring the risotto and then grating some fresh parmesan. She wanted to ask him all sorts of questions, but she didn't even know where to begin—and she didn't want to scare him off. She got the sense that he was pretty reluctant to talk about his job or his retirement, and in any case, they were meant to talk about her business... which *she* didn't want to talk about.

Maybe she'd just stand here and enjoy the view, because the fact was Jack Wexler was a very pleasing sight indeed. He was wearing what some might consider a typically boring city banker type of outfit—khakis and a button-down shirt—but the shirt was crisp and emphasized his muscular chest while bringing out the blue in his eyes. He'd rolled the sleeves up over his forearms, and Jenna's gaze kept being drawn to his wrists.

"When did you get that Rolex?" she asked, mainly to distract herself.

He gave a self-deprecating smile. "Do you really want to know?"

"Now I do."

He sighed as he gave a little shake of his head. "My first bonus. I went out and bought it right away, the flashiest one I could, because I thought I was such a hotshot."

Jenna felt a smile sneaking over her face. She could totally picture it. "And were you?"

"Is anyone who thinks they're a hotshot actually one?" Jack asked before holding up one hand. "Don't answer."

"But you still wear it," she observed, and he flashed a quick, teasing smile that made her stomach curl with anticipation—of what, she didn't know, but she was definitely feeling ready for something.

"Yeah, because it's a Rolex," he told her, as if it were obvious, but he was smiling, and she laughed.

"Fair enough," she said as he brought the pot of bubbling risotto to the table. A pleasing aroma of mushroom, cheese, and garlic wafted up as he set it down.

"It smells delicious," Jenna told him. She picked up her wineglass and brought it to the table before sliding into her seat. "And I'm really kind of touched that you cooked for me," she told him, her voice inexplicably dropping an octave as she gazed up at him from beneath her lashes. Whoa, that had sounded—and felt—way too romantic, like this wasn't just a date, but they were actually *dating*. One glass of wine in and she was already more than a little muddle-headed.

She looked away quickly to disguise her embarrassment, and to his credit, Jack took the misstep—if that was indeed what it had been—in his stride.

"Wait until you taste it," he told her, before fetching the wine bottle and topping up both their glasses. Jenna had *meant* to cover her glass and tell him she couldn't have any more, because she was driving, but somehow she didn't and she told herself it was okay, because she could always call an Uber... which really meant a friend, because Starr's Fall didn't have Ubers. But still, it was fine. She'd find someone to drive her home... which meant she could enjoy this second glass with impunity.

"Cheers," she said, and hefted it, clinking it with Jack's before they both took a sip, their gazes meeting over the rims.

Okay, this was starting to feel very date-like, and dare she say it, romantic, and Jenna was pretty sure it wasn't just her. But instead of feeling excited by that prospect, she suddenly experienced a cold sweep of panic because she wasn't ready for date-like, or romance, or falling for a guy who was so much like Ryan in so many ways... even if he wasn't.

Jack was still rich, and confident, and privileged and powerful, and he came from a world that had basically booted her out and then stomped on her, or maybe vice versa, but either way it had *hurt*, and she wasn't ready for another round. Not remotely.

Unsteadily, Jenna put down her glass. "So maybe we should talk business," she said, in a voice as unsteady as her hand.

Jack frowned slightly, but then he nodded. "All right." He waited, and Jenna realized he wanted her to go first.

"My sales have been declining steadily for several years," she admitted baldly, emboldened no doubt by the wine. "And recently the decline has sped up. I know it's happening to everyone in one way or another, but some businesses are managing to stay afloat. Laurie and Maggie both opened new stores this last year, and they seem to be doing okay, so why can't mine?" Realizing she sounded a little petulant, she hurried on, "I've tried different things, admittedly not very well, but that's because I don't have a lot of wiggle room cash-wise. And I don't want to become a copy of something in Litchfield, because—"

"Starr's Fall is not Litchfield," Jack cut in, his voice surprisingly gentle. His mouth twisted in a teasing smile. "Or so I've heard."

"Right." She subsided into silence, feeling subdued by her own litany of woe. Then she tried to summon a smile and inject a cheerful note into her voice as she asked, "So what do you, wise and experienced investor that you are, advise?"

"Well..." Jack heaped risotto on both their plates, his forehead furrowed in thought. "I'm not sure it's as simple as that."

Jenna hadn't been expecting some kind of quick fix, but something about his tone alarmed her, at least a little. "Why not?"

Jack toyed with a forkful of risotto, his gaze lowered, and Jenna's stomach tensed with anxiety. Never mind the risotto, the wine, the flirting—right now she didn't want to be here, having to brace herself for whatever Jack was going to say.

"It's just that," he finally began, looking up to gaze at her with an unsettling mix of both resolve and compassion, "most of the investors I used to meet, who would come to me hoping I'd take them on—they were hungry. Eager, with a million ideas about how they could improve their business, innovate, expand, change..." He paused, and Jenna swallowed.

"And I'm not?" she filled in, because it seemed like the inevitable comparison he was going to make.

"A few investors, though," he continued as if she hadn't spoken, "weren't. They were cautious, tentative, wanting me and my firm to take the reins so they could—relax, I suppose. I think they found it all very stressful. But I usually didn't take them on as my clients. I wanted them to feel that fire in the belly."

Is that what he thought she was doing? Being *lazy*?

"But," Jack continued before she could say anything, "I don't think you fall into either of those categories. You feel like something different... It's not that you're afraid of hard work, but maybe you're afraid of success." He cocked his head. "And I've been trying to figure out why."

"I'm... not," Jenna protested, sounding unconvincing even to herself. "I mean, why would I be?"

"Good question." Jack popped a forkful of risotto into his mouth, and Jenna did likewise, even though her appetite had vanished. She'd been expecting some ideas from Jack, along the lines of get rid of the sofa on the porch and get a credit-card machine that works, not a psychological evaluation. *Afraid of success?* Why on earth would she be afraid of success?

"I'm not sure what to say to that," she said finally, swallowing her mouthful of risotto. It was delicious, even if she was no longer hungry. "I mean... it would be kind of self-defeating, to be afraid of success."

"Yes, exactly." Jack reached for his wine, his gaze steady on her.

"What, are you now an armchair psychologist, now that you're no longer Mr. Venture Capital?" Jenna asked scoffingly. She'd meant to sound playful, but she hadn't been able to pull it off.

Jack raised his eyebrows. "Feeling a little defensive?"

"All right, yes," she admitted. "I mean, wouldn't you? Why do you think I'm afraid of success?"

"I don't know, but... this whole resistant-to-change thing you've got going on?" He shook his head slowly. "I'm not buying it."

"What..." She really didn't know what to say to that. It had become her *thing*, to be averse to change. It was what she was known for. It was comfortable as well as comforting, a shabby old outfit she protected herself with, to avoid pretty much anything.

Which, now that she thought about it, was not sounding all that healthy.

"You moved to San Francisco and then to New York," Jack told her. "You have a degree in marketing. According to Zach, you've been on the forefront of some major changes in the town—lobbying to get the streetlights fixed, restarting the Christmas festival, chairing the Business Association last year... So you're not trying to keep Starr's Fall in a time warp." He paused. "Just the store."

Jenna reached for her wine, just to have something to do. There was too much truth in what he'd said. She'd had no idea he'd learned so much about her or had been so observant. She felt as if he'd crawled inside her head somehow, without her even realizing. Okay, she'd been open about not changing the store, but somehow the way Jack said it... it felt way more knowing. Way more personal.

"And it seems very personal," he continued, as if reading her thoughts. "More personal than it needs to be... almost like you can't separate yourself from the store. Almost as if you *are* the store."

"*I'm* the store—" Jenna tried to scoff. What mumbo-jumbo was this?

"Like asking someone to change the store is asking *you* to change," he clarified, "and that's what you're resisting. You don't want to have to change for anybody. And you resent anyone asking you—or the store—to change." He raised his eyebrows, his smile playful but also humiliatingly compassionate. "How is my armchair psychology so far?"

"I..." For a second Jenna couldn't speak. She managed a laugh, barely. "Okay, you might have a point there," she finally said. She felt almost unbearably raw, like he'd scraped off a layer of skin with his words. For a second, the painful memories rushed through her—loving Ryan so desperately, with a kind of frantic hunger that never signified anything healthy or good, changing everything about herself to be what she thought he'd wanted her to be—her clothes, her hair, her *laugh*—being told she still wasn't good enough, and never would be, and not only that, but she was ridiculous to think she ever could be—that he would ever see her that way.

It all came back in a horrifying, humiliating rush, causing her eyes to sting and her stomach to churn. She found she couldn't manage any more words, and so she just shook her head, her gaze on her plate and the barely touched risotto.

"Jenna." Jack leaned over and covered her hand with his own, warm and dry and strong. Jenna liked the feel of it. "I'm sorry. I didn't mean to sound so... brutal. I suppose I'm still used to the corporate world. Cutthroat, remember?"

"You weren't brutal, just honest." She found she had to squeeze the words through her throat. "I appreciate that. And you know what?" Her voice wobbled, and she forced herself to look up at him, even though her eyes were swimming with tears. "You're right. I have equated the store with myself in a way that I can see is unhealthy and hard to explain." At least not without going into her romantic history, which she really didn't want to do right now. Zach had guessed a little of it, it was true, but he hadn't skeweringly psychoanalyzed her the way Jack just had. She brushed at her eyes. "I'd tell you why I've been doing that, but I'm holding on to my composure by a thread as it is, and I really hate crying in front of people, so..."

"Oh, Jenna." His voice sounded almost tender, along with low and rumbly, and Jenna decided Zoe had been right. It was a very sexy voice, not that she was thinking that way now. She was really, really just trying not to cry, because that would be seriously embarrassing. It was embarrassing enough that he knew how close she was to it.

"Anyway." With what felt like superhuman effort, she drew in a ragged breath and managed to blink the tears from her eyes. Crisis averted... for now. "If you were going to suggest some changes to the store, and assume that I would be willing to make them... what would they be?"

Jack nodded slowly, seeming willing to take this conversational route, which was a relief. She could deal in practicalities. Hopefully.

"You identified some challenges," he began, his gaze narrowing in thought. He'd removed his hand from hers and stupidly, she found she missed it. "The quickness and convenience of online deliveries, and the fact that your store can't stock everything, so people will have to shop elsewhere, as well. Those are significant, although not insurmountable."

"They aren't?"

"I think *you* need to decide what you want Miller's Mercantile to be." He met her gaze directly, and the icy blueness of his eyes made her feel like shivering. "You could go the gift shop route, with candles and blankets and overpriced kitsch, but I wouldn't advise it."

Jenna couldn't keep a gurgle of laughter from escaping her. "That was Zach's advice. He wants it to be all artisanal, a place for local craftsmen and carpenters. And yes, with candles."

"I think his furniture business could do that very well," Jack agreed without missing a beat. "But general stores that don't actually sell anything useful are a dime a dozen around here, I'm afraid, or at least in Litchfield County. Overpriced everything for city slickers like me, who want a candle or some cute sign to remember their jaunt in the country."

"So..." She cocked her head, waiting for more.

"I like that you want a store that is useful," he told her. "With plenty of grocery staples. But at the moment, you're missing a lot of staples. And the space is big enough that you could provide everything a local needs, or almost, and at reasonable prices. And there would be still enough space to offer something a little extra for the out-of-towner—an olive bar, or a buffet station, or a coffee kiosk, or all three. You don't get a lot of foot traffic here, but this *is* the road out to Winsted. There's no reason why you couldn't entice some cars to turn in, to take a break, if you advertised it well."

It sounded obvious when he said it, but Jenna hadn't considered appealing to people traveling to somewhere else, only the residents and local tourists. And the attempts she'd made to do something different hadn't worked out... although admittedly she hadn't given any of them a wholehearted effort. It was a lot to think about. "I'm not getting those cars at the moment," she told him.

"Because you're not trying." Even though she'd basically acknowledged the same thing to herself, Jenna couldn't help but wince, and Jack noticed. "I'm not being mean, just honest," he reminded her as he filled up both their wineglasses. "The sign out front is ancient, and the wood looks rotten. The broken gas pump and the old sofa on the porch are basically functioning as 'Stay Away' signs for *any* tourist, never mind a discerning one. And while the store itself has a lot going for it—a certain rustic charm, shall we say—you're not capitalizing on it at the moment. At all. It's like you're daring people to come in and accept the store as it is, rather than enticing them to a retail experience they'll enjoy. It's got a definite 'take me as I am or screw you' kind of vibe, and that generally doesn't appeal to people, especially people who want to buy things."

There was a hint of gentle humor in his voice, and Jenna tried to smile, even though it was starting to feel personal again. *Very* personal. And yet she knew he was right. The resistance to changing the store wasn't actually about the store at all. It was about her. About how she'd changed herself inside out for a person once and she never wanted to do it again.

How messed up was that, and also... how had she not fully realized that before? How had a man she barely knew seen something she'd been so blind to herself? *Deliberately* blind, and maybe that was the reason why she hadn't seen it.

"Have I overstepped?" Jack asked, sounding wry as well as regretful. "I'm sorry."

"It's okay. You have some good ideas." Jenna took a sip of wine. "And you're right, the store could definitely use a major refresh. I might take some new ideas on board, although putting in a coffee kiosk and an olive bar..." She shrugged. "I don't have the financial resources for any major change, I'm afraid." It was a little humbling to admit that to someone who was obviously *not* strapped for cash.

For a millisecond, she thought Jack might offer to loan or maybe even give her some money, and Jenna tensed, readying herself for a polite but firm refusal. She was not about to become his charity case. But then he sat back, his wineglass cradled in his hand and simply said, "You could always get a small business loan. There are some banks that have initiatives particularly for rural regeneration. I've looked them up, and I could forward you some links."

Relief coursed through her; that had been an awkward moment she was glad to avoid. "Thank you," she said, meaning it, because already Jack had gone above and beyond for her. "I'd appreciate that."

He smiled, and it felt like things were easing between them;

she wasn't going to cry, and he wasn't going to offer her money. Good.

As for what the rest of the evening held... Jenna had no idea. What had happened so far had already wrung her out completely.

11

Jack could have kicked himself when he'd seen Jenna's golden-green eyes fill with tears. He really had not meant to make her cry, but when it came to businesses and whether they were workable or not... well, he tended to see things in a brutal black and white, and, truth be told, he'd supposed Jenna was made of tougher stuff. It was kind of nice to know she was softer than he'd thought. Even so, he was glad they'd moved past that uncomfortable moment, as well as the ones earlier when, like a total loser, he'd basically told her he had no friends.

It still made him cringe to consider how she must view him—some sad, lonely rich guy rattling around in a big, empty house on his own, desperate to be of use to someone. Pathetic. And yet... there had also been something surprisingly refreshing about how unfazed Jenna was by his wealth. His Rolex was a joke to her, she hadn't seemed particularly impressed by the size of his house, or the fact that he'd made his first million nearly twenty years ago. It was so different from the women he'd known back in New York, who, at least in the circles he'd traveled in, seemed more interested in the particulars of his bank account than his personality.

But he really hadn't wanted to make her cry, although she'd looked even more beautiful with her eyes sparkling and luminous with tears. A couple of times tonight, it had felt like they were flirting, and yet the "maybe later" joke about his bedroom had caused her to blush and stammer. It was hard to gauge how she felt about him; she seemed guarded about her own emotions, but then he was about his, as well. He wondered what was so painful, that she couldn't talk about it in regard to the store, and why she was reluctant to change anything. There was clearly some serious history there, but he wasn't about to press.

"So why Starr's Fall?" she asked as she took another bite of risotto. Outside the moonlight was silvering the surface of the lake, and the kitchen yawned all around them, the recessed lighting creating pools of light and shadow. Despite the size of the room, it felt intimate. "I mean, why not stay in New York?" she asked. "Or go to the Hamptons, or I don't know..."

"Somewhere more my type?" he filled in, and she gave a slightly abashed smile.

"Well, somewhere that *seems* more your type, but I'm coming to realize I shouldn't stereotype you, or anyone, I suppose. *Mea culpa.*"

"I'm glad to hear I'm confounding your assumptions." He settled back into his seat. "I picked Starr's Fall," he told her, "because my mother is in a nursing home in North Canaan."

"Oh." Her mouth made a perfectly rounded O of surprise as her eyes widened. "I'm sorry, I didn't realize..."

"Why would you? I didn't tell you." He paused as he felt a familiar sadness steal over him at the thought of his mother—wispy-haired, vacant-eyed, an uncertain smile curving her lips whenever she caught sight of him. *You look like someone I once knew... You aren't the guy who redid my kitchen, are you?*

"She has Alzheimer's," Jack explained. "Fairly advanced now, unfortunately. I spent the last twenty years too busy to see her much, even after my dad died, and I guess I'm trying to make up for lost time. A brush with death really makes you seriously rethink your priorities."

"That sounds so tough." Her voice was soft and compassionate in a way he'd never heard before, and he realized how much he liked it. He *liked* someone caring about what he was going through, how he felt, even just a little bit. It had been a long time, way too long, since he'd felt like anyone did.

"It can be hard," he admitted. "She doesn't always know who I am. Sometimes she does, though. It just depends on the day. I had the idea that she could come live with me here, in time, but her neurologist said to leave it for now. She's settled in the home and any change could make things worse, so..." He spread his hands wide, looking remorseful.

"Oh, Jack." Jenna shook her head, full of sorrow. "Annie Lyman is going through something similar with her mom, but it's nearer the end, I think." She let out a sigh as she finished her wine. "Why does life have to be so hard sometimes?"

"Just the way it is, I guess." He took a sip of wine before asking, "What about your parents?"

Jenna made a rueful face. "Well... they're living their best lives in Florida, having retired from the store nearly five years ago."

He cocked his head, curious. "You don't sound entirely pleased about that."

A breath escaped her, long and low and gusty. "I should be, I know. They worked hard and they deserve a break. It's just... they've never been all that *interested*, as parents. In their children, I mean." She grimaced again. "Which sounds kind of pathetic, coming from a thirty-nine-year-old woman. I mean, I should be over that kind of thing, right? So my parents were a little hands-off. Most parents were of their generation, anyway. It's just... they were so wrapped up in each other and their own romance, and sometimes it felt a little... lonely, watching it from the outside. Plus it caused me to make some bad choices, not that I blame them for that. It was just... hard." A sudden laugh, almost like a bark, escaped her. "I don't know why I'm telling you all this. I wouldn't normally." She paused before admitting with another laugh, this one sounding uncertain, "I think... I think I might be a little drunk." She gave him a direct look, a small smile playing about her mouth, that had Jack's senses flaring to life. The way she'd spoken... it had almost sounded like some kind of invitation.

"Well, it's good wine," he finally remarked, keeping his tone light. "I can always call you a taxi, you know, so don't worry about that."

"A taxi?" She let out another bark of laughter. "There are no taxis in Starr's Fall. There was once, but the driver, Harry McCall, got too many speeding tickets and lost his license. Anyway." She straightened in her seat. "I can call Annie or Maggie to give me a lift. Don't worry about that." She checked her watch as she gave a laughing grimace. "But was that a hint to get going?"

"No, it definitely wasn't." Instinctively he reached over and caught her wrist, enjoying the feel of her warm skin beneath his fingers, the slight indrawn breath of surprise at his touch. "I don't want you to go," he admitted quietly, sounding far more heartfelt than he'd meant to, and then deciding he didn't care.

Jenna's eyes widened and the moment spun out. His fingers were still on her wrist, his thumb touching her pulse which was beating hard. Finally, after what seemed like a very pleasant, very *expectant* eternity, Jenna let out a shaky laugh and gently withdrew her wrist.

"Well, in that case..." she said. "I suppose you can pour me another glass."

Jack did.

He was hoping the mood would melt into something relaxed and languorous, spin out a little more as they saw where this might take them, but before Jenna had even taken a sip of her wine, he saw her expression tense and he felt the atmosphere shift to something uneasy and far less pleasant, like a chilling of the air.

"I probably should call Annie or Maggie," she said a little unsteadily. "Just to give them a heads up."

"All right," Jack replied, because what else could he say? He wasn't going to make her stay, even if he wanted her to... and he'd just told her so.

Jenna rose from the table to get her phone from her bag, while Jack sipped his wine and tried to regroup. For a few seconds there, it had felt like something might happen between them. Now it no longer did.

Jenna went out into the hall to make her call, which stung, stupidly, because of course she'd want some privacy. Still, Jack suddenly felt like an interloper in his own empty home. He sighed and put down his wineglass. His head was feeling muddled enough already; if he hadn't had a couple of glasses himself, he would have offered her a ride, so she didn't have to call a friend.

It was all starting to feel kind of teenaged and *awkward*, he reflected glumly, which was not the vibe he'd been going for at all.

The minutes stretched on with Jenna still in the hallway, so Jack decided to clear their plates and get out the dessert—a raspberry mousse he *had* bought in Litchfield. His culinary skills extended only so far. As he scraped plates into the garbage disposal, he wondered what he'd been hoping for, from the evening. To help Jenna with the store, or get to know her better, even a *lot* better?

Maybe, he mused, it would be better for both of them if he just focused on the store. If she really was willing to start changing things, he knew he'd like to help her. He'd like to have a project to sink his teeth into, after six months of kicking around as he'd tried to get his health back. But would Jenna be open to accepting his help?

* * *

Shoot. Jenna stared at her phone as if it had the answers to the universe, or at least to how she was going to get home tonight. This could become seriously awkward. In fact, it probably already was, because she'd been standing out in the hallway for about fifteen minutes, trying to figure out what to do.

Briefly, Jenna closed her eyes—and remembered how Jack's fingers had felt on her wrist. Warm and strong and sure. That little touch had shaken her far more than she was comfortable admitting, even to herself. Had Jack seen how she'd been affected? Probably.

Which was why she needed to figure out how she was getting home. She'd enjoyed the little bit of light flirting, but this wasn't going anywhere, and she wasn't willing to entertain the notion that it might. Ten years on, you'd think she'd be able to risk her heart again, and she thought she might be, but not with a self-assured city slicker like Jack Wexler. What did they say the definition of insanity was? Doing the same thing over and over again and expecting different results.

Once was enough for her. It had to be.

She could hear Jack moving around in the kitchen, and she knew it was time to go back in and face the music. She just wished she had a plan.

Taking a deep breath to steel herself, Jenna slipped her phone back in her bag and rounded the corner. Jack smiled as she came in, but she saw a question in his eyes and knew he must be wondering why she was acting so weird.

"Hey, sorry about that," she said.

"Everything all right?" He gestured to the table, on which he'd set two dishes of what looked like raspberry mousse, garnished with a sprig of mint and a single, jewel-like raspberry. "Full disclosure, I did buy these in Litchfield."

"I'll forgive you," Jenna teased as she sat down, and Jack joined her at the table.

"So did you find a ride?" he asked, and Jenna managed a wry smile.

"Um, no. That is, not yet. Annie's with her mom and I forgot Maggie and Zach are out at the movies tonight. Laurie doesn't have a car." She paused as she picked up her spoon. "There are other people I could ask, but... let's just say they'd be a little nosier about it all than I'm comfortable with." She didn't want Liz Cranbury or Zoe Wilkinson peppering her with questions or rubbernecking to get a good look at Jack's house. But it was looking like she might have to put up with that, if she wanted to get home.

Jack's eyes glinted with humor. "Understood. I'd drive you myself, but I had as much wine as you did."

"I know." She smiled at him, abashed. "This is a problem of living in the country."

"It's certainly not an issue I encountered in New York." He paused, his gaze on his untouched mousse before offering in a cautious kind of voice, "You know, there is a solution to this problem that doesn't mean involving the whole town with all the ensuing gossip?"

Intrigued, Jenna laid down her spoon. "And that is?"

Jack lifted his gaze to hers. He looked as cautious as his tone had been, but with a gleam in his eyes that made Jenna's stomach give a little flip. "You could stay the night," he said, and her stomach flipped again, like she'd just crested a rollercoaster. "In one of the guest bedrooms," he continued hurriedly. "Obviously."

Obviously? Jenna didn't know if she was offended or relieved.

Jack must have sensed how that sounded because he continued quickly, "I just meant... I have the space. Unless you have a burning need to sleep in your own bed, you're welcome to choose any one of the five spare bedrooms."

"Wow, *five?*" She raised her eyebrows as she smiled teasingly, and he gave a good-natured grimace.

"I bought this house as an investment."

"You do realize that everyone in Starr's Fall will collectively lose their minds once they've realized I spent the night here?" she said, feeling compelled to point out the obvious. "And they'll jump to all sorts of conclusions."

Jack raised his eyebrows. "I didn't actually see any binoculars in the bushes, and the house is on a private drive. How will they know?"

"Because they'll see my car is missing from my own driveway."

He laughed in soft disbelief. "Do they have your house watched?"

"Basically. Liz Cranbury will be doing regular drive-bys all evening, I'm sure." That might have been a *slight* overexaggeration, Jenna acknowledged, but not much. Not enough.

"It must be nice to feel so important to people," Jack mused. "But like you said a while ago... sometimes a little suffocating."

"Yes to both," Jenna agreed. "But I wouldn't want to live anywhere else." After her years in the big city, it had been a powerful balm to come back to a place where people loved and, more importantly, accepted her for who she was. They weren't asking her to change; they didn't want her to. It was a conundrum that had frustrated her brother Zach, who had *wanted* to change but felt like Starr's Fall wouldn't let him. Jenna had been the opposite... but maybe she needed to take a page out of her brother's book and change a little bit. At least change the store.

And, who knew, maybe herself too.

As for tonight... there would definitely be gossip. Did she care? There would, Jenna realized, be gossip no matter what she did. Kindly meant gossip, but gossip all the same. And yet there was something dangerously tempting about spending the night here, even in a guest bedroom. Something seriously awkward about it, too. What was the morning going to look like? Feel like?

She thought of Jack's hand on her wrist, the low thrum of his voice as he'd said *I don't want you to go.*

She didn't want to go, either. She wasn't sure what she wanted, but at least she knew that. Jack was still waiting for her answer. Outside the night looked dark and cold, and the thought of calling more people at nine-thirty on a Wednesday night to figure out a way home was... unappealing. To say the least.

"Okay," she said at last.

Jack smiled, and Jenna saw—something—flare in his eyes. Heat? No, she wasn't going to think that way. Not yet, and maybe not ever.

"In that case," he said, "let me put the fire on."

He rose from the table and went to the adjacent family room, which had a deep L-shaped sofa in taupe leather facing a massive stone fireplace.

Jenna cleared their dessert dishes and then followed him over to where he was crouched in front of the fireplace, touching a match to kindling. A few tasteful pieces of modern art decorated the walls and tables, including an interesting sculpture made of driftwood. One entire wall was made up of a floor-to-ceiling picture window, overlooking a deck that extended right over the lake. Stepping out on it must feel as if you were walking on water. It really was, Jenna reflected, an amazing house. Maybe she'd get a photo for Liz after all. She didn't think Jack would mind.

Soon the fire was crackling away, with a cheery blaze and a comforting smell of pine, and Jack made them both coffee and brought it over, setting their cups on the coffee table. Jenna curled up in one corner of the sumptuous sofa, feeling remarkably content. Now that she knew she was staying, a sense of relaxation and even peace was stealing through her bones, turning everything inside her molten and deliciously sleepy. No more decisions to make. For a little while she didn't want to have to think about the store or Starr's Fall or the limitations of her life or *anything*.

Jack settled on the same sofa a few spaces away from her, but close enough that if she stretched out her legs, her toes would brush his thigh. He'd stretched one arm along the back of the sofa, and Jenna could almost imagine herself curling into that inviting space, resting her head on his broad chest. She thought about how *nice* it would feel, comforting and exciting all at once. Why she was thinking that way she had no idea... but she was.

For a few minutes, neither of them spoke. Jenna leaned her head back against the soft, sumptuous leather and let her eyes flutter closed, the molten sense of relaxation stealing even further into her bones. The sound of the logs shifting and settling in the grate was a lovely, sleepy kind of sound, and she enjoyed the warmth of the firelight dancing across her skin. She could hear Jack breathing, steadily in and out, and she found that was a nice sound, too.

She thought she should probably say something, but she was so relaxed and still feeling muzzy-headed from the wine, and really, silence was golden. She felt as if she could happily stay like this forever. A soft sigh slipped out from her, and she settled deeper into the sofa, the leather as soft as butter against her cheek, the room warm and cozy, firelight dancing across her closed eyelids, the presence of Jack, silent and steady, like an anchor. She liked knowing he was there.

And somehow, like that, she fell asleep.

12

"Jenna... *Jenna*."

Slowly Jenna blinked the world into focus, feeling as if she were coming up from underwater, swimming toward the surface. Jack's face loomed in front of her, surprisingly close. She could see the golden glint of stubble on his jaw, the way his dark lashes fanned his cheeks as he looked down at her, the intense blueness of his eyes. She took a breath and inhaled his citrusy scent. Her mind swam.

"You fell asleep," he explained gently as he tucked an unruly strand of hair behind her ear, his fingers skimming her cheek. "I deliberated about whether to wake you up, but I thought you wouldn't want to spend the whole night on the sofa. Not when there are five bedrooms to choose from, after all."

"Oh... right." She was feeling weirdly disoriented. She hadn't just dozed off; she'd been deeply asleep. Had she been snoring? *Drooling?* As discreetly as she could, she wiped her mouth. She put one hand to her head and felt that her hair was sticking up in several directions. So much for the smooth, rippling waves Zoe had created with her straighteners. She must look like a total disaster. "Sorry about that," she mumbled, her voice thick with sleep. "I... I guess I didn't realize how tired I was."

"It's okay." Jenna thought she heard laughter in Jack's voice. Great, she probably had been drooling. So much for coming off as sophisticated or even remotely pulled together. Watching someone you barely knew dribble all over your designer sofa had to be a serious turn-off. "Shall I show you the bedrooms?" he asked.

"Okay. Thanks." She pushed her hair away from her face and then glanced down and saw her sweater had gotten pulled down, so she was practically popping out of it. Jeez, she was a mess. Hurriedly she adjusted her top as she clambered off the sofa, only for a wave of dizziness—caused by both sleep and the wine—to overwhelm her so she stumbled.

Jack caught her in his arms, his palms cupping her elbows as he steadied her. "Whoa," he murmured, his hands still on her arms.

"Sorry," she mumbled as she steadied herself. "How long was I asleep?"

"About an hour?" An *hour*? And he'd just been watching her drool on his sofa? "I closed my own eyes for a bit," he told her, which was some small consolation. Still, Jenna felt far too disoriented to make any further remark as Jack let go of her and then she followed him up the sweeping staircase to the bedrooms above.

Some motion-activated low lighting came on as they walked down the upstairs hallway, the carpet so thick Jenna sank into it nearly up to her ankles. Jack pushed open the first door. "There's this room," he said, and Jenna peeked into a massive bedroom all done in gold and cream, with a view of the lake.

She glimpsed an adjoining bathroom with what looked like an infinity shower and felt compelled to admit, "This is nicer than any hotel I've ever stayed in. Do I get to see all the bedrooms?"

"Of course. And choose the one you like the best." He ushered her toward the next one, which was just as elegant and large, decorated in tones of gray and ivory.

"Your interior decorator had a fifty-shades-of-greige thing going on," Jenna remarked.

Jack gave a grimacing laugh. "I know, right? I insisted on blue for my bedroom, though. I wanted a manly color." He rolled his eyes, and Jenna found herself smiling.

"Do I get to see that one, too?" she asked, realizing how provocative the question sounded only after she'd asked it. Well, maybe really a *second* before, but she'd asked it anyway. And now she was gazing at Jack, who was giving her a heavy-lidded look back, and the hallway seemed very dim and their bodies very close as she waited, her breath held, for how he was going to reply.

"If you want to," he finally said, and his tone gave nothing away.

Jenna stared at him for another second as her heart rate sped up and then slowed, and Jack stared back steadily, waiting for her reply. Challenging her a little, maybe; his eyes looked very blue as he stared at her. Jenna's heart felt as if it were tumbling in her chest, and then suddenly her head cleared.

She was on the cusp of making a very, very big mistake, she realized with a sudden, stone-cold clarity. In that moment she had the sure certainty that if she told Jack she *did* want to see his bedroom, and she strolled with him to that chamber, things would get very pleasurably out of hand very quickly. And she wasn't remotely ready for that, no matter how much she'd enjoyed their mid-level flirting.

Composing herself, making sure her expression was bland,

she turned away. "Let's see the others first," she said, inwardly thinking, *chicken*. But she'd rather be a chicken than be stupid, and tired and tipsy as she was, she was very close to being very stupid—and losing her heart to a man who might just grind it under his heel.

"Okay," Jack replied, and once again she couldn't tell anything from his tone.

One by one Jack showed her all the other bedrooms—all decorated in shades of cream or taupe with accents of other muted colors. It was all very beautiful—and also very boring. By the time they'd reached the fifth, she was ready to see *his* bedroom just to have a change of color. And, you know, because it was his *bedroom*. No matter what she'd said—and felt—before.

The master was at the end of the hallway, with a set of double doors like the entrance to a grand salon. With an ironical, mocking bow, Jack pushed them open and ushered her in first. The room was dim, with the same sensor-detected low lighting that cast it in a warm, inviting glow as Jenna stepped in, breathing a masculine scent that was distinctly Jack—soap and aftershave and just him. How did she know his *scent* already? Yikes.

"Wow," she murmured, because there really wasn't anything else to say.

The room, like every other in the house, was huge, with a king-sized bed on a dais like it belonged to an emperor. There was a canopy and a *lot* of throw pillows. The bed faced an equally enormous window that overlooked the lake, now swathed in darkness. Another set of double doors led to a bathroom that looked to be twice as big as Jenna's bedroom at home; she glimpsed a huge sunken tub with jets and the frosted glass doors of an enormous walk-in shower.

"I know it's a bit much," Jack said as he came to stand beside her. "I almost thought of taking another bedroom because I've never slept on a *platform* before. I mean, who has? But... I like the view, especially in the mornings, when the sun rises over the lake."

And just like that, Jenna could picture herself in that bed, slipping out from under the rumpled covers, to watch the sun touch the water with its first golden rays, setting the surface of the lake shimmering. Blindly she turned around and headed toward the hall.

This was definitely getting dangerous.

"I think I'll pick... the first one," she said, mainly because it was the one farthest from Jack's. Jack followed her without speaking, and Jenna knew he had to be wondering why she was so changeable in her responses—flirting one minute, freaking out the next. She really needed to get a grip on herself and her emotions.

"There are some towels in the bathroom, along with a robe," Jack said as he stood at the doorway of the bedroom she'd chosen. "If there's anything else you need, let me know." He paused. "I could lend you a shirt and sweats, if you want, for pajamas."

For a second, Jenna was torn. She could refuse, because wearing his clothes seemed weird, but then she'd have to basically admit she'd be sleeping in her underwear. Or she could accept... which, again, *weird*.

Then she realized she was tired of second-guessing every single thing, and so she managed a smile and a twitchy sort of shrug. "That would be great, actually, thanks."

Jack nodded, seeming relieved to have something to do. "I'll be right back."

Jenna took the few moments alone to mentally slap some sense into herself. "Stop freaking out," she said out loud, only to have Jack reappear in her room at that exact moment. He'd clearly heard, but they both pretended he hadn't as Jenna took the clothes—neatly folded and smelling of fabric softener—with a murmur of thanks.

"Good night, Jenna," he said quietly, and she realized how rarely she'd heard him say her name... and how much she liked it.

A gusty breath escaped her when he finally closed the door behind him. She felt bereft, but also relieved. Whoever would have thought that the guy she'd been so sure was nothing more than a rich jerk would end up being her most dangerous temptation?

And it *was* dangerous... because of all the types of guys on the planet, rich jerks were definitely her nemesis. She should be inoculated against them, considering her experience with Ryan, but obviously she wasn't. And she'd rather have her heart broken by a poor, simple farmer than a man like Jack Wexler, because if she let a man like that break her heart? Well, then she really was stupid... to let it happen twice. And somehow she had a feeling it would hurt more the second time.

With another sigh, Jenna pushed such thoughts away. She was tired and still a little buzzed and she just needed to go to sleep. Tomorrow morning she'd be in better shape to figure out how she felt and what she should do about it... if anything.

* * *

Sunlight was streaming through the window when Jenna woke the next morning, dressed in Jack's t-shirt and sweats, spread-eagled in the middle of a very comfortable bed, feeling pleasantly groggy and thankfully not hungover. She took a breath—and inhaled one of the best morning smells, that of fresh coffee and frying bacon.

Bliss.

For a few seconds, she simply lay there, enjoying everything about the moment—the sunlight streaming through the window, the luxurious comfort of the huge bed, the smell of bacon and the knowledge that it was an attractive and interesting man who was frying it for her.

There really was just so much to enjoy about this.

Jenna lay in bed for a few more minutes, simply savoring every aspect of the experience, and then, feeling a sudden burst of energy, she jumped out of bed. She couldn't resist the walk-in shower, but she kept it quick, conscious that Jack had to be waiting downstairs. Wearing the same clothes from last night wasn't ideal, but it could have been worse.

When she stepped out into the hallway, she saw he'd left a new toothbrush and tube of toothpaste outside her door, and she smiled before quickly making use of both.

As she headed downstairs, her stomach leapt with a pleasant sense of anticipation. She was looking forward to both coffee and bacon... and seeing Jack. Even if she still felt confused about... well, basically everything.

As she stepped into the kitchen, she saw he was standing at the stovetop, freshly showered and wearing new-looking jeans and a plaid flannel shirt.

"Are those your country clothes?" she teased, and then worried that she'd sounded snarky when she really hadn't meant to be.

Jack glanced down at himself before laughing wryly. "Do I look the part?"

"I think they need to be a little more well-worn." She slid onto a bar stool at the huge marble island. "Maybe go outside and roll around in the dirt for a few minutes?"

He grimaced good-naturedly. "I think I'll pass and just own my newbie, city slicker status. Coffee?"

"Yes, please." Jenna propped her chin in her hands as he poured her a giant mug from the coffeemaker. This all felt surprisingly *un*awkward, considering the fair few floundering missteps of last night. "And is that bacon I smell?" she asked as he handed her the mug.

"It is, indeed."

"I would have thought bacon wasn't on your approved list of foods, post-heart attack," Jenna remarked as she took a sip of coffee.

"It isn't, but my doctor said I could have a little of what I love, so..." He shrugged, giving her an abashed smile that was pretty endearing. "It might seem like a small thing, but I really love bacon."

"I understand completely," Jenna assured him. "We're talking about bacon, after all."

"Everything's better with bacon," Jack agreed, and for a second they just smiled at each other.

"Has it been very hard?" Jenna asked as she put down her mug. "I mean, recovery? It seems like it required a major lifestyle shift."

"It certainly did. Complete one-eighty." He sighed as he raked a hand through his hair. "I really fought against it at first, which is why I was so grumpy that day in the store, trying to find something I was actually allowed to eat—"

Jenna held up a hand to forestall him. "Clean slate, remember?"

"Right." He gave her a rueful smile of acknowledgment. "Anyway, I was resisting having to change anything about my life for a long time. My doctor told me if I went back to work, the stress would kill me before I was fifty. He was serious, but I didn't want to believe it, although I knew I should."

"Goodness." Jenna shook her head slowly.

"What's so crazy is that I would have kept going even if it cost me my health, my *life*. But..." He sighed. "I'd lost my mojo," he confessed. "That world is so ruthless. One hint of weakness, *any* kind of weakness, and investors lose faith. People immediately start looking elsewhere. And your credibility crashes. When that happens, it's basically over, and so I decided to walk away before I was booted. But I wasn't happy about it. Not by a long shot."

"I don't blame you," Jenna replied feelingly. "That sounds so tough."

"It was." He paused before continuing briskly, "Well, I know there's nothing more boring than someone talking about that kind of stuff, so I'll shut up. But let's just say that with the ulcer on top of the heart attack, and having to have *two* separate surgeries... I finally got the wake-up call I needed. I'm choosing to live differently... even if I don't always like what that has to look like right now. I know I need it."

"And what *does* it look like?" Jenna asked, intrigued.

Jack turned back to the stove to flip the bacon. "Boring," he replied succinctly and then, almost to himself, "Lonely." He turned back to her, shaking his head slowly, almost as if in wonder. "You know, I was never lonely in the city. I was too busy. I had meetings all the time and when I didn't have meetings, I was still doing something productive—going to the gym, reading the news, keeping up with everyone and everything. I didn't have a moment to think, except when I went sailing, and then I enjoyed the peace and quiet because I had so little of it in my life, and it was an active kind of thinking, anyway. You're pretty busy when you're sailing solo." He blew out his cheeks in a gust of a sigh, shaking his head once more.

"Not so much now, I guess?" Jenna filled in softly. She felt sorry for him; it sounded like he'd had a very full life, and just about all of it had been taken away from him. She knew what that felt like, even if her experience had been about heartbreak rather than health.

Jack's gaze moved to the view outside the huge window with its endless vista of lake and sky, sunlight sparkling on water. "I'm not about to complain," he told her, nodding toward the window. "I know I'm one seriously lucky guy, in all sorts of ways. But... I miss having a purpose, even if that purpose ended up being not so great for my mental or physical health, which I didn't even realize until I was in ICU, being prepped for surgery. Talk about needing a wake-up call."

"So you feel like you need a new purpose now?" Jenna clarified, and he cocked his head, as if waiting for more. "Well..." She felt as if she were edging out onto a diving board, high above the water, about to do a swan dive when she barely knew how to swim. "I could help with that," she offered uncertainly, already half-regretting putting herself out there.

Jack raised his eyebrows. "You could?"

"I can't pay the big bucks, or even any bucks at all, but you don't seem like you're hurting for money." He nodded his acceptance, looking intrigued, waiting for more. "You could be the consultant on my store revamp," Jenna explained a little stiltedly, because she felt so nervous. What if he shot her down? *Uh, thanks, but I'm not that bored...* "You've already given me good advice, but I know I'll need some help putting it into practice. A lot of help." Especially since she took everything about the store so personally. She really needed to get over that. Now that Jack had so helpfully pointed it out to her, hopefully she would... with some continued guidance. "That might not be the kind of thing you had in mind," she backtracked when he still hadn't spoken. "To help out a Podunk store in a Podunk town."

"No, it's not that..." he said quickly before clarifying, "I mean, it's not what I was expecting, but that's not a bad thing. At all." He gave a little laugh, although Jenna still couldn't tell what he really thought about her idea. "I'm honored you'd want me to be a consultant," he told her. "I... I get the feeling that the store isn't just you, it's also like your baby."

"Ye-es," Jenna acknowledged. "And it's struggling. A baby in distress." She tried to smile. "So I know I need help, serious help... and here you are, an expert on everything—"

"Hardly—" Jack began to scoff.

"I mean that sincerely," Jenna told him. "I'd be stupid not to ask for your help... that is, if you were willing to give it." As she said the words, she realized how true they were. Jack Wexler was a goldmine of information and experience. No, he didn't have a lot of history with Starr's Fall or even small towns, but Jenna had come to realize that he had the acuity and intuition to understand both the town's—and the store's—needs and challenges.

And at the base of all this pragmatic problem-solving was the exciting and uncomfortable knowledge that really she just wanted to spend time with him.

Was he aware of that?

Whether he was or not... he still hadn't spoken. He was just looking at her thoughtfully, and a sudden, scorching mortification swept over her. "Sorry, I realize how this must sound," Jenna blurted, horrified by what she was sure he must think. "I just basically asked you to work for me for free and then acted like I was doing you a favor." She shook her head, briefly closing her eyes in intense mortification. Here he was, a millionaire businessman, and she was offering to let him paint shelves. "Forget I said anything, please."

"I don't want to forget you said anything," Jack replied, a smile in his voice as well as his eyes. "I like the idea. A lot. In fact... I'd been thinking of something similar myself. And I'd like to work with you. Not for you," he clarified with a wry grin. "I think that would be difficult for both of us. But... if you want someone to help you with a vision of what Miller's Mercantile could be, and help you achieve that... then, maybe I could be your man."

Your man. The words went through her with a pleasantly thrilling ripple of awareness. Of course, Jack Wexler *wasn't* her man, not in any sense of those two words. But she still liked hearing him say it.

"Okay," Jenna told him, a smile spreading across her face like warm butter. "It sounds like it's a deal."

13

"So, *spill*." Laurie's eyes danced with amusement and expectation as she leaned over the kitchen counter, waiting for Jenna to confess to all manner of things. "What's going on with you and Jack?"

Jenna leaned back against the counter as she took a sip of wine, mainly to stall for time. It was three weeks since she'd asked Jack to be her unpaid consultant, he'd accepted, and they'd got to work. Three weeks since all of Starr's Fall had been buzzing with friendly gossip, having clocked—as Jenna had known they would—that she'd spent the night at Jack's house on Bantam Lake. Three weeks of everyone in the town wondering what was going on... including her.

"There's nothing to spill," she told Laurie with regrettable honesty. "He's helping me renovate Miller's Mercantile, which is wonderful, but that's all."

"That can't be all," Laurie protested, sounding both disbelieving and disappointed. "There are *vibes* between you two. And that date that lasted all night..."

"Laurie," Jenna protested, part-scoldingly. "You know it wasn't like that."

"So you say," Laurie replied teasingly as she turned to check on the casserole in the oven. Jenna had come over to Laurie's for dinner, along with Joshua, Zach, and Maggie. She'd arrived early unknowingly—Laurie had invited her to come half an hour before everyone else so she could dish the dirt.

Sadly, there was no real dirt to dish.

In the three weeks since he'd started helping her, Jack had behaved like a perfect gentleman. More to the point, like the perfect *businessman*. Jenna had left his house practically floating on a cloud of deliciously nebulous possibilities, imagining cozy tête-à-têtes and long, lingering lunches while they chatted about everything *other* than the store. They'd get to know each other. They'd bond. They'd even *kiss*, maybe.

Yes, she'd thought that way. Vaguely. Sometimes not all that vaguely. Sometimes not vaguely at all. She'd had *hopes*, and she'd felt those start to unfurl, even as part of her still wanted to keep them completely closed up and guard her heart as she always did. She'd still dreamed... of Jack. Of them flirting and then bonding over sanding floorboards or ripping out shelves or any of the number of things they'd been doing, helping to turn Miller's Mercantile into a going proposition.

And the reality had been...? Not that. Definitely not that.

The very day she'd made the suggestion they'd headed straight over to her store, and he'd paced the floor, firing off suggestions about how to change its layout, initiatives to get the town more involved, creating a community hub in the space... All of it had been invigorating and exciting, making Jenna see the store in a whole new way, not just as a building but as a community.

"You need to cater to every customer," Jack had told her seriously. "So you could look at creating a food pantry here—I don't think there's one in Starr's Fall? As well as stocking a few key luxury items for the more well-heeled customers. And coupons are always a great way to bring people in, changing them every week, which keeps things fresh. People get excited when they feel like they've gotten a deal."

She'd loved his suggestions, and even more excitingly, they'd sparked her own, so they'd riffed off each other, building on each other's ideas, ending each other's sentences. The sense of camaraderie and mind-melding had been even *more* exciting, and yet... all the while, Jack had acted every inch the corporate CEO. Every time Jenna thought they might share some kind of moment, he'd turned away, pointing out another part of the store that needed work.

Jenna had managed to let go of her prickly self-defensiveness —mostly—when it came to Miller's Mercantile, but his laser focus—when it wasn't on her, but rather her struggling store— had felt dispiriting. Like he cared more about rehabilitating it than getting to know her, which maybe he did.

And yet, Jenna told herself, trying to rally her flagging spirits, she'd known she needed the help, and Jack was being incredibly generous with his time. And so she'd gone along with it all happily enough... even if she was half-hoping that at some point Jack would relax and they'd go back to that fun, flirty vibe they'd had at his house.

It hadn't happened.

Jack had made a list of things she needed to do and a timeline for her to do them in, and he was strict as a schoolteacher about her meeting her targets. She'd started feeling like he was her boss and not her boyfriend, not that she'd been thinking that way at *all,* and yet... she sort of had. Stupidly, and against her own better judgment.

And yet could she really begrudge him his free time and advice? She couldn't, especially because Jenna recognized how valuable it was. Jack had even gotten his hands dirty, ripping out shelves and sanding floorboards, shifting boxes and inventorying stock, pricing out a salad bar and a coffee kiosk.

Jenna had enjoyed their work-focused camaraderie, and especially how the store had felt like something they were doing *together*, but... it hadn't felt anything like the flirtatious possibility that had sprung up between them the night they'd had dinner. Jack treated her like a cross between a colleague and employee, and even with the occasional banter, the quick smile that made his eyes sparkle... she'd started to feel a little pathetic, always hoping for crumbs of flirtatiousness—a secretive look, a hint of innuendo, *anything*.

There had been nothing. Not one thing. Even when she'd felt like they were on the same page when it came to the store, they *weren't* on the same page when it came to each other.

Which was *fine*, she told herself—again and again—because she wasn't looking for a relationship, and especially not with a man like Jack Wexler. Yes, she'd liked the flirting, but she wasn't sure she wanted it to go anywhere, so the fact that he clearly didn't want it to was actually a *relief*.

Still, his seeming obliviousness to her person as he focused on the store had been... humbling.

"There really is nothing to tell," Jenna told Laurie with a sigh, and then, in an embarrassing moment of weakness, admitted, "Unfortunately."

"What?" Laurie stared at her, shocked as well as disappointed. "Are you telling me that for the last three weeks Jack Wexler has been coming over to your store pretty much every day and *nothing's* been happening?"

"He hasn't come every day," Jenna felt compelled to correct, "and lots of things have been happening. You should see the store." Except of course Laurie wouldn't, not until mid-December anyway, because Jack had been adamant that there needed to be a grand opening. So Jenna had closed the store for the last two weeks and the plan wasn't to re-open it until the Winter Wonderland Weekend. Five weeks of lost revenue wasn't as much of a concern as it should be, Jenna knew, especially because she'd applied for a small business regeneration grant and received it, thanks, she suspected, to Jack's influence. Still, she was grateful. Grateful for his tireless work on the store, his expert advice, his steadfast commitment... to the store. Sometimes she just wished he was a little more interested in *her*.

"I'm not talking about the store," Laurie exclaimed. "I'm talking about *you*."

Jenna let out a tired laugh. Once upon a time, she'd conflated the store with herself. No longer. Now that Jack was so very interested in the store—and *not* in her—she had been able to keep the two very separate in her mind. Funny, that.

Or not.

"I know you are," Jenna told her friend. "And, as I've said, I'm afraid there's nothing much to tell you on that front."

"Nothing?" Laurie exclaimed, so clearly disappointed, before her eyes narrowed. "Wait, you're *afraid*?"

"In a manner of speaking—"

"And before you said 'unfortunately,'" Laurie recalled with laser-like focus, before trumpeting triumphantly, "You *like* him!"

"*Laurie.*" Jenna looked around furtively, even though there was no one in Laurie's apartment save for her and Laurie and her dog, Max, who was watching their conversation with a certain alertness, probably because he thought there might be food involved. "Don't."

"Don't what?" Laurie challenged, unfazed. "State the obvious?"

Jenna sighed and reached for her wine. "It doesn't matter," she told Laurie. "Jack and I are very much on a professional footing only. He's been great with the store, giving me all kinds of advice and getting his hands dirty, but that's it. Really."

Laurie frowned. This was not, Jenna suspected, the fairy tale her friend wanted. It wasn't the one she wanted, either. Not exactly, anyway. She might not be ready for a relationship, but the faint, buzzy *possibility* of one would have been welcome.

That lovely, even magical, evening at Jack's house three weeks ago now... well, technically nothing had happened, but it had felt like so much *had*. She'd sensed and seen depths to him that she hadn't realized before. She'd acknowledged afresh just how attractive he was. They'd flirted. Low key, yes, but still. There had definitely been a spark there.

The three weeks since then had been depressingly sparkless, at least on Jack's side. On her side, there had been all sorts of inconvenient sparks. As soon as Jack walked in the door of Miller's Mercantile, Jenna's senses swam. She had an irritatingly intense awareness of him as a person. She'd come to recognize every facial tic and habit—she knew when he was about to launch into a lecture, after he'd drawn a significant breath; she recognized that quirk of his mouth when he gave her a half-smile of rueful acknowledgment; she understood he was frustrated when he ran a hand through his hair and then let it fall to his side. She even understood the faraway look that came into his eyes whenever he talked about his former life, and she suspected just how much he missed it.

She felt like she knew this man, and yes, she *liked* him. But he had not given her even the smallest sense that he liked her back, in that way. No smiling, no sideways glances, no quick, flirty smiles. No laughing innuendoes, no accidental brushes of the arm. Nothing. Three weeks was a long time to hope for some small sign. That he thought of her the way she knew she was thinking about him, even if she wasn't ready for it to go anywhere.

The truth was, her feelings for Jack both scared and depressed her, because hadn't she learned *anything*? She'd fallen so hard and fast for Ryan, had spent the same ridiculous amounts of time looking for clues that he felt the same way... and here she was, doing it all again, and to what purpose?

None. None whatsoever.

It needed to stop. Now.

"Okay, well, tell me about the store then," Laurie said, and Jenna was both relieved and disappointed that her friend was willing to let it go so easily. Clearly Laurie had believed her that there was nothing going on. Either that, or it really was that obvious... to everyone.

"We're doing a complete refurb," she told her, trying to inject a note of enthusiasm into her voice. "Low budget, admittedly, but you'd be surprised at how many little things you can do to improve the place without breaking the bank."

"I'm sure there are lots of ways," Laurie replied, which Jenna decided not to take as an insult.

She started detailing some of the ways Miller's Mercantile had improved—the sagging sofa and broken-down gas pump were both gone, the floorboards had been stripped and revarnished, the old metal shelves replaced by wooden ones custom-made by Zach, on a rush order. Jack had agreed they should keep some of the individual, old-fashioned touches—the antique cash register, the barrel of pickles, the popcorn machine.

"But make sure it works," he'd told Jenna, with some exasperation. "There's nothing that says 'has-been' more than sporting a major feature that doesn't work."

Which Jenna pretty much had to agree with. She'd called in Mike the Mechanic, and he'd managed to get the popcorn machine working in about five minutes. She was both amazed and ashamed to think she hadn't called him in earlier. Sometimes it took another person—in this case, Jack—to show you your blind spots.

"Well, it all sounds amazing," Laurie told her. "I can't wait until the grand opening. When is it?"

"December, at the start of the Winter Wonderland Weekend, before Christmas." Jenna was planning to decorate the whole store with festive evergreen and holly, have a nativity scene, and Mike the Mechanic as Santa Claus, if she could convince him. She thought she could. Jack had also suggested she stock some Christmassy food items—locally made cranberry sauce, Christmas cookies from The Rolling Pin. She'd riffed off that idea with her own "Christmas Dinner in a Basket"—everything needed for the festive meal, wrapped with a big crimson bow.

"I can't believe we're already talking about Christmas," Laurie said. "It's barely November."

"It'll be here before you know it." Jenna was not actually a big fan of Christmas anymore. She'd loved it as a kid, when her parents had decorated the house and store and the whole town had gotten involved, but in the last five years, it had just been her and Zach. Their parents spent the holiday in Florida, and this year Zach was going to be with Maggie and Ben. They'd invited her along, but she wasn't sure she wanted to third wheel quite so obviously, and so it would be her alone with Netflix and a tub of Ben and Jerry's, which was fine. Who wanted to cook a roast turkey for one anyway? Now *that* would be depressing. She wondered, very briefly, what Jack would be doing, and then pushed that unhelpful thought away. Nothing with her, obviously.

"And I'm excited for the Winter Wonderland Weekend," Laurie continued. "Lizzy Harper has big plans for it this year. Not just the tree lighting and decorating, but a whole evening of stores opened at night, craft and artisan events, food stalls... I think it could be really fun, as well as bolster the community spirit here."

"Definitely," Jenna agreed. At the last Business Association meeting, Lizzy had been in full throttle with plans for the weekend. Even though she wasn't a big fan of Christmas anymore, Jenna had felt excited... especially as her new-and-improved store was going to be part of it all. "Anyway, how are you?" she asked Laurie. "How are things at Max's Place?"

"Things at the store are fine," Laurie said firmly, but there was an emphasis to the word store that made Jenna pause.

"And with Joshua?" she asked after a moment.

"Wonderful," Laurie replied, and judging from the sparkle in her eyes and the faint flush to her cheeks, Jenna had no reason not to believe her.

"So why do I feel like there's something else going on?" she asked, trying for a laugh.

Laurie let out a sigh as she checked on the casserole once more, unnecessarily, before turning to Jenna. "I heard from my mom again."

"You did?" Jenna knew that Laurie's biological mom, Rose, had grown up in Starr's Fall, gone to the same high school Jenna herself had, although she'd never known her. Laurie had been so excited to meet her last year and then had been devastated when Rose had told her in no uncertain terms never to contact her again. Then, surprisingly, Rose had been the one to get in touch months later and arrange a meeting—only to not show up. Jenna had thought Laurie had decided to cut all contact after that, but judging from her unhappy and troubled expression, she was now feeling torn. "What did she say?" Jenna asked.

"She apologized for not meeting before, and asked if we could meet again."

Hmm. Jenna was not overly impressed by the sudden change of heart. "And what did you reply?" she asked.

Laurie sighed. "I haven't replied yet. She only messaged me yesterday, and I haven't even told Joshua about it." Her mouth turned down at the corners, the sparkle gone from her gaze. "I know what he will say, though: that she's had enough chances."

"Well..." Jenna hesitated, wanting to speak gently. "I thought you had agreed not to get on that emotional rollercoaster again?"

"I know I did, but... she's my *mom*." Laurie's voice wobbled and Jenna saw she had to blink back tears.

"Your biological mom—" Jenna began.

"The *only* mom I'll ever have," Laurie cut across her quietly. "I didn't have anyone else growing up."

"I know," Jenna said softly. Laurie had told her how she'd grown up cycled through foster care; it was completely understandable that she'd want a connection to the woman who had given birth to her. "I just don't want you to get hurt again," she explained with a squeeze of her hand. Making the same mistake not just twice but three times? Laurie didn't need to go there. And neither did she, with her love life, or lack thereof.

"She seemed really sorry that she'd backed out before," Laurie explained as she knotted her fingers together. "She said she was scared because her husband doesn't know about me, but she really did want to meet me."

"And is she going to tell him now?" Jenna couldn't keep from sounding a little skeptical. How many chances did you give a person to hurt you? She'd given Ryan too many... which was why she wasn't keen to go down that road again. For her friend's sake, she didn't want Laurie to, either.

"I don't know. She didn't say. But I understand why she would have been nervous, Jenna. Don't you?" Laurie thrust her chin out, looking a little mulish, so clearly wanting to believe the best of her mom. Laurie was an eternal, determined optimist, unlike Jenna. She'd rather be realistic, brace yourself for the smackdowns. If you did, they might hurt less.

"I suppose she would have," Jenna replied carefully, "but it's you I'm concerned about, Laurie, not your mom." She paused. "It sounds kind of like you've already decided, though, and obviously it's your decision to make."

Laurie nodded slowly. "I think I have." She frowned, biting her lip. "Do you... do you think less of me for it? I mean, I get that I probably seem a little pathetic and desperate, chasing after her like this—"

"*Laurie.*" Jenna laid a hand on her arm. "There's absolutely nothing pathetic or desperate about wanting to connect with your mom. Nothing at all."

"What about you, then?" Laurie asked with a small smile as she discreetly dabbed at her eyes. "I know you and your parents don't get on all that well. Maybe you should reach out."

Well, that was unexpected. Jenna hadn't thought they were talking about *her*, or her parents. "I'm fine with the way things are," she stated, even though she knew she wasn't, not entirely. Zach had reached out to their parents recently, and now they had regular video calls. He'd encouraged Jenna to join in, but so far she hadn't. She hadn't even been tempted, not really, and now she wondered why not. Was it just about protecting herself—or was she angry at them for the indifference they'd shown her when she'd been growing up, simply because they'd been so wrapped up in each other? It was both, she supposed, although she was cordial when she spoke to them. But sometimes it was better not to mess with the status quo.

"Let me know how it goes," she told Laurie, who smiled wryly in understanding, thankfully getting the memo; they were not talking about Jenna's mom, just Laurie's.

"I will."

They didn't have a chance to say anything more, because someone was coming up the stairs, and moments later Joshua came in, waving cheerily at Jenna before greeting Laurie with a kiss. Laurie smiled up at him, slipping her arm around his waist, and they looked so blissed-out with each other that Jenna felt an uncomfortable pang of envy. She longed for that with someone, even if she'd long ago given up hope, or at least told herself she had. Spending time with Jack had shifted something inside her, chipped away at her hardened cynicism and made her remember how exciting it was to like someone. To feel that flutter, to have someone give you that sparkle in your eye and spring in your step... and more than that, to really *get* someone, and have them get you. But none of that mattered, because for the last three weeks Jack really hadn't seemed interested. At least, he'd seemed far more interested in the store than in her, which was just as well, because like she'd told Laurie, she was fine as she was. Really.

Zach and Maggie came in then, looking as loved up as Joshua and Laurie did, and Jenna had to keep telling herself she didn't mind all the laughing looks, the casual arms slung over the shoulders, the way Maggie leaned into Zach, or Joshua dropped an unthinking kiss on Laurie's forehead. She kind of wished Laurie had invited someone else to this dinner, so she didn't feel like such a fifth wheel, but that could have been awkward too, if it had turned into some sort of semi-date situation. She was good on her own. She really, really was.

"I thought maybe you would have invited Jack tonight," Zach remarked when they were all seated for dinner and Laurie was dishing out the chicken casserole. Jenna couldn't tell if he was addressing her or Laurie, and so she stayed silent.

"I thought about it," Laurie replied easily, "but I thought maybe he and Jenna needed a little break from each other." She gave Jenna a teasing look. "Considering they're spending twenty-four-seven together as it is."

Twenty-four-seven? Where was *that* coming from? "We are not," Jenna said in as dignified a tone as she could muster, "spending that much time together." In fact, Jack hadn't been to the store in several days; he'd said he had some other stuff to catch up on, and in any case, Jenna knew she was perfectly capable of managing the work on her own. It had just been nice to have someone to do it with.

"No?" Zach raised his eyebrows. "I see Jack's Porsche parked outside the store most days."

Which meant, Jenna knew, that most other people did too. Well, she'd already known that everyone in Starr's Fall was talking about her and Jack. It didn't mean anything was actually happening... or even that she wanted it to. There was a big difference between enjoying a little light flirting and wanting a relationship.

"Because he's helping me in the store," she told him. "And he hasn't been there *most* days," she added. *Some* was more like it. Maybe *quite a few*, but not *most*.

Zach gave Maggie a laughing look before he nodded slowly at Jenna. "Whatever you say, sis," he told her. "Whatever you say."

Jenna decided silence might be the best policy, and she focused on cutting a piece of chicken, giving it far more focus than she would normally. She wasn't going to convince her brother or anyone else that there was nothing going on between her and Jack, so she might as well not try. It was just particularly aggravating that everyone seemed to think she was the one who was in denial when they so clearly were.

For whatever reason, Jack Wexler had decided he was not interested in her, no matter what sparks she'd felt between them during their one and only sort-of date. And that was fine, because she wasn't interested in him.

Really. End of.

Jenna looked up to see four people all giving her knowing smirks, as if they'd all been party to her entire thought process—and didn't believe it.

And then Jenna wondered if maybe she just didn't believe herself.

14

"Meeting come to order!" Lizzy called out cheerfully, banging the gavel a few times for good measure. Jenna sat down at the end of the table, dropping her bag down next to her. She'd come late to the meeting, so she only had time to shoot everyone there a quick welcoming smile before Lizzy started talking. She let her gaze skate over Jack, who was sitting at the front near Lizzy, telling herself not to mind when he didn't even seem to meet her eye. He was completely focused on Lizzy and what she was saying.

Jenna suppressed a sigh. It had now been a month since she and Jack had started refurbishing Miller's Mercantile—in addition to the lovely new wooden shelves and varnished floorboards, there was space for a self-serve coffee station and a salad bar that was being installed next week, sourced mainly from local farmers. Jenna had enjoyed getting to know more local suppliers, and was working on some new agreements for local honey, maple syrup, and jam, in addition to the fresh produce.

A new, hand-painted sign would be delivered tomorrow, and new stock was arriving daily. The store was starting to look pretty good, and Jenna was very grateful for it. Once she'd stopped trying to keep it exactly the same, she'd found the process of change liberating, and she'd seen even more areas than Jack had mentioned that could use a pick-me-up.

Dried flowers in a vase on the windowsill, an armchair from the barn that looked antique rather than dilapidated and provided a welcome place for people to sit down for a moment... a chalkboard above the cash register suggesting favorite items, a bulletin board by the door advertising local services and organizations... All these touches added something special to the store that she knew had been missing.

So yes, she was grateful to Jack for getting the process started, but she just wished she hadn't more or less ceased to exist in his eyes, because that was what it had started to feel like.

He had been so focused on making her store a success, throwing himself into every project, that he sometimes seemed to forget she was even part of it. And then, in the last week, he'd only stopped by the store once, just for a few minutes, seeming distracted when he did, almost impatient, jangling his keys the way he'd once used to. Jenna had tried not to take it personally, but he'd barely met her eye, and she'd started to wonder if he was annoyed or maybe just bored with her and her poky little store.

He'd told her herself, back when they had dinner, that he still wanted some purpose in his life. Why should her little store be enough for him? In any case, he certainly hadn't wanted to stay, and for the first time he hadn't promised to stop by again soon; he'd just walked out without a backward glance.

Which was *fine*, she'd told herself, because the consulting part of the project was pretty much done, and it wasn't like she needed him to hold her hand forever or anything. And while they'd certainly gotten along, they weren't really friends... except

Jenna had sort of thought they had been. At least, she'd become used to him being around, which was dangerous, so really it was good he wasn't coming by anymore because she needed to get back to the status quo.

Yet no matter how many times Jenna told herself it was all better this way... it didn't feel like it.

"So, first item on the agenda, the Winter Wonderland Weekend!" Lizzy announced. "It's only three weeks away, and Christmas really is around the corner. We need to start decorating! Planning! And so I'd like to nominate Jack Wexler and Jenna Miller to chair the weekend's organization."

Say what? Jenna jerked her gaze back to Lizzy, who was giving her an innocent, beatific smile. "I thought *you* were organizing the weekend," she said blankly. "I mean, I thought you'd already organized it." Since it was now mid-November, Jenna had assumed most of the work was already done. Although, to be fair, any planning in Starr's Fall tended to be on the haphazard side. But Jenna had already started making her Winter Wonderland Weekend plans for the mercantile, which were coming along nicely.

"Well, I've got a lot on my plate right now," Lizzy replied breezily, "and it's true, much of the groundwork *has* already been done. But in terms of the final details... making sure all the stores are on board, the decorating, organizing the caroling and the big Saturday night event... I thought you and Jack could work on it together."

"The big Saturday night event?" Jenna repeated. She didn't recall any such event. Last year, the weekend had been the lighting of the Christmas tree and one night of stores being open till eight. This was starting to feel like an even bigger upgrade than Jenna had realized.

"Yes, didn't you read it in the minutes?" Lizzy asked, her eyebrows arched. "A few of us discussed it after the meeting last month." Lizzy looked at her expectantly, but Jenna just shook her head. She hadn't been at this spontaneous discussion, and she never read the minutes. Who did? "We're planning to hold a barn dance for the whole town," Lizzy explained. "Zach volunteered your barn. And the other day he suggested you and Jack could organize it, since you obviously work so well together. Everyone agreed."

What? Jenna swiveled to stare at her brother, who gave her a bland smile back. She was sensing a stitch-up. A serious stitch-up. The Starr's Fall Business Association was busy matchmaking... but there really was no point.

She glanced at Jack, who, no surprise there, wasn't looking at her. Was he embarrassed at how obvious everyone was being? Did he think she'd put Lizzy up to it, because she wanted to spend more time with him now that he'd finished helping her? Heaven forbid. "Why doesn't Zach organize the big Saturday night event?" she asked Lizzy, a little mulishly as she threw her brother a glare that bounced right off him.

"Not really my thing," Zach told her. "And I'm already organizing some local woodworkers to do some workshops throughout the weekend. That's keeping me pretty busy."

"I'm pretty busy too—" Jenna began, only to have Jack interject.

"I don't mind," he said, his voice quiet but firm. Jenna turned to look at him and saw he was frowning at her, looking confused and maybe a little annoyed. "I think it could be fun," he said to the group, but Jenna thought the discontented look in his eyes said otherwise.

Still, to continue protesting would be ungenerous as well as embarrassing, and so she just gave a nod, folded her arms, and sat back in her seat. She glanced again at Jack—still frowning. She looked away.

The meeting lumbered on, with yet more talk about the streetlights that were continually going on the blink despite Jenna's efforts over the years to get them fixed, everyone's plans for late-night openings all through December, and then forward-looking hopes for some kind of springtime event around Easter. Jenna started to tune out, because she was thinking about planning a barn dance and who knew what else with Jack and bracing herself for spending yet more time with him, while judging from the last week and his virtual disappearance, he was seeming even less enthused. It was not a particularly enticing combination. The last thing she needed or wanted was to be around someone who seemed to have decided he didn't want to be around her. She knew what that felt like, and it wasn't good. She had no intention of feeling it again, and especially not with someone like Jack.

She hadn't even realized the meeting had broken up until Jack dropped into the empty seat next to her, giving her an uncertain smile as his gaze scanned her face. He was wearing a gray fleece and the usual khakis, his hair slightly ruffled. He hadn't shaved that day, and stubble glinted on his jaw. Basically, he looked scrumptious.

"Hey," he said.

"Hey." Jenna managed a tight smile in return, determined to rein in her emotions. "Sorry you got railroaded into organizing this barn dance," she said. "I know you've had stuff going on."

"I don't mind." He continued to scan her face, as if looking for clues. "But you seem like you do...?"

"No," Jenna said quickly. Too quickly.

Jack cocked his head. "Okay," he said after a moment. "Well, how about we go out for a drink and talk about it? If you have time?"

"Okay," Jenna said after a moment, knowing she sounded reluctant. She could feel everyone's beady eyes on them; Liz Cranbury wasn't even trying to hide the fact that she was unashamedly eavesdropping; she practically had a hand cupped to her ear. "If we go to The Starr Light, we'll have half the town listening to us, though," she added, like a warning.

"Don't we always?" He gave her a glimmer of a smile that Jenna did her best to return. All right, she needed to get over herself. So Jack wasn't being flirty anymore. He wanted to talk shop, nothing else. She was a grownup. She could take it.

"Fine," she said, and Jack frowned again. Okay, she was going to need a little time to get over herself, clearly, but she'd get there.

They headed out into the crisp night, the streetlights—those that were working, anyway—glimmering in the darkness, the air holding a touch of frost. Thanksgiving was next weekend, and the weather had definitely turned; it felt like winter, Christmas on the horizon just as Laurie had said.

"How have you been?" Jenna asked diffidently as they walked toward The Starr Light. "You seem like you've been busy this last week or so."

"Yeah, there's a few things going on," Jack replied repressively, and Jenna tried not to feel rebuffed. So he didn't want to tell her. Fine. Again, she could take it. She *would*.

They walked in silence the rest of the way to the diner.

* * *

Something was clearly going on with Jenna. Jack kept sneaking her sideways glances, wondering why she'd turned so prickly. He'd thought they'd gotten along pretty well over the last month;

he'd enjoyed helping her with the store; diving into a project had really invigorated him, and she'd seemed to appreciate it. Now he wondered if he'd been too high-handed with some of his suggestions. Maybe Jenna resented his interference. Maybe she wished she hadn't asked for his help at all. She was certainly acting like it right now.

And yet, the truth was, Jack had loved having a project to sink his teeth and even his spirit into. Six months of doing mostly nothing had taken even more of a toll on him both mentally and physically than he'd realized. Being *involved* in something, figuring out a way to make it work, even if it was just a rundown general store in the middle of nowhere... he'd *needed* that. It had energized and focused him, in a way he'd forgotten he used to feel all the time. Mental muscles that had atrophied had sprung back to life, and he'd felt wide awake and ready for action.

But maybe, in his invigorated interest, he hadn't clocked just how bossy he was being? Maybe Jenna was annoyed with him... It felt almost, but not quite, like they were back to that tense stand-off of the summer, when they'd more or less disliked each other.

Except he didn't dislike Jenna. At all. So what was going on?

They didn't speak again until they were seated in a booth in the back of the diner, and Rhonda had handed them menus with an over-the-top wink. She'd certainly softened toward him, after that first aggressive introduction, for which Jack was grateful.

He perused the menu disinterestedly, knowing he'd only have a beer. "All things in moderation," his doctor had said at his check-up last week, which had felt like a major step forward.

"So this barn dance," he remarked. "It's a new thing?"

"Yes." Jenna was studying her menu with what felt like unnecessary concentration. "The whole Winter Wonderland thing was shelved for years because some city type had objected to the Christmas tree, saying it was a hazard. We only brought it back last year, and I guess it's still evolving."

Some city type? Why did that feel personal? "And so now Lizzy wants to make it an even bigger deal?"

"I guess." She shrugged, deliberately not meeting his gaze. At least that's what it felt like.

Suddenly impatient, Jack put a hand over the laminated menu that hid her face and deliberately drew it down. "Jenna, what's going on?" he asked, quietly enough so no one nearby could hear, or so he hoped. "Why are you acting like you're angry with me?"

She shrugged, a twitch of a shoulder. "I'm not." So unconvincing.

"Yes," he told her, trying to smile, "you are." He willed her to meet his gaze, but she wouldn't, keeping it firmly fixed on the table. "*Jenna*... did I do something to offend you? Have I been too over-the-top with the store? I'm sorry if I took too much control. I guess I'm used to being in charge—"

Jenna sighed and glanced up, meeting his gaze with the resolution of someone facing a firing squad. "It's not that," she said, and then did not elaborate.

Okay. But her tone suggested it was *something*. "What is it, then?" he asked.

Another sigh, this one more angsty. "Look, Jack, can we... not do this?" she asked in a pleading voice. "Let's just focus on the barn dance, okay? I'm thinking Christmas lights strung among the hay bales... not that we have hay bales, because we don't have any animals, but I'm sure one of the local farmers might have some and we could decorate with some evergreen and holly as well..."

"I don't want to talk about hay bales," Jack said. "Or holly." Jenna seemed agitated, and he wanted to know why. Was she mad at him? She didn't seem mad, not exactly, but there was definitely something going on that she didn't want to talk about... So what was it?

"Jack," she said quietly. She was looking down at the table, her hair falling in front of her face. She didn't say anything more.

"Jenna..." he answered back, and then fell silent, because he wasn't sure what to say. What he wanted to say. He'd spent the last month focused on helping her, totally committed to her store, trying to be purposeful and professional and not to notice how her hair smelled like strawberries, or how the freckles on her nose seemed to dance when she laughed, or that he actually liked her overalls with the purple patches. No, he had definitely not noticed any of those things. Much.

And now... now she didn't want to tell him why she was annoyed with him? Jenna, who always seemed willing to tell him, or anyone, why she was annoyed? Was that a good thing, or a really bad thing? He really wasn't sure what was going on, and he had a seriously sneaking suspicion that he might be reading this situation completely wrong. In which case...

"Okay," he said at last. "Let's talk hay bales."

Before Jenna could reply, Rhonda sashayed over to them, a smirking smile on her thin face as she flicked her thin blonde ponytail over one bony shoulder. "All right, lovebirds, what can I get you?"

"*Rhonda.*" Jenna shook her head, seeming despairing. "Come on."

Rhonda's pencil-thin eyebrows rose. "What?"

Jenna just shook her head again. "My usual, please."

"I'll have whatever's on tap," Jack said, only for Rhonda to roll her eyes.

"This is a diner, not a bar," she said as she wagged a finger in front of his nose. "There's nothing on tap."

Of course there wasn't. "I'll have a Heineken, please."

"Good choice," Rhonda approved. "Anything to eat?"

Mutely Jenna and Jack both shook their heads, and Rhonda whisked the menus away before heading back to the kitchen.

Jenna sighed. It was the kind of sigh that suggested she'd rather be doing anything else than sitting in The Starr Light with him, and Jack didn't know whether to be hurt or hopeful. He was kind of both, at the same time, which didn't make sense, but...

Nothing about right now made sense. He really hadn't expected this, although *what* he expected he couldn't have said. The last month had been enjoyable, invigorating, *fun*. He had thought things between them had been going well, but clearly he had not been picking up all the signals.

"Okay," he said at last. "If you want to talk about the barn dance, let's talk about the barn dance, but..." He hesitated before finishing with a wry smile. "It would be nice if you didn't act as if you were being tortured while we were doing it."

"I've hardly been acting like that," Jenna protested. Feebly.

"You've been annoyed, though," Jack replied, fixing her with a level stare. "Sorry to keep harping on about it, but why won't you tell me why?"

Jenna was starting to look as tortured as she'd sounded. "I thought we were talking about hay bales."

Jack lifted his shoulders in a shrug, unrepentant. "Well, now we're not."

She held his gaze for a moment and then she let out another sigh as she just shook her head. "This is stupid."

"It doesn't feel stupid."

"Why," Jenna burst out in exasperation, "are you going all emo on me now, when for the last month you've basically ignored me?"

Wait, what? Jack stared at her in shocked surprise while Jenna snapped her mouth shut, shook her head, and then rose from the table.

"Look, this wasn't a good idea," she said, doing her best not to look at him. "Let's just... talk about it later."

And then, while Jack and what felt like half of Starr's Fall watched, she stormed out of the diner.

15

Nice way to make a scene, Jenna thought in a mixture of fury, despair, and pure panic as she practically sprinted down the street, slipping on some ice and nearly doing a face plant, which would have really rounded out the evening nicely. *Why* had she had to flounce out of the diner like a teenager throwing a hissy fit? Why did she have to be so stupidly *emotional*?

Everyone in Starr's Fall was going to think she was losing her mind. More to the point, *Jack* was. Why on earth had she acted so over-the-top and basically unhinged about something she couldn't even articulate? And yet she knew she couldn't go back into the diner. The whole thing had just been way, way too embarrassing. And it brought back way, way too many memories.

"*Jenna!*"

Jack's rumbling baritone carried all the way down the street. As tempted as Jenna was to keep running, she knew that was a bad idea. She'd embarrassed herself enough for one night surely, and yet there was almost certainly more to come.

Slowly she turned around to face Jack, who had stopped

about ten feet away and was gazing at her in confusion. "Jenna, what's going on?" he asked.

She gestured to the diner behind them. "Sorry about that—"

"Seriously," he cut her off, sounding impatient now. "What's going on? We're both adults, and I thought we were friends. Why can't you tell me why you've been acting so touchy?"

Because I'm hurt that you don't like me the way I like you. No way was she saying those words. No way was she humiliating herself more than she already had.

"It's just been... kind of a day," she half-mumbled.

Jack shook his head, looking even more exasperated. "*Kind of a day?*"

Okay, she really did need to act like a grownup. But not here in the street, with who knew who looking on, making all sorts of assumptions. Or in the diner, where people would practically be handing out the popcorn.

"Can we go somewhere more private?" she asked. "So we can talk sensibly?"

Jack made a sweeping gesture with his hand. "Be my guest."

And so they ended up walking, mostly in silence, back to Jenna's house. Jack had never been in her house before, although he'd been in her store plenty of times. She felt self-conscious and slightly embarrassed by how shabby and small it was, compared to his behemoth of a lakeside palace. As he stepped inside, she had to sweep a pile of papers off the table and push a basket of unfolded laundry into the mudroom. At least the clothes were clean.

"Sorry, I wasn't expecting company," she muttered. "Coffee?"

"Sure."

She set about making coffee while Jack stood in the middle of the room, rocking back on his heels and seeming to take up all the air. She snuck a glance at him and saw how *assessing* he looked, his gaze moving slowly around the small room with its ancient cabinets, the weathered kitchen table, the piles of papers, the calendar tacked to the wall that was from last year.

How on earth was she supposed to explain herself, Jenna wondered in both panic and misery. Anything honest would be humiliating as well as make her sound seriously desperate. And yet she already suspected Jack would know if she was lying before she even began.

What to do? What *did* one do, when honesty was definitely not the best policy, at least not for her mental wellbeing or maybe just her pride?

"So," Jack said, when the coffee had started brewing, the heady aroma of it filling the air.

"So." Jenna let out a shaky laugh as she focused on getting out coffee cups. "I fully accept that I have acted kind of crazy tonight and seemed like I'm annoyed or even angry with you, when I'm absolutely not." Well, not *really*. Not in a way she could easily explain, at any rate.

"Okay..." Jack cocked his head, clearly waiting for more.

"I guess... I'm just a little sensitive," Jenna began shakily. She couldn't make herself look at him. "To, um, feeling... ignored."

He didn't say anything for a long moment, and her toes curled up inside her hiking boots because *why* was he not speaking?

"Are you saying I've been ignoring you?" he asked eventually, sounding incredulous.

"Well... kind of? In a way?" She snuck a glance at him; he looked completely bemused. "I mean, I know you've been helpful with the store, very helpful, but... that's the *store*."

He shook his head slowly. "And yet you said you and the store were pretty much the same thing."

"In my *head*," Jenna burst out in a well-duh tone. "Not in yours. And not in real life."

"Okay." Jack was now looking befuddled as well as bemused, and Jenna could hardly blame him. She barely made sense to herself, never mind another, far more reasonable person. "Can I ask... without inciting your ire... how I ignored you?"

Inwardly Jenna cringed. Jack's level tone, his genuine confusion and curiosity, well... it made her feel ridiculous and childish, along with petty. Not a good combination. Not a good feeling. And did she really want to explain how she'd felt ignored? *If you don't see it then I can't explain it to you.* No, she couldn't go there.

The coffee had finished brewing, and so she took a moment to pour them both mugs, conscious of Jack's stare burning into her back as he waited for her to make sense of something she really wasn't sure she could make sense of. Not, at least, without admitting some pretty humiliating truths.

And then, suddenly, like a lightning bolt to her heart, jolting her awake, Jenna suddenly thought *why not*? Why not lay it all out there, admit how she'd been feeling—a little bit ignored, yes, but also kind of hopeful that maybe something could happen between them one day? Bruised by past experiences, very much so, but also wanting to be different. To *choose* to live differently. Could she say all that to Jack?

Okay, yes, the risk of embarrassment was high, but there were worse things than embarrassment. There was heartbreak. There was the soul-deep disappointment of missing out because you weren't brave enough to try. There was living alone for the rest of your life because you were a coward.

"I suppose..." she began slowly as she handed a mug to Jack, "I just thought... that things would feel..." Goodness, but this was hard. Her throat was dry, and her heart was starting to hammer. Memories of brokenly telling Ryan how much she loved him were rushing through her in a towering wave of remembered humiliation and hurt. And Jack was gazing at her with narrowed eyes and pursed lips; he looked a lot like he had the first time she'd met him, and suddenly she couldn't do it.

She couldn't lay herself out there, not again, not when the memory of telling Ryan in a trembling voice how much she loved him while he stared at her with the very same expression that was on Jack's face right now... *no*! She was not a masochist. She was *not* doing this. Not again. Whoever had said it was better to have loved and lost than never loved at all had not known what they were talking about. At all.

"It's just the last week or so, you've been kind of MIA," she said finally as she buried her nose in her coffee mug, unable to meet his gaze. "And I wondered if you were getting a little tired of the store or of—of me." That was as far as she was willing to go with her confession. "And if you are," she continued, trying now to sound briskly practical, "please just say so. We don't have to organize the Winter Wonderland Weekend together. I don't want you to be working with me on—on sufferance or something. And you've been so helpful already, I want you to know I really appreciate it." The last was said in a rush, in case he thought she was ungrateful.

"I'm not tired of you," Jack said after a moment. She couldn't tell anything from his tone. "Or the store. I've really enjoyed working on it, to be honest. But... the last week was kind of busy with—various things." He paused before continuing, "Maybe I should have told you what was going on, but my mom had a fall at her nursing home, and I had to take her to the doctor, as well as have a meeting with the care staff to discuss next steps in managing her decline. It was pretty intense, all things considered. And then I had a couple of doctor's appointments of my own, in the city, to assess my recovery. And you know how I don't like talking about my health stuff." He smiled crookedly, which just about melted her heart.

"Oh." Now she felt like a complete heel, complaining about him not showing up when he'd obviously had so much else to deal with. Why hadn't she considered that? She'd been too wrapped up in her own pity party even to think about it. "I'm sorry," she told him, heartfelt. "I should have thought about what you might be going through." She gave a grimacing sort of smile. "How is your mom?"

"Well." He glanced away, his jaw bunched, and she had the sorrowful sense that talking about personal stuff was difficult for him, which was probably why he hadn't told her what was going on. He had emotional baggage too; hers had made her jump to conclusions while his had caused him to retreat. "There's only one way this is going," he said at last. "When you have Alzheimer's. So any decline is not unexpected, but... it can be challenging."

"I'm sorry," Jenna said again, more softly.

"It's the regret that is the hardest to deal with," he admitted in a low voice, without looking at her. "I spent twenty years being too busy to see my own mother. And part of that was motivated by how I saw my dad live—stuck in some mid-level job he hated, counting down the days until retirement, and then he died of heart failure just three years into it. I was so dismissive of them both, of the choices they'd made, and yet... he and my mom were so *happy* together, that whole time." His voice choked, and tears stung Jenna's eyes. Slowly Jack shook his head. "I thought he'd missed out all these years, because of his job, and it wasn't until I had the heart attack that I realized maybe I was the one missing out, all along." He turned to give her a bleak, level stare that made Jenna ache with sympathy for him. "Do you know, I haven't had a single serious or meaningful relationship in twenty years? I mean, a couple of dates, a few casual things, but nothing memorable. Nothing *real*. I was just too damned busy."

"Oh, Jack..." Jenna shook her head, her heart breaking for what he felt he'd missed. He'd been so painfully honest with her... how could she still hide from him what she'd been feeling? "I know what it feels like to worry you've missed out," she said quietly. She hesitated, and then, compelled to an emotional honesty by his own, she confessed, "When I was twenty-six I fell in love with a guy who... who broke my heart, but worse than that, he crushed my confidence." She swallowed, still unable to look at him as she continued, "And I've spent the last decade trying to get over it and also telling myself it isn't worth it, to try again. Not that there have been a lot of options, but maybe there haven't been because I haven't been willing to look. To try, simply because I was too scared of getting hurt." She fell silent, wondering if she should have said all that, and yet also strangely glad she had. "At least," she tried to joke, "you've made millions in the process. I'm still broke."

"They're cold comfort sometimes," Jack replied with a crooked smile. "They don't keep you company, I've learned that much. I didn't realize how lonely I was until I moved to Starr's Fall." Something in his tone made Jenna finally turn to risk looking at him. He was gazing at her with a new intentness that made her catch her breath.

In a single second, it felt as if the mood had completely shifted between them, from heartfelt and emotional to... exciting and expectant. It was a lot to take in.

"So this guy who broke your heart," Jack said after a moment. "What was he like?"

Jenna smiled crookedly. "A rich city slicker."

"*Ah.*" The single syllable held a wealth of understanding.

"We dated for nearly three years. I thought it was going somewhere. He just saw it as... I don't know. A distraction?" She shook her head slowly. "Nothing serious, anyway. Nothing remotely what I'd thought it was. The night he broke up with me I thought he was going to propose. It turns out he'd actually gotten engaged to someone else... more suitable."

Jack pressed his lips together, anger on her behalf flashing in his eyes, which was kind of a nice feeling. "He sounds like a total jerk."

"He was, but I only realized that in retrospect. He could be very charming when he wanted to be. And I was heartbroken, but worse than that..." Jenna paused. She had thought she wasn't brave enough to go into all this, but maybe she was, after all. Maybe Jack had helped her to be. "I was just so *mad* at myself, both for convincing myself this guy was worth it and also for— for changing myself for him. I tried so hard to be what he wanted —this sophisticated city woman, and that just wasn't me. So... when I came back to Starr's Fall, I doubled down on being me. Country bumpkin who refuses to impress anyone. And that's when I started to get personal about the store... and feel like it shouldn't have to change, either. That no one should, and especially not for some rich jerk." The words burst out of her, and she bowed her head.

"I understand why you would react that way," Jack replied after a moment, his tone gentle. "No one should feel like they have to change to be loved."

Loved. The word seemed to shimmer in the air between them, with possibility, with promise. Jenna was afraid to say anything, to break that golden silence. Words, any words, might spoil it, and even though she felt emotionally flayed right now, she wanted to enjoy the sense of hope and even expectation that Jack's words had caused her for just a few seconds...

"Jenna..." Jack began. His eyes seemed bluer than ever, and his expression was both intent and serious. He took a step toward her, one hand reaching out. Jenna's heart lurched with hope—

and terror. What was he going to say? Was she ready for this... whatever it was?

"Hey, sis!"

Jack took a jolting step back as Zach waltzed through the back door, insouciant and oblivious—until he caught sight of Jack.

"Oh. Uh, hey." He laughed, cleared his throat, laughed again. "Did I, um... interrupt something?"

"Just some brainstorming about this barn dance," Jack replied lightly. He sounded remarkably unaffected by what, Jenna was fast realizing, had been essentially nothing. Nothing had happened between them. Nothing had even been said.

And yet...

Zach looked between her and Jack, seeming as if he was trying to assess the mood, and then he raised his eyebrows and gestured to the door. "You want to have a look at the space? It's got some junk in it at the moment, but I can clear it out."

"Okay." Jack glanced back at Jenna before turning to Zach. "Sounds good," he said, and with Jenna watching, he strolled out of the kitchen with her brother, as if seconds ago he hadn't been about to tell her he loved her... which of course he hadn't.

What had just happened? Nothing, Jenna realized, and for the first time in a long while, she wasn't at all relieved. She was just disappointed.

Which, in its own way, was progress. Unfortunately.

16

The hammering on the front door had Jenna calling out only slightly irritably, "All right, *all right*, I'm coming." She stood up from where she'd been making a display of Christmas baking items, dusting off the knees of her overalls before hurrying to the front door of the mercantile.

It had been nearly a week since she'd seen Jack, since they'd had that almost-nothing, which was the only way Jenna could let herself think about it. He'd texted her the next day to say he wouldn't be around this week, as he was going into the city to see friends and then spending Thanksgiving with his mom, but he hoped to see her when he got back... whatever that meant.

Jenna had no idea anymore. She'd worn herself out, over-analyzing her conversation with Jack, the things they'd both shared, the things they'd almost said—or not—and whether any of it actually *meant* anything. Why, on the verge of what had felt like something wonderful, had he gone out so readily with her brother to see the barn? Had he been looking for a reason to leave? Had he been *relieved*?

She couldn't let herself obsess about it, even as she recognized she already was. It was hard not to, but she had so many other things to think about—especially getting the store ready for its grand opening during the Winter Wonderland Weekend, just two weeks away.

Already Starr's Fall was transforming itself into something like a Norman Rockwell painting—wreaths on every door, lights spangled along the lampposts on Main Street, and this morning Jenna glimpsed a hard frost on the ground, sparkling like silver. It really did feel like Christmas was around the corner.

"Well, it's about time," a voice harrumphed before Jenna had completely opened the door. She blinked, surprised to see Henrietta Starr standing on her new-and-improved porch. Instead of a lumpy old sofa, there were Adirondack chairs, as well as an American flag and a sculpture of a grizzly bear that Zach had sourced from a local artist, and a hand-carved welcome sign by the door.

"Miss Starr..." Jenna greeted her in surprise. She peered out into the empty parking lot, looking for a car. "Did you come with Laurie?"

"No," Henrietta replied in the same tetchy tone. "I walked on my own two feet." She glanced down at her feet, encased in sensible brogues, her wool stockings pooling in wrinkles around her ankles.

"You *walked*?" Jenna didn't manage to hide her surprise. Miller's Mercantile was half a mile from the center of town, and Henrietta had told her at the boardgame night it was too far for her, which had been something Jenna had no trouble believing.

"Why do you sound so surprised?" Henrietta demanded, straightening her tweed skirt before she admitted grudgingly, "It took me some time. But if I don't move these old bones every so often, I'll never be able to. Or so Laurie keeps telling me."

Jenna smothered a laugh. "Wise advice," she told Henrietta.

"Would you like to have a look around? Or rest for a minute." She gestured to the armchair by the window. "We're not quite open yet, so things are still a little jumbled, but if I can help you find anything..." She trailed off, for Henrietta was already shuffling through the store, leaning heavily on her cane. Jenna watched her go with a funny little ache in her chest. There was something both so dignified and desperately sad about Henrietta Starr's careful steps through the store, the way she stopped and peered at something on a shelf, before giving a little harrumph.

"Let me know if you need anything," Jenna called, before heading back to where she'd been working. Now that the store was finally coming together, she was feeling positive and even excited about its re-opening. The resistance she'd felt to changing it seemed silly now, the temper tantrum of a child, although Jenna knew herself well enough to accept that it hadn't been childish stubbornness that had kept her from renovating Miller's Mercantile, but simple fear. An unexpected bonus of this whole endeavor had been how much she'd enjoyed it. Despite her resistance, it hadn't been nearly as painful a process as she'd feared, and she'd really enjoyed the creative challenges. Although if she let herself, she still felt nervous that the whole thing would be a flop; the customers wouldn't come, she wouldn't be able to repay the regeneration grant, *and* she'd be eating the salad bar leftovers every night.

Most of the time, though, she could talk herself down from that particular ledge. She had reason to be optimistic; Jack, with all his investment experience, seemed confident that the changes she'd made to the store were the right ones. And she trusted Jack...

Which was why she wished he'd said something *slightly* less oblique in his text message. Something she could pin some possibility, some *hope*, onto. But never mind, because she wasn't obsessing.

"The store looks different from what I remember," Henrietta remarked as she stumped toward Jenna. She was carrying a nylon shopping bag that had a few lumpy items in it which looked like soup cans. Jenna hoped she'd found the ones she'd stocked with more heft to them, as Henrietta herself had suggested.

"I've been giving it a makeover," Jenna told her cheerfully. "Do you like it?"

"Hmm..." Henrietta looked around critically. "Better selection of food, I suppose." She turned to Jenna with a narrowed, bright-eyed gaze that was close to a glare. "Although I *don't* like beef in canned soup. The meat is always so stringy."

"Noted, thank you," Jenna murmured. "May I take that for you?" She reached for the bag, and Henrietta handed it over, somewhat grudgingly.

"What happened to your parents?" she barked as Jenna took the soup cans out of the bag. "How come they're not running this place anymore?"

"They retired," Jenna replied. "They're living in Florida."

"Hmm." Henrietta pursed her lips. "I'd thought they'd died."

Jenna smothered a startled laugh. "No, not yet," she replied as she rang up the first can of chicken noodle with vegetables.

"Your father was always a bit of a looker, wasn't he?" Henrietta remarked. "Charming with the ladies, as I recall."

Jenna's eyebrows rose. That was the first time she'd heard *that*, although admittedly her father had been—and still was—a handsome man, charming to his customers. "I suppose he was," she told Henrietta. "He and my mother love each other very much."

"Well, your mother certainly loved him," Henrietta replied

shrewdly, before adding quickly, "I always thought they were a good-looking couple."

What, Jenna wondered, was the old lady implying? What had she noticed—or maybe even *seen*? All Jenna's childhood, her parents had been wrapped up in each other, often to the exclusion of their two children. At least it had felt that way to Jenna... but it *had* been that way, hadn't it? Her memories couldn't be that messed up.

"In any case," Henrietta resumed, "I hope they're enjoying their retirement. Life is short enough." She paused before continuing in a trembling voice, "In fact... I just learned my daughter died."

Jenna nearly dropped the soup can she was holding. "Your... your daughter?" she exclaimed, startled, before quickly adding, "I'm so sorry."

"I never knew her." Henrietta's expression turned distant; every wrinkle and line in her face seemed to be etched even more deeply. "I gave her up for adoption when I was just a young woman, barely all of twenty." The corners of her thin lips turned up in a wry, crooked smile, although her eyes drooped with sorrow. "I met a man in New York and fell in love with him, more fool me. It ended up being rather inconvenient... for him especially, as it turned out."

"I'm so sorry..." Jenna didn't know what else she could say. She could hardly believe Henrietta Starr, the matriarch of the town, was sharing such painfully intimate details of her life.

Henrietta shook her head, in both acceptance and dismissal. "It was a long time ago. I let it affect me for far longer than I should have. And it took me nearly seventy years to try to find my daughter... and then it was too late. I just found out she'd died a year ago, of breast cancer. Her son wrote me after he'd checked her—oh, what is it called, Face-something?"

"Facebook," Jenna filled in quietly.

"That's right." She nodded and then straightened. "In any case, life is too short for regrets. You should learn from your mistakes, not let them fester, and worse, affect your future." She gave Jenna an uncomfortably beady look. "Don't you agree?"

"Yes," Jenna said after a moment, swallowing hard. "I do." Henrietta had sounded like she'd meant the remark personally. Had even she heard the gossip about her and Jack, or was Jenna just projecting? She glanced down at the cans of soup. "That'll be four-fifty."

Henrietta reached for her voluminous pocketbook, taking out a little embroidered change purse before counting out the amount in quarters with painstaking precision.

"I could give you a lift back," Jenna offered once she'd taken the money, "if you'd rather not walk?"

Henrietta gave her an imperious look, her nostrils quivering. "I am perfectly capable of managing the walk back, thank you," she said, and, throwing back her bony shoulders, she strode out of the store.

Jenna put the money in the register before slowly walking back to the shelves she'd been stacking. Her mind was buzzing with all Henrietta had said—both about her own life and Jenna's. What had she meant, saying that about her parents? It almost had seemed as if she'd been implying that Jenna's mother loved her father more than he loved her back, and that thing about her father being a looker and so charming...

Jenna had always assumed her parents' marriage had been mutually consuming. It had certainly felt that way as a child. But what if she'd been wrong? What if it had been more one-sided than she'd ever seen or felt? And why had Henrietta talked about regrets as if she knew Jenna's own history? If the gossip had reached Henrietta Starr's ears... well, it was all part of living in a small town, Jenna supposed. And as far as regrets went, she definitely didn't want them to affect her future, and certainly not for seventy years...!

Quickly, before she could overthink it or chicken out, she texted Jack.

> Hope you're having a good week.

She hesitated, wanting to say something more, but still instinctively reluctant to put herself out there too much. Then she thought of Henrietta again and decided to be at least a little bit reckless.

> I've been thinking of you and wishing we could have continued our conversation from the other night. There was more I wanted to say.

She pressed send before she could have second thoughts, and then let out a shaky sigh, tossing her phone aside and then rubbing her face with her hands. She didn't regret saying what she had—not much, anyway—and really she hadn't admitted that much, even if it was more than she had before, but she knew she'd be checking her phone compulsively until Jack replied, trying not to obsess and doing it anyway.

* * *

By the next afternoon, as Jenna headed over to Maggie's for Thanksgiving dinner, she was feeling more than a little anxious about the whole affair—or *un-affair*, as it so happened. Jack hadn't replied, although she'd seen, with a plunging sensation in her stomach, that her text had been delivered and read... just three minutes after she'd sent it. And still, twenty-four whole hours later, nothing but silence.

Jenna had given herself several stern talking-tos, insisting it wasn't a big deal and that he was busy, or maybe thinking about his reply, or maybe he'd let his phone run down and had forgotten to bring a charger.

These were, she told herself, all reasonable scenarios... as was the possibility that he'd blanked her because he didn't know what to say and being with his city friends had reminded him of everything he'd missed about his former life, and so he was trying to figure out a way to let her down gently.

That, really, seemed like the most probable scenario of all.

She tried not to tie herself up in knots over it, especially with Henrietta's words about her parents still fresh in her mind. She really, really didn't want to love a man more than he loved her. She didn't even want to *like* a man more than he liked her. Not anymore. And if that's where things were at with Jack... well, she'd focus on all the things she liked about her life instead, especially her friends, and do her best to forget all about Jack Wexler if she could.

"Jenna!" Laurie enveloped her in a warm hug as Maggie waved from the kitchen and Zach and Ben both gave her a grin from the desk, where they were hunched over the computer, playing the fantasy role-playing game they both loved, RainQuest. Jenna had been shocked to learn her brother had loved the game, and had played it somewhat compulsively when he'd come home to help their mother through a cancer scare many years ago—she'd been in San Francisco, and her parents hadn't even told her her mom was sick, something that still stung if she let it. She wasn't going to right now.

"I hope you're both slaying orcs or whatever it is you do," she told them as she brought the pumpkin and apple pies she'd made over to Maggie before shedding her coat.

"It's wyverns, thank you," Zach replied with a grin. "Get your fantasy creatures right, please." He peered behind her as if expecting someone else to appear. "Where's Jack?"

"Not here," Jenna replied as blandly as she could, wondering why her brother had assumed Jack would be accompanying her. It wasn't like they were *dating* or anything. "He was in the city for the weekend," she told him, "and he's spending Thanksgiving with his mom. And in any case, he wasn't invited."

"Oh, but he would have been," Laurie protested. "All you had to do was say the word! And I can't help but notice," she added teasingly, "that you seem to know his movements." She frowned thoughtfully, tapping her chin. "Hmm... I wonder why."

Jenna shook her head good-naturedly. "I know all of Starr's Fall is dying for us to get together, but if it happens, can we please just let it happen naturally?"

"Ooh, that sounds promising!" Maggie exclaimed before laughing when Jenna stuck her tongue out at her.

Once this kind of gentle ribbing would have annoyed or even alarmed her, made her feel like she'd admitted too much, but now she found she was almost enjoying it. If only Jack would reply to her text...

But she wasn't going to overthink it. Definitely not. Even so, Jenna slipped her phone out of her pocket for a discreet peek, and had to suppress a sigh when she saw there had been no new messages. Never mind. She'd sent that text for her sake as much as Jack's, to prove to herself that she'd both moved on and could be brave. Whether Jack replied or not was immaterial.

Sort of.

Maggie was taking the turkey out of the oven, and others were decanting vegetables and sauces into serving dishes, and so

Jenna slid her phone back into her pocket to help bring the meal to the table.

"This all looks amazing," Zach told Maggie as he slipped an arm around her waist and kissed her cheek. "*You're* amazing."

"Well, thank you," Maggie replied, flushing with pleasure while her fifteen-year-old son Ben rolled his eyes and pretended to make gagging noises, although Jenna knew as well as anyone that Ben was secretly—or not-so-secretly—thrilled that Zach was in their lives.

"So I'm meeting my mom on Saturday," Laurie told Jenna in a low voice as she mashed the potatoes and Jenna added butter to the boiled carrots.

"You are?" she said in surprise. "You got in touch, I'm guessing?"

Laurie nodded. "I told her I was willing to try again. I mean... I'll be honest, I think I'd give her as many chances as she needs, because... isn't that what you do? There's no 'three strikes and you're out,' right? Although if she doesn't show up, it *will* be three strikes." Laurie sighed. "But I keep telling myself that I don't know what she's been going through. Maybe she'll tell me, though, and then I'll understand more."

"I hope so," Jenna replied, "for your sake." And she hoped this time Laurie's mom turned up.

"Yeah." Laurie gave a little grimace as she started spooning the potatoes into a serving bowl. "If she lets me down again... well, it will be hard, I know that much. But I still want to try, because she seems to *want* to try, you know? And that's enough for me."

Jenna lightly touched her arm. "I get it," she said sincerely. Maybe wanting to try really was enough. Maybe that's where Jack was... although she needed to *not* be thinking of Jack right now.

"And I'm glad for you," she told Laurie. "Let me know how it goes, okay?"

Laurie smiled and nodded. "I will."

Annie and Mike arrived then, Annie looking a little pale and tired and Mike protective and bear-like, his arm around her as they came up the stairs. Barb had taken a turn for the worse recently, and Jenna knew her friend was on high alert, checking her phone even more than she was. Everyone embraced them warmly, especially Annie, and for a second it felt like a lovefest before Mike announced he was hungry, and Maggie said she just had to make the gravy, and the crowd scattered with a few people discreetly wiping their eyes.

Everyone started pitching in to bring the meal to the table—carrying dishes, pouring wine, putting on music. Jenna quickly checked her phone again—nothing.

"So how's your Jack?" Mike asked her as they all went to sit down, the table heaving under the platters of delicious food—green bean casserole with crispy onions, sweet potatoes with a golden-brown marshmallow topping, glistening, jewel-like cranberry sauce, and of course the turkey—beautifully browned and smelling delicious.

Jenna smiled and shook her head. "He's not my Jack, Mike, as I think you very well know," she told him teasingly, "and he's fine as far as I know." Not that she'd heard from him since he'd left for New York, but still. He was probably fine.

"Man should get a move on," Mike stated authoritatively. "Life is short and none of us is getting any younger."

It was more or less the same sentiment as Henrietta Starr's. "True enough," Jenna agreed wryly, hoping to leave the conversation there. She sat down and reached for her wine as Mike turned to say something to Annie. Everyone, she mused, seemed to take it for granted that she and Jack would get together. It felt like a foregone conclusion, and only a matter of time. As cautious as she tended to be, it was hard not to start believing their hype; even now part of her was half-expecting Jack to bound up the stairs, throw open the door, and take her into his arms in the grandest of gestures. This, despite the radio silence on the text front. She surely wasn't delusional.

She sighed and took a sip of her wine as she told herself to stop mooning. Henrietta had been right; life was too short, as well as too precious, to waste on regret of any description. If Jack wasn't interested, well, then, she'd get over it. She still had a good life—plenty of friends whom she adored and who adored her back, a business that was ready to re-open and have a roaring trade, her health...

Okay, it wasn't the *longest* list, but it was long enough. She would let it be enough. For once, she would let it be enough. At this realization, Jenna felt something settle inside herself. The cynicism as well as the yearning, the regret along with the self-defensiveness... All the brittle emotions she'd clung to after the breakup with Ryan melted away, at least in this moment. She didn't need Jack to text back, as much as she wanted him to. It really had been enough that she'd been brave enough to text him in the first place.

She was happy just as she was, Jenna realized, with her friends, her business, her brother, her whole life. She really was thankful.

* * *

Later, as she tottered home, only slightly tipsy, with still no reply from Jack and yet still holding on to the feeling that all was okay with the world, Jenna had the sudden, surprising thought that maybe she'd call her mother. She couldn't even remember the last time they'd spoken; it had been months, at the very least. Over dinner, Zach had mentioned he'd had a video call with her that morning, and, thinking of Henrietta's oblique comments about her parents' relationship, Jenna had felt a sudden pang of —something. Longing or regret, she wasn't sure which, but she knew she wanted things to be different with her parents.

And so, as she let herself into the house, she reached for her phone. Nope, still no text from Jack, which was *slightly* soul-destroying, despite her insistence on optimism. It had been over twenty-four hours now, and the radio silence was starting to feel a little hurtful. Never mind. Life went on.

Defiantly, she swiped to call her mom.

"Jenna...?" Her mother sounded hesitant and a little incredulous that she'd called.

"Hi, I thought I'd wish you a happy Thanksgiving," Jenna greeted her in a tone of slightly forced joviality. "Zach mentioned you guys were spending the day with golf friends?" Somewhat weirdly, her parents had discovered golf upon their retirement and become semi-obsessive about it.

"Ye-es, some friends of your father's." Jenna didn't miss the emphasis, like they weren't her mother's friends. What exactly did that mean? Did it relate in any way to what Henrietta had said, or was Jenna reading way too much into offhand comments? Her mother let out a little uncertain laugh. "It's so nice to hear from you."

"I'm sorry I haven't called sooner," Jenna said, and her mother let out the same little laugh.

"Well... I wasn't expecting it," her mom told her, and instead of feeling stung, as she might once have, and snapping something back, Jenna just sighed.

"I know," she said quietly. "I'm... sorry."

"Oh, Jenna." Her mother sighed too, the sound full of

sadness. "You don't need to be sorry." She paused. "If anything... I'm the one who should be sorry, and I am."

Well, this was brand-new territory for them, Jenna reflected wryly. Her conversations with her parents had tended to be staccato-short, snapped-out phrases rife with unspoken hostility, at least on her side. On her mother's side she'd assumed indifference, but now she wondered.

She wondered about a lot of things.

"Why, Mom?" she asked quietly. "Why should you be sorry?"

"Oh, just..." Her mother's voice wavered. "I know you've been angry with us for years now, and I've never really done anything about it, even though I know I probably should have."

Also brand-new territory, and it left Jenna momentarily speechless.

"I don't know what to say," she said at last, because she really didn't.

"I'm not sure I do either," her mother replied, and they were both silent for a moment, in a way that *didn't* feel hostile. Finally her mother spoke. "I suppose... I just want to let you know that I'm glad to hear from you. After talking to Zach recently... I realize maybe your dad and I... we hurt you without meaning to. I did, by being so..."

She stopped then, and Jenna wondered how she might have finished that sentence. She decided not to press. "I just thought you didn't care all that much," she admitted, an ache in her voice because it felt exposing, to say that much.

"Oh, Jenna." Her mother gave a soft sigh. "Of course I cared. I still care. But I let... other things... get in the way of that. Of us." She paused, seeming like she was going to continue in that vein, before suddenly switching to a new tack. "I suppose," she said, "you always seemed so independent to me. You were scheming to get out of Starr's Fall since you were tiny. You had such big dreams about seeing the world, going places..."

That had all come crashing down. "I know I did," Jenna replied, "but you and Dad, Mom... you've always seemed like you had this fairy-tale romance, and somehow that didn't translate to a fairy-tale family." She felt her throat thicken and she forced herself to plow on. "You and Dad have always been... your own unit. Totally contained and... consumed with each other. Zach and I felt like we were on the outside, looking in, rather than part of something." She'd never verbalized how that had felt, and saying it now only made her feel sad. Did it even matter anymore?

Her mom was quiet for a long moment. "I never meant to make you feel that way," she finally said, sounding unhappy. "But I accept that I—we—did."

Which wasn't all that much of an apology, really, yet Jenna recognized it was perhaps all her mother could give in this moment. She thought of Laurie, willing to give her biological mother so many chances, because she didn't know the full story. Maybe Jenna didn't know the full story with her own parents. Maybe loving someone was about loving the worst or weakest part of themselves and not just the strongest or the best.

It was a lot to think about.

"I'm glad we've talked," she said at last, and her mother clutched at her words like a lifeline.

"Me, too. And I... I hope we can talk again. I love you, Jenna. I know I haven't said it nearly enough, but I do."

Jenna was silent for a few seconds, absorbing the throb of emotion in her mother's voice that she didn't think she'd ever heard before. "I love you, too," she said.

They said their goodbyes, and Jenna stood there for a moment in the darkened kitchen, the phone in her hand. She glanced at it again, out of habit rather than hope. No reply from Jack.

And that, amazingly, really was okay at last. Mostly. She wasn't going to let it define her, or them, if there even *was* a them, which right now it didn't seem like there was. Which was also okay.

Mostly.

17

"This turkey looks nice, Mom." With a determined smile, Jack prodded the slice of rubbery turkey on his mother's plate. "With a little cranberry sauce?" He speared a single, gelatinous cranberry and sawed off a bite of the turkey before proffering the fork hopefully at his mother, who stared at him without speaking, her expression vacant.

Today had not been a good day for her. With a sigh, Jack sat back in his seat and looked around the nursing home's dining room, decorated in shades of bland beige and olive green, with cheerful, innocuous-looking prints of flowers interspersed on the walls. Other residents of the memory care unit were enjoying their Thanksgiving dinner—or not. Most of them had the same vacant stare as his mother's, although one woman was eating with gusto. Jack would not have realized she had dementia save for when she leaned over to him, winking, and asked, "Hey, hon, do you know how much I have to tip in this joint?"

He'd almost laughed, except there was something so desperately sad about the calculating expression in her bright eyes. She obviously had no idea she was in a locked memory unit.

"I don't think you need to tip here," he'd told her with a small smile, and she'd beamed at him, delighted.

"Really, no tip? Wow." She'd shaken her head. "Classy place."

Indeed, Jack thought with a wry weariness. His mother had picked this nursing home back when she'd first been diagnosed with Alzheimer's three years ago, and she'd still possessed the cognitive acumen to plan her own care. She'd grown up not too far away, in southern Massachusetts, and she'd wanted to be near her childhood home, never mind that nobody was still around from those days.

Back then, Jack had visited the home with her; to his shame he remembered checking his phone several times during the half-hour tour, jangling the keys in his pocket, and generally, he feared, acting like an ass. Looking back, his mother must have been both hugely shaken and afraid to be facing such an overwhelming challenge in life, and Jack knew he had not been there emotionally for her. At all.

He'd been impatient to focus on what he'd thought *really* mattered... his latest investment, making money, the New York Stock Exchange. They'd been more important to him than his frail mother. He felt a deep shame that he'd been that man, and not even that long ago. It was, he reflected, hard to excuse.

"How about another bite, Mom?" he suggested gently as he handed her the fork. She took it listlessly, holding it in her hand without taking a bite, so a crimson droplet of cranberry sauce fell back onto her plate. "And pumpkin pie for dessert," he told her jovially, like he was coaxing a child, and he was rewarded with a heartbreakingly small smile.

Jack sat back in his seat, a soft sigh escaping him. The last few days had been particularly jarring; they had been the first time he'd left Starr's Fall for any appreciable length of time, and he'd found he missed the little town he'd once been so determined to avoid, which had surprised him, because he'd really been looking forward to a long weekend with old friends in New York—if friends was really the right term. Former business colleagues and friendly acquaintances might be a more accurate description, but when his old colleague Will Bryant had reached out, asking him to come to a last-minute house party, Jack had agreed more on principle than anything else. He was enough of a hermit as it was, so he really felt he should accept any invitation. And he'd been deeply curious as to whether he could slot back into his old life like he'd never left.

He'd got his answer to that question pretty quickly. He couldn't. Not easily, anyway, even though he'd wanted to. All Will and his wife and their so-called friends seemed to want to talk about was money, or the trappings of money. Their new summer house, the trips to the Italian lakes or Dubai, the latest Wall Street gossip, every guy checking the NYSE on their phones every two seconds like he had a physical tic. *No one* had seemed happy —the men restless, impatient and shifty-eyed, the women high-strung and nervous, braying with laughter at things that weren't funny, and everyone drinking way too much, to anesthetize themselves in the midst of their smugly happy lives—Bloody Marys or mimosas at breakfast, a bottle of wine or three at lunch, whiskey and cocktails in the evening, another nightcap to round off the day. It was the way Jack had lived once upon a time, and happily so, but that weekend he discovered he'd wanted to leave about five minutes after he'd arrived.

Perhaps the worst part of the whole experience had been the way all these former friends had treated him—like he'd died, and they'd managed to resurrect his corpse. No one asked him about his new life, just disparaged having to live so far away from everything. Several people had assumed he'd be "back in the game" as soon as his doctor gave the all-clear, because of course that had to be what he wanted... right?

"We're just waiting to see what you do next," Will had said as he'd thrown back his single malt. "Don't stay away too long, buddy, all right?" he added, clapping him on the shoulder. "We need your energy."

"I'll see," Jack had murmured. There had been a complicated part of him that had so desperately *wanted* to slot back into what everyone else was doing. Had longed for it to be that simple, that easy. He still missed the energy of his old life, the sense of purpose and power, the simplicity of skating over so much of life in order to completely focus on a job he knew he could do, and really well at that.

Actually living—being, relating—was a lot harder. Especially after the text he'd got from Jenna yesterday.

While his mom took another bite of turkey, Jack slid out his phone and stared at the message he still hadn't replied to.

> I've been thinking of you and wishing we could have continued our conversation from the other night. There was more I wanted to say.

It had been enough to make his whole body tingle, his heart leaping with both excitement and hope, because he knew it must have cost Jenna a lot to admit so much. She was one of the most emotionally cautious people he knew. And he'd been all ready to fire a "me too, when can we talk"-type response before he'd hesitated. Not out of reluctance, or even caution, but simply because when it came to Jenna he really didn't want to mess this up.

She'd obviously been very badly hurt by the city schmuck who had messed with her heart years before. Jack didn't want to do the same thing, by rushing in with possibilities or promises he couldn't deliver on, because he didn't have everything figured out

—about Jenna, about their situation, about his own life or his own heart.

It had been his MO as a venture capitalist, never to take that leap before he knew everything about what he was getting into. He'd known some guys who liked to latch on to the latest hot thing and run with it wherever it took them, enjoying the leaps and dives, weathering the plunges and exulting in the highs. They'd thrived on the risk-taking, treating venture capitalism like an extreme sport, willing to sustain a few bruises and breaks in the process. Jack had always taken a more cautious, cool-headed approach. He observed, he researched, he considered all the angles and then, and only then, did he make a move. Fast. And he succeeded. Always.

He was emotionally astute enough, if, he acknowledged, if only just, to recognize that comparing an investment to a relationship might not be the healthiest thing to do, but there *were* similarities. And Jack needed to figure out just what he wanted from Jenna, what he could offer her, before he promised or even told her anything. But he was conscious it had now been nearly twenty-four hours without a reply, and she was understandably most likely waiting for something from him.

"You're a good boy, Jack." His mother's voice was soft, and Jack jerked up from his phone, feeling guilty for ignoring her, as she put down her fork and patted his hand. "A good boy."

He so wasn't. He'd seen his mom *maybe* once a year before the Alzheimer's diagnosis. After his dad died, Jack had actually had his assistant help with the arrangements, rather than doing it himself. He had a vivid and now extremely uncomfortable memory of asking his assistant to call his mother back about the message she'd left regarding what casket they should choose for his father, and whether he should be buried in his best suit. The memory of just how callous he'd been, and worse, without even realizing it, still made him cringe.

Funny how a life-threatening heart attack could put everything into startling perspective. And sitting here with his mom as she waited out her days... well, it made him want to jump on living his own life to the full.

But was that with Jenna? And was he crazy, thinking this way? Why not just have fun and see where it went? That's what most men would do. But already Jack knew that wouldn't work. Not with Jenna's history and not the way he operated, and in any case, neither of them was getting any younger. Who wanted to waste time, especially if, on the fringes of his mind, he had some hazy ideas about marriage and children? Which maybe *was* crazy.

"Mom..." Jack asked suddenly, "how did you know that Dad was the one? For you, I mean?" His parents, Jack had always thought, had lived very humdrum, middle-class lives, and yet they'd been so very obviously happy together, in a quiet, uncomplicated way, and there was, he was coming to realize, nothing at all humdrum about that.

"Your father..." his mother replied, her voice wavering as her expression clouded. Jack's heart lurched. Did his mom even remember his dad? The thought was heartbreaking.

Then her face cleared, and she gave him a beatific smile. "I knew he was the one because when he saw me his expression changed." She let out a little, girlish laugh, so unlike the usual sounds she made—weary sighs, the occasional groan. "His eyes sparkled, and he looked so *happy*. And I knew I wanted to be with someone who was always so pleased to see me." His mother cocked her head, her vacant gaze, for a brief moment, turning both gentle and shrewd. "If you can't put a spring in her step, Jack, then you're looking in the wrong place."

Did he put a spring in Jenna's step? Jack realized he had no idea... but maybe he could find out. With a chuckle, he patted his mother's hand. "Wise advice, Mom," he told her. "Wise advice."

* * *

Later, he drove through November's bleak and wintry landscape back to Starr's Fall. Night was falling, and the day seemed cold and cheerless, although maybe that was just his mood, knowing he was returning to a vast and empty house. Again.

As he drove by Miller's Mercantile, Jack noticed the new sign, the refurbished porch, everything looking ready for the grand opening during the Winter Wonderland Weekend, and he felt a rush of pride for what he and Jenna had accomplished together. He also saw a light on in the kitchen and before he could over-think it, or even think at all, he jerked the steering wheel hard enough to cause a spray of gravel as he pulled his Porsche Spyder into the store's empty parking lot.

He still hadn't come up with a plan as he walked toward the kitchen door. He was a man who *always* had a plan, with multiple bullet points, and right now his head was empty, without a single coherent thought rattling around inside. Still he kept walking. Tapped lightly on the door and waited.

It took Jenna a few moments to come to the door, and then undo the bolt, and then stare at him in obvious stupefaction. Was there a sparkle in her eye, a spring in her step, at the sight of him? Jack hadn't seen either, but it was dark.

"Hey." His voice was a rumble, and he had to clear his throat. Heaven help him, but he was nervous. And he still didn't even know what he was here to say.

"Hey." She cocked her head, her hair in a long loose braid over her shoulder, gleaming almost gold in the dim lighting. She was wearing a wildly patterned shirt in purple and red with a corduroy skirt and striped wool tights, and she looked so vibrant and alive, Jack had a sudden urge, a *need*, to take her into his arms.

He put his hands in his pockets instead.

"Can I come in?" he asked.

"All right." She stepped inside, and he came into the kitchen, which was as small and homely as he remembered, cluttered with dishes and papers.

"I just got back from Thanksgiving at Maggie's," Jenna told him as she closed the door. "I don't know if you'd heard, but Barb, Annie's mom, is nearing the end."

"I'm sorry," Jack said quietly. "I hadn't heard."

"It's a long time coming, but still... when it does come, I know it will feel like a shock." She glanced at him uncertainly, before lowering her gaze, so quickly that he hadn't been able to gauge her expression, never mind whether there was a sparkle or not. "Would you like a drink?"

"Uh... sure." He let out an uncomfortable laugh as he admitted, "I didn't really have a plan in stopping by. I just did it."

"Oh?" Jenna sounded diffident as she went to fill the kettle. "And why was that?"

"Because I haven't responded to your text," he stated baldly, "and I didn't want to leave it any longer."

"Ah." She nodded, her back to him as she stood at the sink. "Well, I appreciate your consideration," she remarked as she set the kettle on the stove and then turned to face him, her hands on her hips. "But please don't feel beholden, Jack, or pressured, or something like that." She gave a little shrug, her gaze skating away from his. "I wrote that text right after I'd... talked to someone." She let out a little laugh. "Henrietta Starr, as a matter of fact. She gave me some advice and I guess I felt a little reckless, thinking about how regret is *not* the most powerful force I want to have in my life." She drew a quick, agitated breath. "And... the truth is, the other day, before my annoying brother came in here and did not seem to read the mood, I thought..." She blew out the breath she'd just taken, her cheeks turning pink. "I thought something might have been about to happen between us. And maybe I read that really wrong—"

"You didn't," Jack inserted quickly, and her gaze moved to his, widening as her cheeks flared pinker, which delighted him.

"So why haven't you answered my text?" she asked unsteadily.

"Because I wanted to be sure—" he began, only to have her cut him off.

"Of what, exactly?" Her voice had turned sharp, and Jack decided total honesty was needed, even if he wasn't entirely sure how to explain what he'd been thinking.

"I know you've been hurt before," he stated carefully, "and I didn't want to be like that other city putz who messed around with you."

"So blanking me was the more considerate option?" she surmised, sounding both wry and a little hurt. She held up a hand to forestall his reply, although he didn't even know what he was going to say. "You know, I was actually okay with you not responding. It's Thanksgiving, a time to reflect and feel grateful and that jazz, and I *was*. I'm happy running this store, being on my own, living in this place. I've spent way too long being bitter and cynical about something that happened years ago, and I'm over it now." She grimaced. "I'm getting over it, anyway. So I'd really decided that you blanking me was no big deal, and I could move on."

"I wasn't actually blanking you," Jack felt he had to object. "I was considering how to respond."

Jenna gave a theatrical wince. "You do realize that might sound even worse? Like, how to let her down easily? You could have googled it. ChatGPT probably has some good breakup lines, not that we were even breaking up, because there was nothing to break in the first place—" Her voice had risen higher and higher, ending on something close to a gasp.

"Jenna." Jack kept his voice gentle. "It wasn't like that, I promise."

A breath rushed out of her and then she nodded. "Okay." She regarded him uncertainly for a moment as the kettle began to whistle. "Well, that's good, I guess," she finally said, and then turned around to set about making a pot of tea.

"Whenever I've made an investment," Jack told her, wanting her to understand, "I've taken my time. Really gotten to know the situation, the investment potential, analyzed all the pros and cons, so when I *do* make a decision, I'm going in with my eyes open, fully committed to the enterprise."

Jenna turned around, the teapot in her hands. "Okay, so in this situation, am I the investment?"

"Well..." He gave a grimacing grin. "Yes? I guess? In a manner of speaking."

She smiled, a flash of humor lighting her eyes, which filled him with relief. "Well, I've been compared to worse things, I'm sure." She put the teapot down before folding her arms and leveling him with a look. "But where is this explanation going, Jack? You ran a cost-benefit analysis and what did you come up with? Or is the data not all in yet to make an informed decision?"

Once again, he heard the hurt in her voice, and he understood it. Relationships *weren't* financial investments, to be decided with a spreadsheet; they were far more important than that. They were *life* investments, and yet at the end of the day... maybe his mom had been right. It was more elemental than anything he'd been deliberating.

Because Jenna put a sparkle in *his* eye and a spring in *his* step. And if he did the same for her...

Suddenly it was simple.

And so, with Jenna staring at him with a mixture of hurt, hope, and exasperation, Jack closed the space between them, took her into his arms, and kissed her.

Which was, he reflected, maybe what he should have done when she'd first opened the door. Or better yet, several weeks ago.

But, he decided as Jenna's arms came around him and he deepened the kiss, at least he was doing the right thing now.

18

As far as kisses went, it was pretty great. Totally great, in fact, and entirely welcome. Jenna's whole body buzzed as her mind emptied out and she wrapped her arms around Jack's neck, leaning into him and the kiss that wonderfully kept going on, his lips, warm and firm, moving over hers.

Okay, so she might have convinced herself that she was all right with disappointment, but *this* was amazing.

Then Jack broke it off, stepping back with a wry smile. "Sometimes analysis is overrated," he said, and Jenna let out a little laugh.

"Sometimes it is," she agreed, although part of her would have liked a little, or even a lot, more analysis. Like, had he just kissed her to shut her up or because he'd wanted to or was this actually *going* somewhere? Her once-crushed confidence was certainly doing better, but she still didn't feel brave enough to ask. Sometimes it was better not to know, so you could enjoy the moment.

And she'd definitely been enjoying the moment.

Still smiling, Jack ran his hands through his hair. Jenna knew that gesture. Knew it meant he was thinking through a problem, trying to find a solution, and one wasn't jumping out at him.

She took a step back. "So," she said, apropos of nothing.

"So," Jack replied, in the same tone.

Then they both simply stared at each other, until Jack finally broke the silence. "I'm not sure what to say," he admitted, which was not the beginning Jenna had been hoping for. "I really like you." Okay, that was better. "And I also really don't want to mess you around. And I'm usually a guy who likes to have a plan, who follows it to the tiniest detail, who knows exactly how everything is going to play out." He ran through his hair *again*, clearly agitated. "But maybe relationships don't work that way, and so instead of planning everything in advance, we can just see where —and how—this goes?" The upward lilt in his voice was the sound of uncertainty. Of doubt.

Jenna swallowed the acidic taste of disappointment, telling herself she was being ridiculously unreasonable. They'd only known each other for a few months. Of course he wasn't about to declare his undying love or sweep in with a marriage proposal or something absurd like that. But the sheer *tepidity* of his feelings still hurt. She'd spent three years trying to convince Ryan to love her. She didn't want to go into another relationship where she felt she cared more than he did at the outset.

And the truth was, she already knew she cared about Jack. A lot. But he didn't need to know that.

"That sounds... reasonable," she finally said, knowing she needed to respond.

"If less than thrilling?" Jack filled in with a grimace, and Jenna let out a little laugh of acknowledgment. He'd read her thoughts so perfectly. "Sorry, I am a facts-and-figures type of guy," he told her. "And it feels like there are a lot of variables here... I don't know what my future will look like. Having a heart attack was a major setback, but whether it changes things forever..."

What, Jenna wondered, was that supposed to mean? What *variables*?

"But..." he continued, his smile adorably crooked and endearing. "I really do like you."

Okay, she could go with that. "I like you, too," Jenna replied with an answering smile.

It was, she told herself as Jack pulled her close for another kiss, a good start. And just as before, she was going to let that be enough, even if she knew she already wanted more... and feared she might not get it.

* * *

As soon as Thanksgiving was over, it felt as if it was going to be Christmas in about two minutes. Jenna drove into town the next week, unable to keep from smiling because it had been a *very* nice weekend, spent mostly with Jack. After he'd kissed her—again—they'd curled up on the sofa in her kitchen and drank tea like an old married couple, *not* that she was thinking that way, of course. But it had been nice and something about it had felt simple and right in a way she knew she'd never felt with Ryan. And not that she was comparing them, either, but... it was kind of hard not to. She'd only had two serious relationships in her life, after all.

On Friday, she'd gone over to Jack's, and they'd done a hike around Bantam Lake; she'd teased him about his hiking boots, which had looked far more broken in than before, and he'd held her hand. They were adults, but she'd felt like a giggly teenager... as well as an old married couple again later that evening, when they'd watched Netflix on Jack's huge sofa, her legs in his lap. It was kind of a nice mix, Jenna reflected, and she was glad they weren't rushing things. Spending time together, cuddling on a sofa, the occasional—or often—amazing kiss... it was all wonderful. And like Jack, she was willing to wait and see where it went... or so she was telling herself.

The truth, Jenna acknowledged ruefully, was that she was falling fast and hard and she knew it. She just pretended she didn't.

As she drove into the town, she couldn't help but notice that the world had definitely got the memo it was coming onto Christmas, and the sight of Starr's Fall decked out in all its seasonal glory lifted her spirits. All along Main Street, brightly colored Christmas lights were strung along the holly wreath-bedecked lampposts, and Mike had already set up the thirty-foot-high Christmas tree on the village green, bushy and glorious, ready for its lighting on Friday. Midnight Fashion had color-coordinated Christmas outfits in the window—"perfect for your holiday party!"—and The Starr Light was strung with garishly festive red and green sparkly tinsel.

The Winter Wonderland Weekend was in less than two weeks, and Jenna was excited for it, more than she ever had been before. Miller's Mercantile was going to be a big part of the festivities, kicking off the weekend with its grand opening and hosting the dance on the final night. She and Jack had worked all day Sunday, decorating the barn with hay bales and Christmas lights, setting up tables for the potluck dinner food and laying in gallons of eggnog and mulled wine. Afterwards, they'd gone into the kitchen where Jenna made hot chocolate and Jack built a fire.

"Are you going to get a Christmas tree?" he'd asked as Jenna had handed him a mug.

"I don't know, maybe?" She'd frowned in thought. "I don't usually." Even if this year she was definitely feeling more festive.

His eyebrows had risen. "Why not?"

"When you're on your own... Christmas isn't all that fun." She'd curled up on one end of the sofa, cradling her mug in her hands. "What about you? What did you do for Christmas all these years?"

He'd grimaced slightly. "Worked straight through last year. Year before was a solo sail in the Everglades."

"Why do you look like you regret it now?" Jenna had asked curiously. "It sounds better than Christmas-for-one in New York, if that was the alternative."

"Well..." He'd paused, staring down into his mug. "I really should have been with my mother. She was all alone for Christmas... and I don't think I really realized back then how she would decline so much, so quickly. I... I wish I'd had that time with her. I hate thinking of her in that depressing nursing home, alone at Christmas, but back then... I didn't even give it a thought."

"Oh, Jack." Jenna's heart had both ached and softened at the sight of his eyes shadowed with sorrow, his mouth turned down in guilty regret. She'd covered his hand with her own. "You're here for her now."

"Yes..." He sighed his agreement. "And I know that's what I need to focus on. The present as well as the future, not the past, which I can't do anything about."

"Very true." It was advice Jenna had known she needed to heed herself... and she was trying.

Now as she pulled up in front of Laurie's store, Jenna told herself to focus on the plans for the weekend, not her burgeoning relationship with Jack. Although she suspected Laurie would want to talk about that more than the Winter Wonderland Weekend, if she knew her friend at all.

"Hey, stranger." Laurie's smile was wide, her eyes bright as Jenna let herself into the pet store. Laurie's dog Max trotted up to her, wagging his tail hopefully, and she bent down to scratch his ears.

"Stranger?" she repeated with a laugh. "I saw you for Thanksgiving."

"I know, but then you were AWOL all weekend, and I have it on good authority that your car was not in front of the mercantile *all day* Saturday."

Jenna laughed again, shaking her head. "Good authority? And who might that be?"

"Liz Cranbury. She came in here for some dog treats for Froufrou and she told me all about it. So." Laurie leaned her elbows on the counter as she regarded Jenna with hopeful eagerness. "Let's hear all the details."

"About the plans for the weekend?" Jenna answered innocently. "The barn decorating is coming along nicely—"

"Jenna." Laurie rolled her eyes. "I couldn't care less about that right now. Tell me about Jack."

"How do you know there's anything to tell?"

"Because you look," Laurie told her with a grin, "like the proverbial cat who got the cream—or is it a canary?" She frowned. "Or a canary dipped in cream, I don't know, but I can tell you are practically floating five inches off the ground, so *spill*."

Jenna couldn't help but laugh then. She did feel happy, and she didn't mind her friends knowing it. It was a fun, fizzy feeling, to be excited, to share her happiness. "*Well...*" she began, her voice laden with meaning, and Laurie's eyes widened as she leaned forward.

"Yes?"

"Jack stopped by on Thursday night, when I'd got home after our Thanksgiving dinner. And... one thing led to another... well, basically we argued, and then he just... kissed me." Jenna let out a happy little giggle.

"That sounds so romantic," Laurie breathed, her eyes like stars. "And so...? You're officially dating?"

"Well..." They hadn't talked about the status of their relationship beyond Jack's suggestion they "see where this goes," which was slightly less definitive than Jenna would have liked. "Yes," she told Laurie. "I guess. Pretty much."

Laurie frowned. "Pretty much?"

"We're just seeing how things go, no pressure," Jenna explained as lightly as she could. "I don't think either of us wants to rush anything, you know? And I'm trying to be relaxed about it all because before, when I dated Ryan..." She swallowed. She hadn't told Laurie all that much about her relationship with Ryan, although like everyone else in Starr's Fall, her friend had probably guessed. Still, talking about it was hard. "I was so intense about it, you know?" she began hesitantly. "I just really, really wanted it to work, and so I became pretty needy and awful, in retrospect. Clinging even though I knew that he hated it. I definitely don't want to be that way this time around."

"But last time, the guy was a jerk, and Jack isn't," Laurie pointed out. "Besides, you need to be yourself, whatever that looks like."

"Well... I want to be the best version of myself," Jenna said, trying to ignore the sudden fluttering of panic in her chest. She knew Laurie had a point; she'd been thinking the same thing herself in regard to her mother, that love was about accepting the worst version of someone, and not just enjoying the best someone could put on with a lot of effort, but...

She and Jack didn't *love* each other yet. And at the start of a relationship, it was best foot forward, right? Time to show the other person how great you were?

"We're just enjoying what we have for now," she stated firmly. "And that's enough."

"Okay," Laurie replied. "That works." She grinned and reached over to squeeze Jenna's hand. "I'm so happy for you! And... I've got news myself." She bit her lip, her eyes still bright, before admitting, "I saw my mom yesterday."

"What!" Jenna gaped at her. "Where? And how did it go?"

"We met in the city. I went for the day, and we had lunch like we were meant to before, but this time it was so much better. She explained some things... She married this guy, a real Wall Street type, you know?"

Jenna nodded, swallowing hard. She knew Wall Street types all too well. Ryan had been one, and so was Jack, although he'd changed, or at least was trying to... right?

"And she never told him about me," Laurie continued. "He has a thing about keeping up appearances, and I guess she was afraid. And when I contacted her, she panicked."

"And panicked again the second time she arranged to see you?" Jenna reminded her gently. She was doing her best to let go of her cynicism, but she didn't want to see her friend hurt.

"Yes, and you know what? I get it." Laurie lifted her chin in defiance. "It was hard, and she was trying, and she's still trying. She's going to tell him about me... I have two half-brothers, can you believe it? They're just teenagers, but she wants me to meet them. Eventually."

"I'm happy for you, Laurie," Jenna said sincerely. Laurie didn't need to hear any more of her cautious concerns. Just as she was enjoying this time with Jack, and seeing where it went, so Laurie could enjoy the same with her mother. You lost the pleasure of the moment by worrying about the possibilities of the future.

"All right, let's talk about Christmas," Laurie said as she pushed up from the counter. "Thursday and Friday night all the stores are open till nine, and the Christmas tree lighting is at six on the Friday. Mike is handing out presents to all kids under the age of twelve—Liz and Zoe have been wrapping them up all weekend. It's a choice of a coloring book and box of crayons or a mini basketball hoop and ball. Lizzy got them in bulk and paid for them out of the Business Association's budget."

"Sounds great," Jenna told her.

"Rhonda is doing free hot chocolates for the Christmas tree lighting," Laurie continued, consulting her notes, "and she's bulking out the food for the barn dance, although it's advertised as potluck, right? Has she been in touch?"

"We've been texting, but I'll check in with her after this. She says she's got everything under control."

"Lizzy's providing bagels and coffee on Saturday morning. She's setting up a stall on the green, and Bella and Ben are manning it so Lizzy and Michael can stay at the bakery. Maggie's got a Christmas crossword to hand out, too... anyone who completes it gets entered in a draw for a free monthly membership to Your Turn Next. Hopefully Main Street will be hopping!"

"Hopefully," Jenna agreed. "It's sounding like it already is."

Laurie put down her notes, her eyebrows raised. "And when is your grand opening?"

Nerves fluttered in Jenna's middle at the thought. "Friday afternoon, right before the Christmas tree lighting. Mike is going to arrive as Santa, hand out some lollipops, and then go on a float to the tree. Everyone's encouraged to walk behind, like a parade." She hoped the half-mile wouldn't feel too long.

"That's so cool!" Laurie's eyes sparkled. "I think it's going to be a fantastic weekend. Zach's been doing lots of advertising online... I really hope we get some interest from outside of Starr's Fall."

All those elusive tourists, Jenna thought wryly. "Me too," she told Laurie. Starr's Fall certainly needed it, and Miller's Mercantile in particular. A lot was riding on this one weekend.

* * *

After seeing Laurie, Jenna continued on her rounds, making sure that every business owner in Starr's Fall had something planned for the weekend. Midnight Fashion was offering 15 percent off all holiday wear; The Rolling Pin had created a special Christmas bagel, complete with red and green sprinkles, and the barber shop, run by the taciturn Ed Howes, who had never come to a Business Association meeting in his life, had agreed to give a 20 percent discount to anyone who got their hair cut there before Christmas.

As she walked back to her car, Jenna's spirits lifted. Under a winter-blue sky, Starr's Fall looked idyllic, the homes and stores that lined the street touched with golden sunshine, the windows rimmed with frost. The Business Association, with the aid of many able volunteers, had sprung for some sprucing—the planters that lined the street had miniature evergreen trees in them, and Christmas lights were twined through the bare branches of many of the trees. A brightly colored banner hung over the top of the town, by the green, advertising the Winter Wonderland Weekend. Lizzy had really upped the town's game, Jenna thought in admiration. This felt like a proper, important event.

Her mood remained buoyant as she headed back home. Jack had invited her over for dinner that night, supposedly to discuss the last-minute details of the weekend, but also, Jenna hoped, to simply be together. They'd spent a lot of time together since that first kiss, and Jenna was savoring every moment... and trying to do that and only that, rather than worry.

As she pulled into the parking lot of the mercantile, her heart gave a little flip at the sight of Jack's ridiculous Porsche Spyder. He was standing on the porch as she got out of her car, and for a second she feared he had some bad news. He looked so serious, his hands in the pockets of his parka, the wind ruffling his hair.

"You have a key, you know," she reminded him lightly. She'd given him one when they'd first started working on the renovations.

"I know, but I just got here, and I saw your car, so I thought I'd wait." His eyes crinkled at the corners as she climbed the porch steps and then he pulled her in for a quick but deliciously thorough kiss. His lips were cold, his hair ruffled, and Jenna's heart fizzed with both joy and relief. It couldn't be bad news if he was kissing her like that.

"I was just checking up on all the preparations for the weekend," she told him as she unlocked the front door. "Everyone seems on board."

"Great." He followed her into the store, whistling under his breath as he looked around. "I haven't been here in a week, and the place looks amazing. You've done such a good job, Jenna."

"So have you," she reminded him, but he shook his head.

"It was mainly your work. I love these touches." He pointed to the armchair and then the community bulletin board.

"Well, I thought about what you were saying at the start—how this store should be for everyone. I thought it could be something of a hub. In fact..." She dropped her keys on the counter as she turned to face him. "Starr's Fall's post office closed last year, so I've applied to be a contract postal unit, which can offer basically all the same services. It's not nearly as hard as I thought it would be; and it should increase footfall too."

"That's great." He took a step toward her and then slipped his arms around her waist. Jenna put her arms around him, resting her head against his shoulder, and for a second they just stood there, enjoying the moment. "You've really done amazing things," he murmured against her hair.

"Well, I wouldn't have done any of it without you," Jenna replied as she tightened her arms around him, leaning into the hug. "Thank you, Jack." She tilted her head to smile up at him. "Why did you come here, anyway? We're seeing each other tonight."

"Well..." He looked abashed. "I just wanted to see you."

Jenna smiled and then stood on her tiptoes to kiss him. That was the kind of answer she loved to hear.

19

Butterflies swirled in Jenna's stomach, but they were happy, excited ones. Mainly. It was the Friday morning of the Winter Wonderland Weekend and, more importantly, the grand re-opening of Miller's Mercantile. Jack was coming over for brunch and then to help with last-minute details before the opening at two and then the parade to the Christmas tree lighting.

Jenna had been working flat-out the last week and a half, both with the store and the weekend in general. She'd thought she'd had everything mostly in hand, but there had been so many last-minute details to attend to—a safety check for the Christmas tree lighting, a station to set up for hot chocolate, just-arrived stock to inventory, and seemingly a million other things. In between rushing around like a chicken with its head cut off, she'd spent every moment she could with Jack, and the result was that a mere ten days into their relationship, she was pretty sure she was in love with him.

They hadn't spoken about the future, not even in the haziest of terms, and Jenna had given herself many a stern talking-to about not running before she could walk, relationship-wise. Fairy tales were for movies and children. Time and experience would bear out the strength of their relationship, and she had to trust that. Trust, too, that Jack was being sensible with his approach... even if she, as ever, longed for more. Did she ever learn? Well, at least a little, she told herself. She might feel this way, but she wasn't going to tell him so.

Now, the morning of the store's re-opening, Jenna took time with her appearance. She'd bought a new maxi skirt from Midnight Fashion, in dark green faux suede, and paired it with the red cashmere sweater Liz had gifted her for her first date, creating a colorful Christmas look. Instead of her usual braid, she'd put her hair up in a loose chignon, letting a few auburn wisps frame her face. It was classy, she decided as she gazed at her reflection, but also still unique. She wasn't trying to be something she wasn't, just the best version of herself.

The doorbell rang, and she gave her reflection one last fleeting look before hurrying downstairs to open the door.

"You look amazing," Jack said as he kissed her hello. "I think the sight of you in that sweater had me hook, line, and sinker the first night."

Jenna laughed as she returned his kiss. "Zoe said I'd be able to knock you over with a feather while wearing it."

His gaze lingered on hers as she stepped back. "You could have. Easily." His smile was so warm, his eyes so blue, that Jenna felt a buzz of joy as well as relief. What was she so worried about? She'd been so happy these last few weeks, but there had also been a constant, low-level anxiety humming in her stomach because part of her, as ever, was waiting for the hammer to fall. For Jack to suddenly turn serious and tell her that things weren't working out the way he'd hoped. That she'd misread all the signals, existing in her own little romantic bubble, and actually that had never been what was going on here.

Sometimes she could almost hear him say it—the low rumble of his voice, the sorrowful tone, the slow shake of his head. She really needed to get over herself and her paranoia that every wealthy Wall Street type was like Ryan. Jack was different, and she was now, too.

"So guess what I made for brunch," she told him as she led him back into the kitchen.

"Pancakes?" Jack guessed hopefully. "Scrambled eggs? Coffee, I'm assuming, judging by the smell, which is a very good thing."

"Ta da!" Smiling a little nervously because she really hoped he appreciated the joke, Jenna brandished the platter she'd arranged earlier that morning, with succulent pink slices of smoked salmon, toasted sourdough, and little dishes of capers and cream cheese as accompaniments.

Jack stared at the platter for one heart-stopping moment, his expression completely blank, and Jenna's stomach went into freefall. Was he sensitive about how he'd come across the first time they'd met? She'd been just as rude, but maybe that didn't matter. Right now he looked…

Then he let out a shout of laughter and pulled her to him. "Amazing," he said, his lips brushing her hair. "I love it."

Once again, Jenna felt that little flutter of relief. Once again, she told herself there was nothing to worry about, and she needed to stop second-guessing every little thing.

Once again, she didn't entirely believe it, as much as she wanted to.

* * *

Today was Jenna's day. Jack stood at the edge of the porch as Jenna, with great fanfare, addressed the crowd.

"Thank you so much for being here today to herald a new era of Miller's Mercantile!" she said, and a raggedy cheer went up from the crowd. "Some of you know me pretty well," she continued, "and you know how resistant to change and frankly ornery about it I can be." This time good-natured—and knowing—laughter rippled through the crowd, and Jack smiled. "So renovating the mercantile has been as much about my own growth as a person as it has been about making this the best store it can be, for all of you."

She glanced at the crowd, smiling, and Jack saw many smiling back before a clap went up, and they were all applauding. Jenna looked taken aback by the praise, and maybe even a little teary. Heck, Jack was a little teary himself. He'd become invested in this place... and its lovely owner.

"But I have to say that I couldn't have done this without all of your support," Jenna continued, "and the support of one person in particular." Her gaze moved from the crowd to where Jack was standing on the side of the porch. "Thank you, Jack, for coming to Starr's Fall and offering me your expertise as well as your friendship—"

"Friendship," somebody scoffed. Jack was pretty sure it was Liz Cranbury. Another laugh rose from the crowd, and this time Jenna grinned.

"Well, more than a friend," she conceded, and Jack figured this was his cue to stride forward and slip his arm around Jenna's waist. She looked surprised and thankfully pleased by his uncharacteristically spontaneous display of affection, and even more so when he gave her a smacking kiss on the mouth.

"And now," he announced to all and sundry, "I think it's time to declare Miller's Mercantile officially open! What do you say, Jenna?"

Laughing and blushing, she pulled away from him to cut the satin ribbon she'd strung across the steps to officially re-open Miller's Mercantile while everyone cheered. There was, Jack noted, a fair-sized crowd gathered for the moment, with the usual suspects as well as a number of faces Jack didn't recognize. As people surged into the store, he smiled at Jenna, and she grinned back.

"That was certainly one way to open the store."

"I enjoyed it," he replied, and she laughed, her cheeks flushed, her hair falling about in wisps that framed her face, that long, sweeping skirt making her look like a schoolteacher on the prairie. It was a look he found he liked, but then he was fast realizing he liked just about everything about Jenna—even her prickly temper, the way she doubted herself, how she lifted her chin when she'd decided she was ready to face the world.

He'd seen her weaknesses, even if she was trying to hide them, and he'd shown and told her his. But today wasn't about weakness, but strength in community, in coming together, in starting over. Miller's Mercantile looked amazing, and Jack enjoyed both the sight of people exclaiming over the offerings— the coffee kiosk, the salad bar, the little gift section—and Jenna moving between customers, smiling and gracious and so very beautiful.

Jack wasn't letting himself think about love yet—they barely knew each other, really—but it felt like a close-run thing. A *very* close-run thing.

"Well, it looks like she's put this place on the map again," a voice said near him, and Jack turned to see an elderly woman nodding toward Jenna. He recognized Henrietta Starr from when she'd come into the boardgame café for Scrabble, although he'd never spoken to her.

"It does look like it," he agreed.

Henrietta Starr eyed him beadily. "I don't recognize you."

"I moved here in June," he told her, and then held out a hand. "Jack Wexler."

Henrietta glanced down at his hand, sniffed, and then touched two of her fingers to his in what Jack supposed was the approximation of a handshake. He smothered a smile.

"Back when I was a girl," Henrietta informed him without any sentimentality, "Starr's Fall had a baker, a butcher, a greengrocer, and a cheesemonger. And your milk and butter were delivered right to your door."

"Those were the days," Jack agreed. He knew Jenna was looking into partnering with a local dairy to offer fresh milk and butter; it was the same farmer who had provided the hay bales.

"They were," Henrietta agreed, heartfelt. "Not that you'd know. You can't be much more than forty."

"Forty-three next month," Jack told her, and she snorted.

"A mere child."

He felt a smile tug at the corner of his mouth. "Sometimes I feel that way."

Henrietta glanced at him appraisingly and then nodded toward Jenna. "And I hope you're going to make a decent woman of her?"

For a second, Jack could only goggle. "Umm..."

"Of course, she's decent already," Henrietta added, before wagging an arthritic finger in front of his face. "But don't break her heart, Mr. Jack Wexler. Having your heart broken once is acceptable and even advised. Gives you wisdom as well as empathy, as long as you don't let it sour you. But twice? I don't know many people who survive it twice."

Jack could not think of a single thing to say. Finally, he asked, genuinely curious, "Have you had your heart broken, Miss Starr?"

"Of course I have!" she barked. "Long before you were born, too. But..." She paused, eyeing him shrewdly. "I can tell you haven't. You've got that shiny, bright-as-a-bandbox glow to you. So you might not realize just how much it hurts." And with that, seeming to have imparted her wisdom, she stumped off toward the soup.

"I see you've met Henrietta Starr," Maggie murmured as she came up to join Jack.

Jack smiled ruefully as he kept his gaze on the elderly lady's retreating back. "Yes, and it was quite an experience."

Maggie nodded. "She has a lot of wisdom."

"She seemed like a savant, or maybe a fortune-teller." He shook his head slowly, still reeling from what the old lady had said. No, he hadn't had his heart broken, at least not in the way Henrietta had meant, but he'd certainly had his fair share of both challenges and disappointments. Still, he took Miss Starr's words to heart. He did not want to be the one who broke Jenna's heart a second time. No how, not in any way, shape, or form.

"It's so great to see her enjoying herself like this," Maggie said as she nodded toward Jenna, who was moving around the store like she owned it—which, Jack supposed, she did. But he knew what Maggie meant; there was a glow to Jenna, a purpose that shone from her whole being. She looked radiant, and it filled him with both pride and affection, as well as a yearning he couldn't ignore.

He'd once had that kind of purpose, that joy. All right, maybe it had been unhealthy and ended up almost killing him, but he still missed it. Helping Jenna with Miller's Mercantile had invigorated him, but it hadn't actually *satisfied* him. Rather, it had whetted his appetite for more. He wanted to work again. He'd been good at what he'd done, really good, and he had to figure out a way to fit it into his life again... But in Starr's Fall? How on earth would that work?

It was a problem for another day, he decided, as Jenna started toward him, her face rosy and flushed, her eyes still sparkling.

"Everyone seems to be having a good time," she told him and Maggie. "And the Christmas Dinners in Baskets are selling like hotcakes."

He smiled as he slid his arm around her waist. "It was a genius idea of yours."

"You had plenty of genius ideas too," she replied with a laugh as she hugged him. "I couldn't have done any of this without you."

The rest of the afternoon spun out in a golden thread. Jenna was kept busy chatting to customers, ringing up sales, and generally swirling about the store, the star of the show. Laurie had pitched in, helping with orders, and Jack became the unofficial bagging boy.

Then, at four o'clock, Jenna came up to Jack looking anxious. "Mike has just texted me to say he can't be Santa. Annie needs him... Barb has taken a turn for the worse."

"Oh, no." Jack put his arm around Jenna. "Poor Annie."

"We all knew it was coming, but..." She swallowed. "It's still hard to face." She glanced around at the children milling around the story expectantly, having been promised a visit by Santa. "What am I going to tell these kids? A lot of them still believe in Santa. I can't say he was a no-show!"

Jack hesitated, because while he was more than ready to be the hero of the hour... could he be a convincing Santa? Well, he'd just have to be. "I can do it," he told Jenna, and she looked at him in complete surprise. The notion clearly hadn't occurred to her.

"*You?*"

"I think, with a suit and a beard, I could do an adequate job," Jack replied with dignity, and Jenna let out a laugh.

"Oh, Jack, I didn't mean that. I'm sure you could," she exclaimed. "I just didn't think you'd want to be."

"Well, want and willing are two different things," Jack replied, and Jenna laughed again as she threw her arms around him.

"You're amazing," she told him. "Truly amazing. Come in the back and I'll get you the suit."

The suit, of slightly motheaten velvet and trimmed with frayed white felt, made Jack question the wisdom of his suggestion. It smelled like mothballs and old sweat and clearly had been neither washed nor worn in some time.

"Mike didn't need a beard," Jenna remarked with a frown. "But you obviously do. I'm sure I can find one somewhere..." She dug through the box of Christmas costumes that had come, Jack had learned, from the church basement, where the Starr's Fall Theater Group's costumes were all kept. Apparently they'd once done a Christmas play. "Ah, here we are!" She held up a beard that looked as well-used as the Santa suit. Itchy, too. Jack had to stifle a groan.

"Great," he said, and Jenna stood on her tiptoes to kiss his cheek. "Did I tell you you were amazing?"

"Yes, but you can tell me again."

Laughing, Jenna slid her arms around his waist and gave him a lingering kiss on the mouth as Jack pulled her even closer. "You're amazing," she murmured against his lips, and for that, Jack thought he'd do just about anything.

Still, he couldn't help but feel he made a rather self-conscious Santa as he made his grand entrance, to a chorus of raggedy cheers—and one poor toddler who burst into tears. Fortunately, that wasn't a sign of things to come, and within a few "ho ho ho"s,

Jack had found his Santa Claus groove, asking children what they wanted for Christmas, laughing heartily and even riffing about what the reindeer were up to. He only heard one kid whisper that he thought he might not be the real Santa, but instead "the guy who owned that fancy car," which he counted as a win, although in truth he suspected that every single child knew he wasn't Santa. No one seemed to mind, though; there were presents involved, after all.

Outside dusk was drawing in, and the Christmas lights Jenna had strung along the porch railings began to glow in the misty twilight. Jenna was ringing up last orders as people started to trickle outside to join the parade to the center of town for the Christmas tree lighting.

"You're meant to lead the parade, you know," Jenna told him with a twinkle in her eye as she tucked an unruly strand of strawberry-gold hair behind one ear. "Don't fail me now, Santa."

"I won't," Jack promised. He adjusted his beard as he leaned forward for a quick kiss. "But first I need to ask you what *you* want for Christmas."

To his delight, Jenna blushed pink. "Maybe you'll find out later," she murmured over her shoulder as she went to serve a customer, and Jack gave a very unSantalike grin.

As he headed outside, Jack found himself getting even more into the spirit of the thing, and he held two children's hands as he "ho ho hoed" his way down Main Street, with what felt like half of Starr's Fall following behind, everyone in a jolly, festive mood.

By the time he'd made it to the village green, he was ready for a stiff drink, although he still had to be man—or Santa—of the hour, and switch on the Christmas tree lights. He waited until everyone was assembled, and Lizzy Harper, as chair of the Business Association, gave him the nod before he flipped the switch and a cheer went up as the lights thankfully switched on in a blaze of cheerful color.

Jack took a step back and then, while everyone was focused on the tree, ducked into the church to divest himself of his red velvet.

"Oh, no, Santa's leaving already?"

He was wearing only the pants as he whirled around to see Jenna standing in the church doorway, smiling.

"I think I've done my time."

"You have," she agreed as she walked toward him. "Thank you, Jack. You're a superhero."

"Well, I don't know if I would go that far," he joked, only to have Jenna turn serious on him.

"I mean it. I never would have done any of this without you, Jack."

He laughed lightly. "I think you might have, Jenna. You're a strong woman."

"No, I really wouldn't have." She laid a hand on his arm. "Not to get all soppy or sentimental, but I'm really..." She paused again, her throat working, as the lighthearted mood turned serious—and intense. "Really grateful that you pushed me. Challenged me and helped me. Today definitely wouldn't have happened without you, and I'm so thankful for that. For you." She blushed and ducked her head, and as her cheeks went even pinker he thought he'd never seen her look so lovely.

"Well..." He found he didn't know what to say. Actually, he did know what to say, but he didn't know how to say it. He barely knew how to *feel* it. She was talking about the mercantile, but he felt so much more. He'd changed the store, but she'd changed *him*, Santa suit and all. He wanted to tell her that, to explain everything or maybe just get the words out, but they were lodged in his chest and all jumbled up in his throat, and in any case, now was not the time to say them, when he was half-dressed in a Santa costume and they had the whole town out there. Besides, today had been *her* moment, not theirs.

But he hoped their moment might come sometime soon.

"Jack?" Jenna prompted, a little uncertainly. "Why are you staring at me so ferociously?"

Was he? He let out a little laugh. "Sorry... I'm just so proud of you." And then he pulled her toward him and kissed her, both because he could and because sometimes actions were better than words.

* * *

So what had *that* been about, Jenna wondered as she left Jack in the church to finish changing. He had seemed as if he'd been about to say something, but then he hadn't. Judging from the way he'd been scowling at her, she wasn't sure it had been a good thing. Or was she just still paranoid, because that was all she knew and even though today had been so very wonderful, some part of her was still bracing for the worst?

She wouldn't let herself overthink it, Jenna decided as she went back out to the village green to join the festivities. The mood of the evening was jovial, and a little ramshackle, with kids running up and down the street and Liz Cranbury's little chihuahua barking like crazy, almost as if in accompaniment to the unsteady rendition of "God Rest Ye Merry Gentlemen" that Starr's Fall's three-piece brass band was playing in one corner of the green.

Jack came out to join her, and she slipped her arm through his. "This is really quite something," he remarked, and Jenna laughed.

"This beats anything you'd see in New York, doesn't it?" she teased, and he nodded seriously.

"Absolutely."

"Even the Macy's Thanksgiving Day Parade?" she challenged.

"Definitely. Who needs giant balloons, marching bands, and clown crews," he exclaimed, sweeping his arm toward the straggling scene, "when you have all this?"

"Fred Byars on the trombone is kind of sensational," Jenna remarked just as that instrument let out a sound like a sheep bleating or maybe giving birth.

"It's all fantastic," Jack proclaimed.

She shook her head slowly. "And to think you almost chose Litchfield over this."

"To think you dared me to," he reminded her, and she smiled at the thought of how awful they'd been to each other. It felt like a long time ago now; it had become part of their story, their meeting.

They walked along the village green, saying hello to various people they knew. Rhonda was dishing out hot chocolate from a massive tureen, her scrawny arms flashing fast as she barked at someone to go easy on the squirty whipped cream she'd provided. Main Street looked magical, strung with lights, store windows glimmering from within. Jack squeezed her hand, and Jenna squeezed back, and then her heart felt as if it were expanding to fill her chest.

This was happiness. This was *hope*. No paranoia, no dread of the future, no regret for the past. Just this... and everything that this moment encompassed.

She loved her life in Starr's Fall, she realized with a wonderful ferocity. No matter how suffocating it could sometimes seem, with everyone and their cousin up in her business, she loved this town—and her place in it. She might have come limping back here because she'd had no other place to go, but she was so very glad she had—and that she'd stayed. There was no other place she'd rather be.

She squeezed Jack's hand as they stood on the edge of the village green and, tilting her head up to the starlit sky, Jenna watched the first snowflakes begin to fall.

* * *

It was still snowing when she and Jack walked back to the mercantile, big, fat flakes drifting down in the dark like something out of a movie. Jack was holding her hand, swinging it slightly as they walked along through half an inch's dusting of snow.

Jenna felt tired in a happy, satisfied sort of way, replete from the food she'd eaten, the work she'd done, the friends whose company she'd enjoyed. And Jack... Jack most of all, by her side pretty much the whole evening—smiling, laughing, holding her hand, touching her back, giving her teasing looks, being the best Santa that ever was... because she'd asked him. She'd reveled in it all, in the simple joy of being important to another person.

"Good day?" Jack asked her as Miller's Mercantile came into sight ahead.

"Yes, a very good day." Jenna squeezed his hand. "But, full disclosure, I don't think I should have eaten that funnel cake." She pressed one hand to her middle. "It was so delicious, though."

"It was, as was the hot chocolate," Jack replied with a chuckle. "Though I think Rhonda might have been lacing the hot chocolate for the grownups. There was a decided rum aftertaste."

Jenna laughed. "That sounds like Rhonda."

Her steps slowed as she came up to the mercantile; there was a car parked by the porch, the light dusting of snow on top suggesting it had been there awhile.

"Who—" she began, only to stop when she saw the woman stepping out of the driver's seat with a wobbly, uncertain smile, her hands deep in the pockets of her coat.

"Hey, Jenna." The voice wobbled as much as the smile, and even though she couldn't see the woman all too well in the dark, she still recognized her.

It was her mother.

20

"Goodness, it's been a while."

Jenna didn't reply, watching silently as her mother stepped gingerly into the kitchen, looking around the shabby space with something like wonder. They had already stuttered their greetings out in the parking lot, and Jack had tactfully taken his leave, promising Jenna he'd call her in the morning.

When, Jenna wondered, was the last time she and her mother had seen each other? Maybe eighteen months ago, two years? Her mother had invited her and Zach to come down to Florida awhile back, and Zach had coaxed her into road tripping it. That part had been fun, but the five days sharing the guest bedroom of her parents' condo with her brother had not been. Her father had pretty much played golf the whole time, and her mother had flitted around, more or less waiting for him to come home. Jenna and Zach had ended up going to the beach by themselves, although Jenna was not a fan of it because no matter how much she slathered herself in factor fifty, she always got sunburned.

"It has been a while," she agreed in a guarded tone. "Five years, almost, since you've been back here." Her parents had not returned to Starr's Fall once since their retirement, which had been yet another piece of the puzzle that was her parents that Jenna didn't understand. They'd made this town their home for *forty* years. How could they have turned their backs on it so completely?

Her mother was standing in the center of the kitchen, her fingers pleated together, her expression both abject and pleading in a way Jenna didn't think she'd ever seen before. What on earth was going on?

Jenna opened her mouth to ask just that and instead heard herself ask, "Would you like a cup of tea?"

A look of gratitude came over her mother's face and she gulped and nodded. "Yes, please. Thank you."

Jenna moved to fill up the kettle. "So what brought this visit on?" she asked once she'd filled it and put it on the stove. "I mean, it's nice to see you, and this is, of course, your house still, but..." She shook her head slowly. "I feel like something is going on."

Her mother nodded and then gulped again. "Yes," she agreed, tucking her hair behind her ears—the same auburn hair that Jenna had, except her mother's was in a neat bob and starting to silver. "Something is going on."

Jenna waited for more and her mother started speaking in staccato bursts, like the words hurt coming out. "I came back... because... I think... I might have... left your father."

For a second, the words, spoken in such jagged spurts, did not compute. They were phrases Jenna could not put into a comprehensible whole, even as she recognized them in their discrete parts. She opened her mouth and then closed it again as the kettle began to whistle.

Neither of them spoke as Jenna set about making tea. Her mind was whirling, and it wasn't until she'd handed her mother a cup of tea and taken a sip of her own that she managed to say cautiously, "You *left* Dad?" It still didn't make sense.

Her mother nodded, her gaze lowered toward her mug. "Yes. I think so. I packed a bag and booked a flight and came here, anyway."

"For a visit."

"I... I don't know."

Jenna shook her head slowly. "Mom... you and Dad... you and Dad are..."

"No," her mother said quietly. "We're not. Not anymore. And really, we never have been. I wish... I *wish* we had. Maybe more than I should have."

Okay, this was her mind officially blown. Her parents' marriage had always been the gold standard. How many times had her dad blown into the house with a bouquet of roses and a smacking kiss for his mother? How many times had her mother laughingly let herself get swept up in his arms? And when they'd all been together as a family? Well, Jenna had never been able to shake the feeling that she and Zach were interlopers in the greatest romance in the world, one she'd wanted for herself with Ryan. Her parents had always been a unit, solid, *too* solid.

And now her mother was basically saying that wasn't the case at all?

"I... I don't know what to say," Jenna said at last. "Maybe I should just ask... what do you want to tell me?" And what did she really want to know?

Her mother didn't answer right away, just took a sip of tea. All around them the house creaked and settled, and the snow continued softly down, blurring the view from the kitchen window.

"Well..." her mother finally began, her tone hesitant, her gaze faraway. "The truth is, I probably should have left him a long time ago."

What? Jenna found she needed to sit down. She lowered herself into a kitchen chair, landing with a thud so a drop of tea splashed out onto her wrist, burning her, but she barely noticed. "I always thought you guys had an amazing marriage," Jenna said faintly. "Too amazing, even. It wasn't until I was an adult that I started wondering if maybe there was something… unhealthy… about it." She winced in apology, but her mother was already nodding.

"Yes, there was something unhealthy about it, Jenna, right from the beginning. I loved your father madly, and he—he loved me back, but…" She took a gulping sip of tea, her gaze lowered. "He loved a lot of other people, too."

"Are you saying Dad had *affairs*?" Jenna demanded hoarsely. Was this what Henrietta Starr had been intimating, by saying how her father was charming, and how her mother had certainly loved him? It all made sense, and yet it totally didn't.

Her mother lifted her gaze from her mug to face Jenna squarely. "Yes," she stated quietly. "That's what I am saying. I don't know how many, or how far it went each time. Sometimes not far at all, according to your father, but… I couldn't live with the uncertainty anymore. With never feeling like I was first—"

"But he *always* put you first," Jenna burst out. It was what had hurt so much, as a child. How extraneous she had felt, along with Zach, to her parents' grand romance, like bit players who were resented when they were onstage. Her parents had never seemed all that interested in anything about her—her accomplishments, her interests, her hopes, her fears. Water off a duck's back, every time. She could still picture her father's faint eyebrow raise as he glanced at her across the kitchen table. *Oh, you again?*

"He made gestures," her mother corrected. "Grand, sweeping

gestures to say sorry, and I accepted them and told myself it was enough. That it was love. But I don't think it ever was."

"Mom, Dad loves you," Jenna objected, feeling it from the depths of her being. "Zach and I never doubted that. It was always you two, and so then we felt... extra."

Her mother sighed. "I know, and that is, at least partly, my fault. Maybe a lot my fault. It took me a long time to realize it but, Jenna... your father is a narcissist. A wonderful, charming, handsome, lovely narcissist." She sighed. "He could walk into any room, and everyone would love him... if he wanted them to. If he didn't care, then you basically ceased to exist in his eyes. And I went from one to the other for far too long... existing on the highs and dreading the lows. When I got cancer, the year you were in San Francisco... I was almost *glad*." Her voice trembled. "Because I thought maybe then he would pay attention to me more. Not just sweeping in with the flowers but holding my hand in the dark. And for a little while, it felt like it worked. He was so attentive during my chemo appointments, but then I realized he was more intent on charming the nurses. He loved playing the devoted husband, but it was all just an act. An act everyone bought except me."

Jenna shook her head slowly. It felt like too much to take in. "And the affairs?" she asked hollowly. Starr's Fall was a small town. Who had her father had an affair with? She shuddered to think.

"I don't know," her mother admitted quietly. "He was discreet, at any rate, and it wasn't all the time, but... I always knew when he came in with flowers or took me to the Litchfield Inn for dinner... it was an apology of sorts. And I accepted it every time." For the first time, Jenna heard bitterness spike her mother's voice as her face crumpled. "I was so in love with him, Jenna," she said brokenly as she wiped her eyes. "I would have done *anything* for him. When he had this dream of setting up this store and living off the land, when he decided to move into antiques or collect wine or do whatever it was he wanted to... I acted like it was my dream, too. I became a shadow of myself, bending myself to whatever shape he wanted. And in the process..." She drew a ragged breath. "I alienated and neglected my two children."

A silence descended upon them then that felt like too heavy a weight to bear. How, Jenna wondered, had she not seen all this? How had she been so blinded, thinking her parents had the greatest romance ever, and then, she realized with a lurch, doing the exact same thing her mother had done, and twisting herself into every possible shape to make a man love her? She'd repeated her mother's mistakes, Jenna realized hollowly, without even knowing her mother had made them.

"I had no idea," she finally said in little more than a whisper. "Really."

"I know." Her mother wiped her eyes again. "I'm sorry."

"You aren't the one who should be sorry," Jenna replied, her voice rising. "Dad..." She stopped, because she didn't even know what to think about her dad anymore. She'd always been in awe of him—his effortless charm, the twinkle in his eye, the way he could make you the center of his world for all of three seconds before moving on, but for a moment you reveled in being in the spotlight, even if the darkness afterwards felt awful.

It was, she acknowledged, the same kind of dynamic she'd had with Ryan. How had she not *seen* all this? Just how blind had she been?

"Your father is who he is," her mother said heavily. "And he's not all bad. He agreed to retire because I insisted on it. I needed a new start, somewhere where I wasn't wondering if every woman was someone he'd been with." She pressed her lips together. "I don't know if it was paranoia or not, but I'd started to feel like everyone was *staring* at me. In pity."

"Oh, Mom..." Jenna shook her head, appalled. Had it really been that way? Among her own friends, she didn't *think* anyone had known about this unsettling and unfortunate dynamic between her parents. If they had, they'd certainly kept it from her. But Barb Lyman? Zoe's parents? Joshua's dad? Maybe they'd all known and kept quiet about it. It wouldn't surprise her. The people of Starr's Fall liked to gossip, but they also could be very close-mouthed when they chose, especially that generation.

"He promised he'd be different," her mother continued, "and I think he meant it. We chose Florida because I had this dream of us together on the beach... Well, it was a childish fantasy, and all that happened was your father discovered golf and all the women who play it, and I fell into the same pattern I'd always been in. Nothing changed but our surroundings."

She lapsed into silence, and for a few moments they both simply sipped their tea. Then Jenna ventured to ask, "So what made you decide to leave?" If she had left. Jenna hoped she had, considering all she'd just learned.

"You," her mother said, startling her. "When you called at Thanksgiving, and you told me how you'd always felt left out, as a child. I think I'd known that, deep down, but you'd never said it so directly and it felt... it felt like a slap to the face. In a good way," she explained in a rush. "Because I needed it. How much of my life was I going to waste, chasing after my own husband?" She shook her head. "It took me a few weeks, but I told your father I'd had enough. I don't think he believed me. He told me to go have a visit, but assumes that I'll be back." She sighed. "And maybe he's right."

"No, Mom." Jenna reached over to grasp her mother's hand. "Don't. You deserve more than that. Any woman does. I know, because... I had the same kind of thing going on with... with that man I fell in love with. Ryan. In San Francisco." Her parents had never actually met him, because Ryan hadn't been interested in getting to know her family—a warning sign if there ever was one. "He was my whole world," Jenna continued, "my sun, moon, and stars, and I... I wasn't all that much to him, no matter what I tried to do to make him love me. You know I only moved to New York because he did, even though I didn't have a job, even though he didn't ask me to." She swallowed painfully, remembering the humiliation of Ryan's response. *You don't have to come to New York with me, Jenna...*

How deluded and desperate had she *been*? "And unlike you," she continued in a stronger voice, "I wasn't brave enough to end it. He ended it for me." She let out a jagged laugh. "I'd convinced myself he was going to propose, would you believe it? And he was actually breaking it off. Not only that, but he'd been seeing someone else, and he was getting engaged to *her*. I hadn't even suspected he was cheating, more stupid me."

"Oh, Jenna." Her mother looked at her with tear-filled eyes. "I'm so sorry."

"I am, too," Jenna replied on a ragged sigh. "I spent ten years being bitter about it and letting myself get cynical about everything. It made me more bitter about you and Dad and what I'd thought you had, because I'd been looking for the same thing and destroying myself in the process. But..." She shook her head, her mouth firming. "I don't want to do that anymore."

"Oh, Jenna," her mother said again. "I don't want you to, either. I wish... I wish I'd been honest with you sooner, as well as a better mother. Maybe I could have kept you from making the same mistakes..."

"I don't want regret to be my main emotion," Jenna told her, recalling what Henrietta Starr had said. "And it shouldn't be yours, either. This can be a fresh start, Mom, for both of us."

Her mother's eyes brightened, and her lips trembled. "I would love that," she whispered.

"So would I," Jenna replied, surprising herself. Did she still carry hurt from her childhood? Yes, probably, but it was an old pain, not a fresh, smarting wound. And her mother clearly had her own wounds, which Jenna had never even known about, to her shame.

Impulsively, and also because she wanted to, she rose from her chair and went over to her mother to put her arms around her. Her mother stiffened in surprise before throwing her arms around Jenna in a tight hug, her voice muffled against her shoulder.

"Thank you for giving me a second chance," she said.

"Thank you for telling me all that," Jenna replied, squeezing her gently. "It can't have been easy."

"I should have done it sooner."

"No regrets, remember?" Jenna released her mother, smiling down at her, feeling a sudden, surprising surge of protectiveness for a woman she'd so often low-key resented. It was a new, and not unwelcome, feeling. "New beginnings and fresh starts," she insisted. "For both of us."

Invariably, her mind moved to Jack. She wanted a fresh start there, too, not repeating her old unhealthy patterns of both dread and desperation. Not tying herself into knots trying to please him, or worrying about when, not if, he broke up with her the way Ryan did...

Fear fluttered through her chest at the thought. It was working, wasn't it? What she and Jack had was different. Deeper, and stronger, and better. She didn't need to convince herself of that.

As if she could read her thoughts, her mother suddenly

asked, "What about the man you were with when you came up to the store? You two seemed close."

"That was Jack," Jenna told her as she took their mugs to the sink. "And yes, we are, but it's early days. Very early days."

And they were still seeing where it went, as Jack had suggested back at the beginning. Not a bad thing, but Jenna knew she still wanted some clarity. And maybe, she thought, thinking of her mother's courage in coming here, she'd be brave enough to be the one to ask, rather than wait for Jack to call the shots.

21

In the two weeks before Christmas, Miller's Mercantile was hopping. Jenna had unearthed her Christmas decorations and even bought a few new ones, draping the store in tinsel and Christmas lights and had carols playing in the background, the air spiced with the scent of holly and evergreen, courtesy of a very expensive candle Zach had gotten her as a re-opening present, in something of a joke.

"And it's the only one I'll stock," she'd teased him, and he'd laughed.

"I can certainly believe that, sis."

Jenna might not have gone the expensive-candle route as her brother had once suggested, but she *had* created a whole section in the store for Christmas food and decorations, and it had proved to be a hit. She'd had to restock the gingerbread house kits and red and green sprinkles three times already, and the Christmas potpourri mix made by a local craftswoman was also a big seller.

Her mother had offered to help in the store, restocking and ringing up purchases, admiring all the new changes, and generally being more encouraging than Jenna could ever remember her being... which might be as much to do with her, she realized, as her mother. They'd both changed and grown.

In the store, her mother was unassuming and efficient, always ready to pitch in and surprisingly easy to chat to. Jenna couldn't shake the feeling that her mother was desperate to make up for lost time, which made her feel guilty for fobbing her off for so many years. But her motto now was no regrets as she forged her future, and so she pushed such thoughts aside and focused on the positive—Miller's Mercantile was doing well, she was enjoying her mother's company, and while she hadn't seen Jack as much in the last few days as she would have liked, things were going well there. Life, Jenna decided, was good.

Zach had taken their mother's return to Starr's Fall in his characteristically easy stride, assuming it was just a normal visit; neither Jenna nor her mother had informed him otherwise. It was up to her mom to decide when and if to do that, and so Jenna hadn't told anyone the truth of her parents' marriage, not even Jack.

He'd called her as promised the morning after her mother's arrival, and they'd seen each other a few times since then—for dinner as well as some Christmas shopping in Litchfield, where Jack had half-laughingly dragged her into the dreaded deli, and Jenna had dutifully bought some asiago cheese and kalamata olives, two products she informed him pertly that she did not stock at the mercantile. It had all been fun and good, but she still hadn't worked up the nerve to have That Talk... not that she even knew what That Talk was meant to encompass.

"We've only been dating for a couple of weeks," she told Laurie when she'd dropped by the store for some soup for Henrietta and invariably asked about the status of their relationship. "It feels premature to demand some kind of commitment."

"You don't have to ask for a proposal," Laurie replied with brisk practicality. "Just some clarification. Move from 'let's see where this goes' to 'how do you think this is going?' A kind of relationship check-in. It's *healthy*, Jenna, trust me."

"Yeah, I suppose." It made sense and sounded so very reasonable, and yet Jenna still dreaded the thought of confronting Jack in such a way. Forcing him to make a decision... about her. Yes, it had been an entire decade since she'd last had that kind of conversation, but it had been a doozy, and it had gone so horribly wrong. Who wanted to risk that kind of humiliation and heartache again, ever? Not her.

Besides, she knew she was afraid of rocking the boat when the journey so far had been so pleasant. She didn't want to want more than Jack was willing to give, and she certainly didn't want to *ask* him for it. And while Jenna had told herself she was not going to settle for scraps the way both she and her mother once had, it wasn't as if Jack was *neglecting* her in any way. He was being pretty wonderful. So why couldn't she trust it, *him*, and let their relationship unfold as it was meant to, however long that took? Why did something that should be so easy and instinctive feel so hard?

"I don't think that's asking too much," Laurie continued, her tone turning strident, at least for her. "And anyway, I don't believe it's a big risk. I can tell Jack adores you, Jenna. Everyone can. He'd probably welcome the conversation. He's probably hoping you'll bring it up."

Jenna forced a smile. Laurie was an eternal optimist, and she had a man who did adore her, quite openly. She understandably saw love blossoming everywhere. Her life in Starr's Fall was practically a rom-com, complete with soundtrack.

"I'll think about it," she promised, and Laurie rolled her eyes.

"And we all know what that means."

"I will," Jenna protested. "But right now I'm just enjoying the moment, which is kind of new for me, so I want to do it while I can."

"Well, that's always a good thing to do." Laurie leaned forward, her eyes starting to sparkle. "I'm meeting my mom and half-brothers at Christmas," she confided, dropping her voice even though there was no one else in the store; it was almost closing time, and Jenna's mother had gone into the house, having offered to make dinner, which was a nice change from her usual cup-of-soup in front of the computer.

"You are?" Jenna exclaimed. "Laurie, that's amazing."

Laurie nodded. "She finally told her husband, and he was totally okay with it. Which just goes to show," she added, pointing a finger at Jenna, "that sometimes it's worth taking the risk and being honest with someone, no matter how scary it seems."

Jenna decided to ignore the rather pointed remark. "Laurie, I'm so happy for you," she said. "So you're spending Christmas with them?"

"The day after." Laurie gave an abashed smile. "Joshua's coming with me... They invited him, too. I'm really nervous."

"They'll love you," Jenna insisted. "How could they not?"

"Well, let's hope so." Laurie's smile wobbled slightly before it firmed. "And if they don't, they don't," she said philosophically. "I have lots of people in my life who do. But what are you doing for Christmas?" she asked Jenna as she gathered up her cans of soup.

"Spending it with my mom, I guess." They hadn't talked about the actual day yet, even though it was only a week away, but Jenna knew Zach was going to be with Maggie and Ben.

"And Jack?"

"We haven't talked about that, either," Jenna admitted. Something else she'd been too chicken to mention to him. "He'll probably spend it with his mom. It's a bit early in our relationship to spend a major holiday together, don't you think?"

"No, I don't think," Laurie retorted. "Why not spend it all together, you and both your mothers? That makes perfect sense to me."

And so it would, Jenna thought wryly, because Laurie had this Pollyanna-ish notion that everything always worked out for the best, even though a lot in her life should have surely showed her otherwise. She admired her friend's optimism, even if she struggled to share it. "You should suggest it," Laurie insisted.

"I'll think about it," Jenna replied, and once more Laurie rolled her eyes.

"Life is for living," she told her as she looped the bag of groceries onto her arm. "Not thinking about it."

The door jingled merrily as her friend left, and Jenna glanced around the store, feeling both satisfied and just the teeniest bit restless. Maybe she should do more than think about it. She could call Jack right now, suggest spending Christmas together...

Just as she was having that thought, her phone buzzed. *Was it him?* Feeling as if her heart were turning over in her chest, Jenna picked up her phone only to look down, her heart now seeming to go completely still when she saw the two-word text from Annie.

> She's gone.

Immediately Jenna swiped to call her friend. "Annie..." she greeted her, only to hear a broken sob. Jenna blinked back sudden tears. This wasn't unexpected, yet it still felt like it was. "Oh, Annie, I'm so sorry."

"She hung on for so long," Annie choked out. "I thought she'd make it till Christmas. I wanted to spend the day with her, our last one…"

"She really did hang on," Jenna whispered, swiping at her eyes. "But I think she was ready to go, Annie. She seemed it, the last time I saw her…"

"I know she did." Annie sniffed. "She told me so herself, even though she couldn't use words. She pointed at her wedding ring, and I knew what she meant. She wanted to be with my dad."

A tear slipped down Jenna's cheek at the thought. She could picture Barb perfectly, gazing down at her ring, ready to meet her husband once more, somewhere in the great beyond.

"She took a turn for the worse on the weekend, and then even worse yesterday," Annie continued haltingly. "She stopped eating or drinking, and I think I knew it was the end, but I didn't want to believe it. She'd scared us before, you know? But I always knew it would have to happen. I mean… we've been waiting for it for so long. I thought I would be *ready*."

"I don't think anyone is ever ready," Jenna replied quietly. Why, she wondered, was death always such a surprise? They'd been expecting Barb's for months and yet now the reality of it had the power to make her breathless with shock, everything in her resisting the notion, the brutally painful reality of it, just as Annie surely was.

"Were you with her?" she asked quietly, and Annie sniffed again.

"Yes, I held her hand all the way to the end."

"Oh, Annie."

They were quiet for several moments, the only sound their breathing, and then Annie said softly, "It puts the rest of life into perspective, doesn't it? I mean… why was I ever bored, or irritated, or restless? If I could have just one more rainy afternoon sitting with my mom with a cup of lukewarm coffee, chatting about nothing..." Her voice broke and she drew a quick, ragged breath as Jenna squeezed her eyes shut, aching for her friend. "Or *anything* trivial or seemingly meaningless," Annie continued. "I frittered away so many moments without realizing I was doing it."

"Oh, Annie, we all do," Jenna protested gently. How much time had *she* wasted, being worried or weary or fearful or cynical or *anything* but incredulously joyous that life was such an amazing gift? "You and Barb had a great time together," she told her. "I don't think you frittered away anything."

"It feels like I did," Annie replied, weeping now, openly on the phone. "So much of life just feels like a slog, something to be got through... but every moment is precious." Her voice suddenly turned fierce. "*Every* moment. Don't waste a single one, Jenna."

The words felt both personal and prescient, and in line with what everyone else and the universe itself had been telling her lately. She thought of Jack, feeling like he'd missed out on twenty years of his mother's life. And she'd missed out on she didn't even know how much, by living so defensively, every decision to protect her heart with the hardened shell of cynicism, believing it was better not to expect anything than to be disappointed. She didn't want to live that way anymore. She wanted to make an active choice not to.

"I'll try not to," she told Annie shakily. "And you, too."

"I'm trying." Annie drew a ragged breath. "I *will* try. Mike is coming over later." She let out a shaky laugh. "I know it's kind of ridiculous, but I do love that man."

Jenna smiled. "It's not ridiculous at all."

"Come on," Annie scoffed. "You know it is. The two of us so giant and wild-haired... We probably scare children away when we're together. We're like something out of a fairy tale."

"You look wonderful together," Jenna stated firmly. "I can't wait for the wedding."

Annie guffawed. "Well, we'll see. I think Laurie and Joshua might be heading down the aisle before we do."

"That would be wonderful, too." For the first time in a long while, Jenna didn't feel that painful little pang of envy of her friends' romantic lives. She thought of Jack, and she felt only hope. When she saw him again, she'd say something. Or maybe he would...

"I should go," Annie said on a sigh. "There's all this admin stuff. The to-do list of death."

"If there's anything I can do," Jenna told her, wishing the words didn't sound so trite. "Anything, Annie. Middle of the night, crack of dawn, whatever. I'm there."

"Go give that man of yours a hug," Annie replied. "That's what you can do. And look forward and never back and *live* your life, Jenna. That's all any of us can do. Live our lives... to the full."

After Annie had said goodbye, Jenna stood in the store a few moments more. That had been a heck of a command, she thought with sorrowful wryness. It was hard to ignore Annie's words when she had so much heartache and experience behind them.

Resolutely Jenna picked up her phone and swiped to call. Jack answered after the second ring.

"Jenna? Hey."

"I was wondering what you were doing for Christmas." In her nervousness, it came out abruptly, a little aggressively. Oops.

"I haven't thought about it too much, to be honest," Jack replied after what felt like a slightly startled pause, no doubt caused by her tone.

Jenna took a deep breath. Closed her eyes. And jumped.

"Wouldyouliketospenditwithme?" she blurted, speaking so quickly it sounded like one long word.

"Sorry, what was that?"

Jenna took another breath and did her best to speak more slowly. "Would you..." she began carefully, "like to spend it... Christmas... with me?"

The answering silence felt endless. A cold wave of mortification and dread swept through her. *Why* had she decided to do this again? She'd just told Laurie that she and Jack were not in a spending-a-major-holiday-together stage yet, and then, made reckless by grief and Annie's urging, she'd taken the stupid plunge.

"I'll have my mother with me," Jack said after a moment, in something of a warning. Jenna couldn't tell if this was his polite way of refusing, or maybe he was trying to make her rescind her invitation. Either way, it felt like a negative, far too close to a no.

"I'll have my mom with me, too," Jenna reminded him shakily. "So it could be a with-mothers thing. If you wanted." Which, she realized belatedly, sounded a little weird.

More silence. Jenna squeezed her eyes shut. She really shouldn't have done this. Hadn't she learned *anything* in ten years of stubborn, cynical loneliness? Forget Henrietta, Annie, Laurie, whoever else had told her to live life, like that was so easy to do. Living life *hurt*. It didn't always work out. Right now, it felt pretty awful.

And so she opened her mouth to retract her offer, stumble through something painfully awkward about how they didn't have to spend the day together, it would probably be better if they didn't, all things considered, what with their mothers and so on, and then Jack spoke before she could stammer through a single syllable.

"Jenna." His voice was the low rumble that she loved. "I think that's a wonderful idea."

"You... do?" Her voice came out in a squeak.

"Yes." He chuckled, the sound soft. "I do. As long as you do."

"I do," she confirmed, and then she let out a laugh of pure relief.

She felt as if she was floating as she closed up the store and walked back into the kitchen where her mother was standing at the stove, stirring something that smelled delicious. She glanced back at Jenna, smiling uncertainly.

"You look happy."

"I am happy," Jenna admitted. For once, she didn't feel dragged down by dread or regret. Impulsively, thinking of how Annie could no longer hug her own mother, Jenna went around the table to give her mom a quick hug. "You know what?" she said. "Let's decorate for Christmas."

"The store...?"

"No, the store's already decorated to the nines!" Jenna exclaimed with a laugh. "I meant the house. I haven't bought a Christmas tree in years. Let's buy a Christmas tree, get the old decorations down from the loft."

Her mother smiled shyly, seeming pleased. "All right, then."

Less than an hour later, after dinner, they were heading to the garden center halfway between Starr's Fall and Torrington that sold Christmas trees and loading one up on top of Jenna's car. Then back to the house, where Jenna braved the rickety ladder and cobwebs of the loft to dust off two boxes of decorations she hadn't taken out since before her parents had moved to Florida.

Her mother made some hot chocolate, and Jenna put on Christmas carols and lit the fire. After they'd decorated the tree, they broke out a bottle of wine and sat on the sofa, curled up by the fire and chatting about nothing in particular... until her mom mentioned Jack.

"So, is it serious?" she asked.

To stall, Jenna took a sip of wine. "It feels serious to me," she said at last. "And I think it might be for him, too. But... it's early days."

"That sounds promising," her mother told her with a smile.

"It feels promising," Jenna returned with a smile of her own.

The sound of the kitchen door opening had them both staring at each other, wide-eyed, before Zach called out, "Hey, anybody home?"

Jenna relaxed back into the sofa. "We're in here," she called, just as her brother sauntered into the room.

"Hey, who started the party without me?" he demanded as he clocked their glasses of wine and the half-empty bottle.

"We did," their mother returned teasingly, "but you're welcome to join us."

Zach bent down to kiss her cheek and for a second, Jenna envied how uncomplicated his relationship with their parents seemed... But then he didn't know about what their marriage had really been like. It wasn't Jenna's job to tell him, but she knew Zach would most likely be furious and hurt when he realized what their dad had gotten up to. Jenna was still trying to figure out whether she could have any kind of relationship with him, not that she'd had much of one to begin with, but at least things were better—a lot better—with her mom. That was certainly something to be thankful for.

Actually, she decided as Zach helped himself to a glass of wine and joined them on the sofa, she had a lot to be thankful for. And that was what she was going to focus on from now on, starting with her relationship with Jack. At Christmas, Jenna decided, she would tell him how she felt. She might even use the

L-word. Why not? A sudden, heady sense of recklessness seized her. Annie was right, she decided. Life was not just for the living, but the grabbing, the savoring and reveling. She'd spent far too much time hiding in the shadows. On Christmas Day, she was coming out in full strength... and telling Jack how she really felt.

* * *

"Nice to see you, Jack."

Jack shook his friend Will Bryant's hand firmly as he smiled. "Good to see you, too."

"Come, sit down." They were in Will's corner office at Sterling Fund Managers, near Wall Street. Twenty years ago, they'd both started there. Jack had left after four years to start his own firm, and Will had stayed and worked his way up to VP. They'd been friends for all that time, although occasionally it had veered into a not-always-friendly competition. But Jack genuinely liked Will, had time for him, which was why he'd agreed, less than a week before Christmas, to head into the city to meet him for lunch.

Also because Will said he had something to talk to him about, and Jack was curious. Jenna had been super busy with Miller's Mercantile and her mom, and while he was very glad for her on both counts, it had left him, in the last few days, feeling like he was at more of a loose end than usual, and that was saying something. Six months of cultivating hobbies had been good for his *physical* health, if not always his mental health.

The truth was, Jack wanted to feel busy again. To have something in his life that wasn't just a hobby or helping someone else. If he didn't develop something, Jack had mused morosely, he'd be old before his time, the highlights of his day making model airplanes and doing the crossword, maybe an episode of *Jeopardy* to round out the evening. Truth be told, he was more than halfway there already. He was only forty-two years old. He needed more in his life. He needed a purpose.

"So, I have a proposition for you," Will stated without preamble once they were seated in leather armchairs in front of a picture window that overlooked the Freedom Tower.

"Hit me," Jack replied easily. Already he felt like he was getting into his groove, and it felt good; he was wearing an expensively tailored suit, he'd had an espresso that morning, and the energy in the city had been like an IV straight into his veins, giving him a sense of purpose and focus.

"This is totally confidential," Will told him with a serious look as he steepled his fingers in front of him.

"Of course," Jack replied as he sat back into his chair. "That goes without saying."

"Good." Will paused, and Jack stayed both relaxed and alert, his hands resting on his thighs. What was his old friend about to say?

"You know I've been at Sterling for over twenty years," Will began.

"Yes…"

He cocked his head. "I think it's finally time for a change."

Jack experienced a pulse of adrenaline-fueled excitement as Will gave him a significant look over his steepled fingers. "Fair enough," he replied easily, keeping his tone casual. "What did you have in mind?"

Will leaned forward, dropping his voice, although no one was in the huge corner office but the two of them. "Starting over, doing it my way." He paused. "*Our* way."

Again Jack felt that pulse, but he merely raised his eyebrows in inquiry.

"You've done it once already," Will continued. "I need your expertise, your *energy*, Jack. And this won't be just another boom-or-bust startup. I'm talking about something *intentional*, considered, focusing on ventures that are sustainable and innovative. Cutting edge as well as responsible." He leaned forward even more, his eyes alight. "I don't want to just be the new guy swaggering around the block. I want to be the face of the future. Between the two of us, I think we can do it. You were the first person I thought of, Jack, when I started considering this. I don't want to leap with anyone else but you." Will sat back, dropping his hands to his lap, his eyebrows raised. "Well?" he asked. "Initial thoughts?"

Still Jack did not reply. His mind was reeling, but in a good way. He'd been waiting for something like this, he realized. Waiting and hoping. No matter what he'd told himself—or others—there had been no way he was going to stay in Starr's Fall for the rest of his life, pottering about and helping local businesses here and there. The realization slammed into him, making him realize just how much he'd been fooling himself, thinking he could be happy working on a bunch of other people's projects, staying in Starr's Fall without any purpose of his own. He was *forty-two*. He still had at least twenty years of career-defining work left in him. He was ready for this.

"I know you've been taking a break," Will said into the silence, "for your health. But I hope you're ready to get back into the saddle."

"I am," Jack replied carefully. The last thing he wanted to do right now was bang on about his health woes, but neither did he want to sign his death warrant. "I like what you were saying about being sustainable," he finally said. "I'm not a twenty-two-year-old who can pull all-nighters three nights a week anymore, and I doubt you are, either."

"Absolutely not," Will replied firmly. "It's all about work-life balance, right?" His eyes glinted with humor. "Within reason, of course."

Jack had a feeling that Will's definition of "within reason" might be different from his. Will had never left New York; whereas six months in Starr's Fall had changed Jack, whether he'd wanted it to or not. And, like he'd told Jenna, he *had* wanted it to, but he also wanted a little bit of the old him back. The guy who had straddled the world, who had done deals in his sleep, who had felt important and purposeful.

Was there a way to have both of those things, to *be* both?

Surely there had to be.

"So can I get the ball rolling?" Will asked. "Talk to some investors, draw up some contracts? You know when I leave here, it will be cutting the cord. I need to know you're with me."

Jack hesitated. Could he really make this kind of decision on a whim? He knew how the investment world worked; if Will was thinking about going, rumors would already be starting to swirl, and he needed to jump before he was pushed. They would have to move fast.

He should talk to Jenna, he knew, and yet what would she say? What would *he*? He'd have to move back to New York, at least on a temporary or part-time basis. The work, no matter what kind of balance Will suggested, would be all consuming, especially at the start. There was a reason, a very good one, that Jack hadn't had any serious romantic relationships in twenty years. There simply hadn't been the time.

And would there be time now?

"What does your wife think about this?" Jack asked suddenly, and Will sat back, surprised.

"My *wife*?" he repeated, somewhat incredulously. It wasn't a question, Jack suspected, that he got very often.

"It'll affect her, is all I mean."

Will shrugged dismissively. "As long as the money's flowing in, I think she'll be okay."

Jack nodded slowly. It was the kind of response he'd expected... and yet it wasn't at all relevant to him and Jenna.

Him and Jenna. Just the thought of her—of *them*—caused his heart to give a little lurch. He'd told her they should see where this goes. He'd said there were variables. Would it be really such a surprise if he told her he was moving back to New York, at least on a part-time basis? That he needed to work, to be himself again? And he couldn't see how that could happen if he stayed retired in Starr's Fall...

Surely she could understand that.

And if she didn't...?

They could still make it work somehow, right? On a part-time basis, long-distance for half of the week...

"Jack?" Will prompted, his smile only slightly tinged with good-natured exasperation. "I know this might feel kind of quick, but you know how these things work. Things have to move fast. Are you in, or at least interested?"

Jack felt his hands tighten into fists in his lap, and he deliberately smoothed them out again. Took a deep breath and smiled as a sense of purpose that he'd been missing for so long flooded through his body. "Yes," he told Will. "I'm interested." He paused and then added defiantly, "I'm in."

22

Jenna had never considered herself a huge Christmas person, but that was before she had something to look forward to at Christmas. *Someone.* The last few days had been busy with pre-Christmas preparations for celebrating at Jack's house, which he'd kindly offered, even though he was at a loss when it came to putting on a full Christmas meal, Jenna had suggested she bring the side dishes, and her mother was doing the turkey. Jack had offered to procure several pies from The Rolling Pin for dessert, and so all together they had a Christmas dinner.

Jenna had deliberated long and hard about what to get Jack for a Christmas present. She wanted something special, but nothing too intense. Something that showed she cared without overwhelming him. She'd settled on a book of hikes in northwestern Connecticut—in the hopes that they'd do them together—as well as a paperweight in the shape of a sailboat, and, as something of an in-joke, a platter of high-end smoked salmon. Was it too much? Not enough? Would he even get her a present? She had no idea.

It was challenging, living in the uncertainty, especially when, in her own mind, she'd already decided to be reckless. On Christmas Day, she was going to tell Jack she was in love with him. Or maybe *falling* in love with him, in the process of falling, even. But the L-word would be mentioned.

And, Jenna told herself repeatedly, she was *not* going to expect a reciprocal response, although she already knew she'd feel deflated if he didn't start to gush. But the point, she'd come to realize, wasn't in eliciting that or any other response from Jack. It was simply being brave enough to do it in the first place. This was, she knew, as much about her as it was about him, if not more. She needed to do this for her sake, to show she'd moved on.

But if Jack said he loved her back... well, that would be a serious bonus.

In the meantime, Jenna was enjoying the Christmas spirit. Starr's Fall looked positively magical under six inches of snow and strung with Christmas lights. Mike had rigged up speakers on Main Street, so Christmas carols played in the background during shopping hours, giving the whole town a holiday feel. Miller's Mercantile continued to do a brisk trade, but with the help of her mom, Jenna was still able to take a few hours off to spend time with Jack.

He'd returned from his visit to New York the other day with a spring in his step which gladdened Jenna, even if it also made her the teensiest bit nervous. When she'd asked him about it, he'd said he'd had a nice lunch with his friend Will and left it at that.

"Do you miss it, sometimes?" Jenna had asked hesitantly. "The city? The buzz?"

He'd shrugged, not quite meeting her eye. "Sometimes." Then he'd caught her up in a hug and kissed her, which had gone some way to calming Jenna's formless fears. "But why are we talking about New York?" he'd asked, and Jenna had had to agree.

There were so many other things to talk about, and she knew her slight paranoia about Jack being the city slicker she'd once called him was on her and her history.

Jack, she'd told herself as well as a few other people like Laurie and Annie, was *not* Ryan. And he would not respond like Ryan when she told him how she felt. It was an especially needed reminder as she headed over to Jack's house on Christmas morning, conscious that today was the Big Day. She was going to tell him she loved him. She really was.

"Wow," her mother breathed as Jenna pulled up to Jack's house.

"I know, right?" Jenna rolled her eyes good-naturedly. "Six bedrooms and it's only him in there."

Her mother's eyes danced. "I guess you guys will have to have lots of kids."

"*Mom*." Jenna couldn't keep from sounding scandalized—as well as slightly terrified. "Please do not make those kinds of comments today, okay?"

"Relax, Jenna," her mom told her with a laugh. "I won't whip out the baby booties I'm knitting while Jack is in the room, I promise."

Jenna shook her head, managing a laugh, although the thought of her mother doing any such thing was enough to make her blood run cold. The truth, she knew, was that she was really nervous about taking this step. She didn't need any well-meaning pushes from her mom at this point, not by a long shot.

"Merry Christmas!" Jack greeted them at the door, kissing her mom's cheek before kissing Jenna more thoroughly. "Come in. My mother's in the kitchen. Polly, meet Denise."

Jenna hadn't given a lot of thought to meeting Jack's mom, what with everything else to think about, but now her heart gave a funny twist as they went into the kitchen and his mother stood up at the table, blinking at them nervously while Jack put a protective arm around her frail shoulders.

"Mom," he said gently, "this is Jenna and her mother Polly."

"Oh." His mother blinked a few more times. "Do I know you?" She glanced at her son, seeming anxious. "Do I know them?"

"No, Mom," he said in the same gentle voice, "you haven't met them before."

Jenna took a step forward. "I'm very pleased to meet you, Mrs. Wexler."

His mother let out a girlish laugh as she tucked her wispy hair behind her ears. "Oh, please, call me Denise."

And with that, things suddenly felt surprisingly easy. They all fell into a natural routine, with Jenna's mother talking easily to Jack's as they poured out glasses of sherry and Jenna began unwrapping the food they'd brought.

"I feel like a fraud," Jack told her in a low voice. "I didn't even provide the turkey."

"It was a group effort, which is the best kind." With everything in the oven to warm, there wasn't much to do but sip sherry and admire the view—the crackling fire, the Christmas tree Jack had bought last minute and decorated with gold and silver ornaments bought at Jenna's store, and the snowy sweep of the lake stretching out under a bright blue sky.

"I don't think I'll ever tire of this view," Jenna remarked, and then wondered if that sounded a little presumptuous.

"Me neither," Jack replied, and she decided she was second-guessing herself too much, wondering if every remark meant something or would be taken the wrong way. The sooner she cleared things up and told him how she felt, Jenna decided, the better.

The moment, however, didn't come for several hours. They brought the food to the table, and lit candles and poured wine, and Jack cut up his mother's food in a gesture so tender it brought tears to Jenna's eyes. They chatted and laughed as they ate, and Denise's occasional confusion was taken in stride. Everything felt easy and relaxed even as a part of Jenna was as tightly coiled as a spring, tense with expectation at what was still to come.

By dessert and then coffee, it was clear Jack's mother was starting to flag, and he decided to drive her back to the nursing home while Jenna and her mom cleared up.

"I think," her mom remarked, once they'd put the dishwasher on, "I'm going to start feeling like a third wheel when Jack comes back." Before Jenna could say anything, she continued, "So I think I'll take myself off and Jack can drive you home whenever you like." Her eyes twinkled. "I won't wait up."

"Mom." Jenna shook her head, but she didn't protest. Her mom kissed her cheek and then, gathering up her coat and gloves, let herself out while Jenna drifted through the house, feeling nervous and excited in equal measure.

How was she going to launch into the whole how-she-felt discussion? Should she give Jack her presents first? What if he hadn't bought one for her? For a second, Jenna thought about calling Annie or Laurie for some reassurance, but then she decided to be grownup about this situation and simply talk sensibly to the man she loved, yes, *loved*.

Twenty minutes later, Jack let himself in. "I thought you'd gone," he remarked as he came into the kitchen, his hair ruffled, and his cheeks reddened from the cold. Outside, the sun was just starting to sink below the fringe of evergreens on the far side of the lake, sending long golden rays across its frozen and snowy surface.

"My mom took the car," Jenna explained. She went to the fire to put another log on, more to have something to do, watching it settle in the grate with a shower of sparks. "She said you could drive me home. I hope you don't mind."

"Of course not."

He moved to join her in the family room, the fire casting dancing shadows, the spicy smell of the Christmas tree scenting the air, the shadows gathering outside. It felt like the perfect moment—cozy and Christmassy, intimate and expectant with promise. She was going to tell him.

"You haven't opened my Christmas presents yet," Jenna said, nodding toward the presents she'd put under the tree earlier. She curled up on the sofa, trying not to sound as nervous as she felt. Any moment now...

"Or you, mine," Jack replied with a smile. Was she imagining it, or did he seem nervous too? Now that they were alone, the mood didn't feel quite as expectant... as tense. Or was she projecting her own fears onto Jack, because she was so nervous?

"So who should go first?" she asked, trying for a playful note.

"Ladies first," Jack replied, and he reached for a small, slim box wrapped in heavy gold paper and tied with a silver ribbon. Jenna opened it with both curiosity and trepidation, wondering what it held. Jack leaned forward, a faint smile on his face.

Jenna lifted the lid of the box and looked to see a silver keychain nestled in the white velvet interior. Engraved into the silver were the words "Miller's Mercantile" in intricate script. "Jack, it's beautiful," she said as she lifted it, the silver heavy in her hand. "And so thoughtful. Thank you."

"Well, you've worked hard these last few months," Jack replied, smiling. "You should be proud of your accomplishments, and I thought you could use it for your store keys."

"Thank you," Jenna said again. It was funny, considering how much she'd previously conflated her sense of self with that of the store, but now that it was revamped and doing well, she felt very separate from it. Which had to be a healthy thing, and yet... she couldn't help but feel that as beautiful—and thoughtful—as the keychain was, and it absolutely *was*, there was a tiny part of her that wished Jack had gotten her something a little more... personal. A little more *her*.

"And there's something else, as well," Jack continued as he handed her another box, this one much larger. "Something of a joke, but I hope you'll appreciate it."

"Now I'm curious." Jenna unwrapped the box and lifted the lid, smothering a laugh when she saw what was inside—a framed crossword made of Scrabble letters, all of words that were meaningful to them. Salmon, Porsche, investment, even shrew, as well as a few others, each clearly chosen with care.

"I hoped we could laugh about it all now," Jack told her wryly.

"We certainly can," Jenna replied, smiling. She realized this was the kind of personal, only-between-them present she'd truly wanted, and coupled with the beautiful keychain, it was perfect, and felt like a sign.

"Jack," she said, looking up from the crossword, "there's something I need to tell you."

"And there's something I need to tell you, too," he replied, his tone turning serious in a way that made her heart leap.

"Okay." She let out a laugh that trembled on its last note as she closed the box and put it aside. "Well, let me go first." As much as she wanted to hear what he had to say, she knew she needed to go first because otherwise she might very well chicken out.

"Ladies first again," he replied easily, although his expression seemed alert, and Jenna could not decide if that was a good or bad thing.

"Okay. The truth is... what I've been wanting to say..." She stopped, already at a loss. *Why*, she wondered, did this have to be so hard? She was getting unfortunate and uncomfortable flashbacks to this very same kind of moment she'd had with Ryan, when she'd fumbled through how important he was to her, and he'd told her, flatly and unemotionally, he wanted to break up. Not that he'd even phrased it that way, because apparently their relationship hadn't been significant enough to require breaking up. He'd more clarified that they'd had nothing to begin with. It had been, hands down, the most horrible and humiliating moment of her life, but she was getting over it, Jenna told herself, and *this* was how.

"I've come to care about you," she blurted at last. "A lot. And I know we said we'd see how this goes, play it by ear and all that jazz, but... it feels important to me to let you know where I've been going, as it were. That is, where I hope we've been going. Together." Her face was flaming, and she felt as if she could throw up. As far as declarations went, it had been fairly mid, but it had still meant a lot to her, and she was pretty sure Jack had to know that.

The trouble was, Jack hadn't said a word. Even more worryingly, she couldn't tell anything from his expression, which was as inscrutable as the day he'd first come into her store, although at least he hadn't curled his lip. But why wasn't he *saying* anything? She'd just bared her heart, at least for her, and he was just... *silent*.

"Jenna," he finally said, his voice gruff. "The thing I need to tell you—"

Something about his tone made Jenna's stomach swoop and then hollow out. "Okay," she managed in little more than a croak. Why did she feel like he was not going to tell her that he cared about her a lot, too? His face was too serious. His voice too low. He hadn't jumped in with any assurances, and the mood definitely didn't feel right.

She had a sudden, excruciating certainty that she was about to experience the most hurtful and humiliating moment of her life, part *two*, and this time it would feel so much worse.

"I've been offered a job," Jack told her. "The job of a lifetime really, starting a new investment firm in New York with an old friend. And I said I'd take it—"

That was all Jenna could bear to hear. She lurched up from the sofa like she'd been prodded by a hot poker.

"Don't," she choked out. "Don't say anything more, *please*."

He stretched out one arm toward her. "Jenna—"

"No." She really couldn't take one more syllable. She said she'd cared, and he replied by telling her he'd taken a job over a hundred miles away. No, she definitely did not want to hear anything more. She'd *told* him what had happened before, and here he was, creating the exact same scenario! Either he was a sadist or the most emotionally unintelligent person she'd ever encountered. Or, the more likely scenario, Jenna realized sickly, was that he just didn't care.

How stupid could she be, *again*? Falling for the same kind of guy—rich, powerful, confident, uncaring—*twice*? Knowing all along that she was doing it and yet convincing herself, so very stupidly, that this time it would be different?

"I'm going to go," she announced while Jack just stared at her.

"Jenna—"

"*No.*" She turned on him fiercely, suddenly furious. "*You* don't get to say a word," she told him. "You don't get to tell me what to do or how to feel or *anything*." Suddenly, with a savage clarity that came like a bolt of lightning, she realized she could have a moment with Jack that she'd never been able to with Ryan. With Ryan, she'd been so shocked, so devastated, that she'd simply tottered off without a murmur to grieve in private. She'd never had the chance to tell him how much he'd hurt her, how truly awful he was.

Now she did.

"How dare you," she choked out. "How *dare* you sweep into Starr's Fall and make me care about you, when you had no intention of caring about me? You were a jerk the first moment I met you, but stupidly I convinced myself you were different! I believed you'd changed, but you clearly hadn't. You're still the same self-entitled rich jerk that I thought you were all along." She shook her head, incredulous and scathing. "You clearly have no compunction with messing with people's feelings, or maybe it's just mine." She tossed her head, defiant now, even with tears streaking down her cheeks. "What was I, Jack, just someone to pass the time with, because you were so bored, out here in the sticks? A hobby, like helping with a store that wasn't even your own, while you waited for a better offer? Not a very good investment, as it turned out, huh?" she finished with a sneer. "Well, I guess I can thank you for letting me know what you're really like, before I did something stupid like fall in love with you! Because I didn't," she felt compelled to point out. "I might have cared about you, but I was definitely *not* in love. I could never be in love with someone who is as—as pompous as to drive a Porsche and wear a Rolex!" She threw the brand names at him like the insults they were meant to be. "And," she added, her tone turning savage, "someone who neglected his family for *twenty* years just so he could make a boatload of money and feel like he was a big deal." She said it purely to hurt him, which she knew she had as his face paled, and he pressed his lips together. "You're such an *ass*!" she stormed, her voice breaking, and then, feeling like there was nothing more to say, she stalked out of the family room, grabbing her coat and purse from the hall, and then walked right out of the house, into the icy twilight of a Christmas that, it turned out, had totally sucked.

23

Jack sat where he was, totally still, letting Jenna's words reverberate through him. *That* hadn't gone as he'd expected. As he'd hoped. He'd managed barely one sentence before Jenna had gone full banshee on him and started screaming. And some of the stuff she'd said—well, it had *hurt*. A lot. Was that really how she thought of him? As someone who neglected his family just so he could make money and feel important?

All right, yes, it might have been who he *used* to be, but he wasn't now, and Jenna *knew* that. The fact that she would throw all that at him now felt like a very low blow. When she'd first started her tirade, he'd been waiting for a chance to interrupt her and explain, but the longer she'd gone on, the more he wasn't sure he wanted to. If this was what she really thought about him...

Well, it was hard not to wonder if what they'd had together was remotely real. Maybe she was right, and it *had* been nothing more than a distraction... for them both. A moment out of time, because they were very different people with different ideas and goals. Clearly. Hadn't Jenna shown him just how much by throwing all that at him without even giving him a chance to explain?

A sigh escaped him, low and defeated. He really had thought this day would be going in a different direction, but maybe it was easier like this. Simpler, anyway...

Except it didn't feel either easy or simple.

And, Jack realized, Jenna had played into all his fears just as he'd played into hers. Throwing back all the parts of himself that he was ashamed of and trying to change, while he'd basically re-enacted her worst moment, by fumbling the receipt of her declaration of caring. Definitely not in love, she'd said, which suddenly, improbably, made Jack smile.

Are you so sure about that, Jenna?

She had protested that point repeatedly, which was interesting, and yet... if that was how they both reacted when they felt vulnerable, what hope could they possibly have? Jenna had pointed a mirror at the worst parts of himself, while showing him her own worst parts. It had led, Jack conceded ruefully, to a pretty awful exchange.

And yet... wasn't that what real love was—accepting the worst along with the best, and choosing to love anyway?

With a new purpose firing through him, Jack leapt up from the sofa, and forgetting his coat, strode outside into a winter wonderland that was very cold. Jenna was nowhere in sight, the twisting road that ran alongside the lake into Starr's Fall completely empty and banked with snow.

It was over four miles back to town, and Jack didn't think she'd walk that whole way. She must have *started* walking, though, and so Jack did the only thing he could think of and started heading back toward Starr's Fall. He wished he'd brought a coat, though, because night was falling, and the wind was cutting right through his cashmere sweater.

Ten minutes felt a very long time to walk, his shoulders hunched, his hands jammed into his pockets, as the wind continued to slice through him. It was getting so dark he wasn't sure he'd even see her on the road, and the two of them being out here like this was potentially dangerous. He didn't even know what he'd say to her if he managed to catch up with her, or whether she'd listen.

Then he saw her figure about twenty yards ahead of him, looking hunched and miserable as she plodded along.

"Jenna!" he yelled, his voice a roar ripped away by the wind. She kept walking. Jack started jogging down the road, as he yelled again. "*Jenna!*" Still nothing. Jack drew a deep breath and kept going. If he had another heart attack out here, he knew who to blame. "*Jenna!*"

Finally, thankfully, she turned around. Glared at him with her arms folded and her face still streaked with tears. "What are you doing?" she asked.

"What are *you* doing?" he demanded, exasperated as well as out of breath. "Besides freezing to death?" He gestured to the empty road, resting his hands on his thighs as he struggled to catch his breath. "Or do you want to give me another heart attack?"

Jenna's expression of angry defiance morphed into one of pure panic. "Jack! You aren't!" She rushed to his side. "I'll never forgive myself if—"

"I'm not," he told her wearily as he straightened. "I'm not in that bad shape. But why did you run out of my house like that? You didn't give me a chance to explain—"

She stiffened, her hand dropping from his shoulder. "You explained very well—"

"No, I didn't," he cut across her sharply. "I said I had a job and that I'd said I'd take it. That was it."

"That was enough!" Jenna cried. "I can put two and two together as well as anyone—"

"And come up with about forty-six," Jack interjected. "Look, I'm not saying I handled that moment well. I didn't, and that's in part because I felt so torn about it all—"

"Well, please don't let me get in the way of your emotional conflict," Jenna snapped.

Jack grabbed her hand and held it between his own. "Jenna, please. Can we not argue? We're two reasonable adults. I know I sent you into a panic back there, because it reminded you of that guy from before, and I am truly sorry for that. But can we have a reasoned discussion about this, preferably somewhere warm?"

* * *

Jenna stared at Jack's face, the weary yet determined expression hardening his features, and felt herself relent. She still didn't feel good about any of it, but Jack was right. She could be a reasonable adult. At least, she was trying to despite her recent outburst, and she knew they needed to have a conversation. Besides which, yes, fine, she *might* have overreacted slightly, because she'd been feeling so raw.

"Okay," she told him. "Let's go back to your house."

It was a fairly frigid and miserable walk back through the cold and the dark, with neither of them speaking. Jenna still had no idea what Jack intended to say. Why tell her he'd been offered a job and was going to take it unless he was planning to break up with her? She could not see a single other scenario.

"All right," Jack said once they were back inside. He blew on his hand before stirring up the fire and then pouring them both stiff whiskeys. "Let's try this all again."

Jenna shook her head slowly. "Jack... I appreciate I might

have been more than a little over-the-top in my reaction before, but... you told me you'd decided to take a job in New York City. I mean, what more is there to say?"

Jack handed her a whiskey before sitting down with his own. "I appreciate I shouldn't have led with that," he said quietly. "I've been turning it over in my mind since Will offered me the opportunity last week. I told him I'd do it, and I was figuring out a way to make it all work. The job. Living here, at least part-time. Us." He took a long swallow of whiskey, but Jenna didn't think she could manage a mouthful, and so she just cradled the glass between her hands.

"And so, based on what you told me, you decided to go ahead?" she filled in when Jack didn't seem inclined to say anything more.

"I wanted to," Jack agreed. "I've *missed* that life, Jenna. I've missed who I was—someone important and yes, a big deal." He grimaced and Jenna winced. She had, she knew, said some very hurtful things, and she was sorry for them. "I was good at what I did," he continued quietly. "I enjoyed it. I liked having that kind of purpose, and you know what? You're right, helping out with a store that *isn't even your own* doesn't compare."

Ouch. "I'm sorry," Jenna whispered. "I shouldn't have said all that."

"But it's true, isn't it? I was distracting myself. Because I am only forty-two and I'm not ready for hobbies being the rest of my life, not even worthy ones. I want to do more. Be more. And I was wrestling with all of that over the last week."

Jenna stared down into the amber depths of her whiskey. "I wish you'd told me," she whispered.

"Would you have understood?" Jack challenged her, his voice gentle. "Or would it have sent you into a panic?"

"You mean like it did?" She looked up, trying for a smile even though everything felt wobbly, her lips included. "I'm sorry, Jack. I overreacted and I—I said some hurtful things. I wasn't even thinking, just... just reacting." She looked back down, afraid to see the expression on his face. "I shouldn't have said them."

He was silent for a long moment, forcing her to look up again. When she did, she saw he only looked sad, and that scared her. Had she ruined everything by freaking out the way she had? What an awful thought, that *she'd* been the architect of their relationship's demise, simply because she'd been so scared.

"I'm sorry too," he said at last, and Jenna's stomach contracted at the tone of his voice. He sounded so *final*.

"Please don't tell me," she whispered, her voice catching, "that my freaking out like that has ruined everything."

For a second, as he stared at her, she could barely breathe. Then he cocked his head and said thoughtfully, "I wouldn't say it ruined *everything*."

Was he joking? She felt too fragile to be able to tell. "Umm..." was all she could manage.

"Maybe I should start over," Jack said. "And if you can listen to the end, that would be great." He smiled to take any sting from the words, but Jenna still cringed in guilt.

"I feel like the word 'shrew' is coming to mind..." she murmured.

"Never," Jack told her. He reached over to clasp her hand with his, and his touch was warm and dry and intensely reassuring. "Jenna, I'm sorry I started like that. I do realize that it would have brought back some very unpleasant memories. But what I was trying to explain was... I was offered a job, I wanted to take it, and that's a part of who I am. And I'm very glad you care about me a lot, and that I care about you a lot, which is what I should have led with, definitely." He released a pent-up breath. "I've spent the last week trying to figure out how this can work. How *we* can work."

"You mean if you take this job in New York?" Jenna asked in a small voice. It didn't have to be a deal breaker, but it was kind of a big thing. A very big thing. If Jack moved back to New York to work eighty-hour weeks, well... what kind of relationship could they possibly have?

"No," Jack said, surprising her. "I'm *not* taking the job in New York. That's what I was going to try to explain. I said I would, and then I backed out, because I realized I couldn't go back into the world, not in that way, as much as part of me wanted to. Really wanted to. But I did mean it when I told you before that I didn't want to be that kind of person again. I know myself, and I can't go back into that world without letting it consume me. But... I want some part of that old life, that old me, back. And I just don't know what that will look like, or if that's something you'd want." He gave a little shrug. "Maybe you care a lot about the Jack who potters around his house and has all the time in the world, and not so much the guy who loves working hard and closing a deal. And yes, drives a Porsche and wears a Rolex. That's part of me, too."

"I care about all of you, Jack," Jenna replied, her voice turning fierce in her certainty. She wished they'd both handled that conversation differently, instead of reacting out of their fear and insecurity, but they could have a re-do now... she hoped. "Not just the parts I like better, or you like better, or anything like that," she continued. "Laurie said something to me awhile back about how we have to love the worst as well as the best parts of somebody. And I'm not saying the Wall Street version of you is the worst, but it is part of who you are, and I accept that part along with every other..." She managed a smile. "If you can accept the crazy banshee part of me along with every other."

Jack squeezed her hand. "Funny, I was just thinking the same thing about the worst and best parts. And as far as you are concerned, I think I can. But as for what it looks like..."

"Maybe we can figure that out as we go along." She took a deep breath and decided that this was the moment for the total honesty she should have given him before. "I shouldn't have told you I care about you before, Jack." He looked startled, and she hastened to clarify. "What I should have said is that I—I love you. I'm *falling* in love with you, if that sounds less scary. But the point is, I'm committed. I *want* to be committed. Whatever that looks like going ahead... for both of us."

Jack was still holding her hand, and gently he twined his fingers through hers, which seemed like a good sign. "Not that it's a competition, of course, but I kind of wanted to tell you that first."

She raised her eyebrows, her heart feeling as if it were soaring upwards, as light as a balloon. Her toes were barely touching the floor. "Tell me what?" she asked.

"That I love you," he told her, his voice a warm thrum, "crazy banshee and all. No *falling* about it."

Jenna let out a trembling laugh. "You definitely should have led with that."

He laughed as he leaned toward her for a kiss that felt full of promise. "Yeah, I should have."

They shared a lingering kiss that went a long way to making Jenna feel a whole lot better. But as they eased back, smiling at each other, the question remained.

"So," Jenna said, just as she had the first time he'd kissed her.

"So," he repeated, smiling a little.

"What now?" She had to ask, even though she was pretty sure Jack didn't know the answer, and neither did she.

He shrugged, still smiling. "You tell me. Or I tell you. But whatever happens... we're in it together. We face the future *together*." He reached for her hand once more. "Whatever that looks like." He squeezed her fingers. "Deal?"

Relief flooded Jenna, along with a new, certain joy. Could anyone ask for more than that? Could anyone expect anything more?

"Deal," she said, and squeezed his hand back.

EPILOGUE
SIX MONTHS LATER

"Let me see that rock again!"

Laughing, Jenna raised her left hand only for Laurie to stumble back, pretending to be blinded. Even she couldn't quite believe the bling, and she'd been officially engaged for three whole days.

A lot had happened in six months... Not only were Jenna and Jack engaged after a romantic proposal on top of the Rockefeller Center in New York, down on one knee and everything, but Maggie and Zach were also planning a wedding, and Laurie and Joshua were actually *married*. They'd surprised everyone by running off and eloping just a few weeks ago, coming back from New York as giddy as teenagers and wearing wedding rings.

Other life changes had happened too in little Starr's Fall; Henrietta Starr had been in touch with her grandson, who had promised to visit, much to Henrietta's cantankerous delight. Annie had surprised everyone by selling Lyman Orchards, and had joined Mike in the mechanic business, claiming the need for a new start. Jack had also started his own business, focusing on rural regeneration, with its headquarters in his house.

Jenna had been worried at the start that it wouldn't be enough for all that energy and purpose of his, but the work kept coming and Jack certainly seemed to enjoy it, as well as the slower pace of life "out in the sticks," as Jenna liked to tease him. The truth was, living in Starr's Fall suited them both... which was a good thing, considering they were getting married in three months, and planning to spend the rest of their lives there, and maybe even raise a family, if they were so blessed.

"All right, ice cream sundaes all around," Laurie proclaimed. She, Jenna, Maggie, and Liz were all at The Latest Scoop for celebratory ice cream. It was the middle of June, the sun-drenched days of summer, when Starr's Fall turned into a tourist destination, and everyone remembered just how great it was to live there.

"Coming right up," Zoe called from behind the counter, just as a middle-aged man and his sullen-looking teenaged daughter came into the ice cream parlor. Everyone fell silent as the man looked around with an abashed smile while the girl scowled and flicked her hair. Tourists, Jenna wondered as the man walked hesitantly to the counter. She'd certainly never seen them before.

"May I help you?" Zoe asked with a smile, brushing her bright pink hair out of her eyes as the man frowned at her, looking, Jenna thought, disapproving.

"Just two ice cream cones," the man said as he turned to look hopefully at his daughter.

"I don't want anything," she snapped, crossing her thin arms across her body and looking away from her father, with a glare aimed at nobody in particular. She looked defiant, but Jenna thought she also seemed scared. She couldn't be more than fourteen.

"Sophie..." The man sounded tired as well as sad. He turned back to Zoe, who was watching them both with narrowed eyes.

"Just one vanilla ice cream cone, then," he said quietly, on a sigh. "Thank you."

Jenna glanced back at her friends, who were watching the sad little scene unfold with the same avidity she had been.

"Are you visiting?" Zoe asked as she scooped the ice cream.

"No, we've moved here," the man replied with an attempt at joviality while the girl's scowl only deepened. "Just last week."

"Ah." Zoe glanced between the two of them, clearly curious about who they were and why they'd moved to Starr's Fall. Jenna was curious too, but already she suspected the pair wouldn't be all that forthcoming, but they still deserved a community welcome. "Well," Zoe said with a big smile as she handed the man his ice cream cone, "welcome to Starr's Fall!"

* * *

MORE FROM KATE HEWITT

Another book from Kate Hewitt, *Playing for Keeps in Starr's Fall*, is available to order now here:

https://mybook.to/PlayingForKeepsBackAd

ACKNOWLEDGMENTS

There are so many people who help bring a book to readers, and I must thank everyone at Boldwood for being so absolutely fabulous, starting with my editor Isobel Akenhead. We have worked together for many years, and it's been such a wonderful, trusting relationship. Thank you, Isobel, for all your wise words as well as your confidence in me! I'm also very grateful to everyone on the Boldwood team, especially Marcela, Wendy, Isabelle, and Amanda. Thanks also to my writing friends who cheer me on, especially Jenna and Emma. Lastly, many thanks to my family, for being so patient when I'm in writer mode, and also (finally!) appreciating that this is really a job. Cliff, Caroline, Jacob, Ellen, Teddy, Anna, and Charlotte, I love you all!

ABOUT THE AUTHOR

Kate Hewitt is a million copy bestselling author of historical, contemporary and romantic fiction. An American ex-pat, she lives in a small market town in Wales with her husband and five young(ish) children, along with their two Golden Retrievers.

Not ready to leave Starr's Fall? Get an exclusive short story by signing up here for Kate Hewitt's newsletter!

Visit Kate's website: www.katehewittbooks.com

Follow Kate on social media here:

- facebook.com/KateHewittAuthor
- x.com/author_kate
- instagram.com/katehewitt1
- bookbub.com/authors/kate-hewitt

ALSO BY KATE HEWITT

The Starr's Fall Series
Coming Home to Starr's Fall
Playing for Keeps in Starr's Fall
Snowflakes Over Starr's Fall

Boldwood

Boldwood Books is an award-winning fiction publishing company seeking out the best stories from around the world.

Find out more at www.boldwoodbooks.com

Join our reader community for brilliant books, competitions and offers!

Follow us
@BoldwoodBooks
@TheBoldBookClub

Sign up to our weekly deals newsletter

https://bit.ly/BoldwoodBNewsletter

BECOME A MEMBER OF
THE SHELF CARE CLUB

The home of Boldwood's book club reads.

Find uplifting reads, sunny escapes, cosy romances, family dramas and more!

Sign up to the newsletter
https://bit.ly/theshelfcareclub